Bloodthief

Robert W. Streeter

October 2011

Published by

Robert W. Streeter
691 Stoner Trail Road
Fonda, NY 12068

ISBN: 0-9791-1061-0
ISBN 13: 978-0-9791106-1-0

Dedication

For my family and T.P. McGloin wherever you are!

Coming soon!

BLOODKING —the next adventure of Nicholas Bonecutter.

Shout at the Darkness

Ryan shifted the truck into drive and slammed his foot on the accelerator. Bonecutter looked back and saw the side door fly off of its hinges, as the dead man burst into the parking lot.

"Go, Father, he's gaining on us!" Bonecutter yelled, looking out the back window in disbelief as the dead man ran, closing the gap on a truck that was moving over forty miles per hour down the old warehouse road. He leaned out the window and emptied the rest of the .45's clip at La Baptiste. One round hit the dead man in the knee and spun him off his feet.

Ryan managed to get the truck onto the main road and ripped down the highway at eighty miles an hour for several miles before he finally calmed down.

"What the hell is that thing? What is he? I killed that guy, I killed that son of a bitch, and he got up and ran after us. What the hell is he?"

Ryan's face went white, for he knew all too well what had run from the warehouse after them. Worst of all, he knew this was far from over.

Acknowledgements

I would like to thank my family, for putting up with all my eccentricities, including the writing business —especially my wife Bonnie. I also received plenty of help and encouragement from a mentor—Debrah Morris, through the lengthy process of leaving the world of fact for the realm of fiction.

Prologue

(From the journal of Father John Ryan)

They tell me I did the right thing; I was doing the Lord's work. Well, my little Irish mother always said that we alone were responsible for what we have wrought. Mom was right. I lie awake at night trying to go through the events, back to find some way to change the ending, find the exact place I went wrong. I never seem to be able to find a way to change the outcome. This is my story. This was what I have wrought. It is my curse.

I alone am to blame for putting a fine young man in the path of an unspeakable horror—scarring him forever by what he had to see and what he had to do. Nicholas Bonecutter was born in a ramshackle Adirondack town. From his birth, much more by circumstance than by choice, he became a fighter, a soldier. Nicky had a difficult youth, an outsider in our backward little town—a place that, at the time, was too close-minded to accept his Native American side, and his being half white still wasn't good enough. Yet, by the time he reached adulthood, even the town had grown up. He became a valued and respected citizen of Wilmington Notch, even had friends.

That which made him different from others didn't hold him back; it made him excel. He was trained in the martial arts, first by his grandfather (as a means of defense against the town's bullies), then by other masters of these arts, after his grandfather died. He studied several disciplines from what he told me, but to me, that stuff is mainly something from grade B movies. In spite of what I tried to teach him about God, my attempts at spreading the faith didn't work. His training was his religion. It taught him to believe in himself and do right in everything he did. He didn't need my church to make him into a good man.

In the end, he walked away from war and his service as a Navy SEAL, settling into a peaceful life, even taking over his grandfather's outdoor guiding service. Peaceful, that is, until I came along and begged for his help, knowing full well he would never say no.

He was the best at everything he did. I sent the best man I had ever known to stop something no one should ever have to know is real.

This is how it all began.

Father John Ryan

Book I
The Missing

Book I
Chapter I
Rensselaer, New York—April

Steven Deusler glanced at the glowing green numbers on his car clock for the fifth time in less than ten minutes. From his parking spot on the dark hillside above the Port of Rensselaer, he could see the Empire State Plaza directly across the Hudson River in Albany, New York. A crescent moon lit the white marble façades of the buildings. He gazed at the Plaza from the window of his beat-up Honda Civic, taking in the odd mixture of architecture: the agency buildings, the tall Corning Tower, and the Plaza's unique marvel—the Egg, an egg-shaped structure that served as a convention center.

Were it not a Monday night, the gravel road where he sat would usually be filled with parking teenagers, fumbling and groping their way through sex, or simply just getting drunk or high, far from the watchful eyes of their parents. Deusler would have welcomed the sight of another car, any other car, even one that was rocking up and down as a couple of teenagers banged away. At least he wouldn't be out here alone.

In spite of the cold, a trickle of sweat slid down the back of his neck, falling on the ratty ponytail he'd worn since college. Moderately overweight, he hadn't changed his look since high school. When he wasn't at work, he always wore T-shirts embossed with the name of some rock band and ratty looking blue jeans. A greasy, pockmarked face, sharp nose, and flitting brown eyes gave him the same expression as a pet store ferret. Although you couldn't tell by looking at him, Deusler had a privileged upbringing.

None of this parenting took, though, because he exuded little in the way of class. One more black sheep from a far more successful flock.

He left the engine off in spite of the cold. His nerves kept him warm enough. If he could only keep his cool for another half hour, he would be on his way to Antigua, with enough cocaine and cash to be set for life.

His plan was deceptively simple. Give the boss man a case filled with fake drugs, and leave with the cash for the next shipment. Then pick up the real shipment of coke. He only needed a few minutes lead time before La Baptiste figured out he'd been had, and it was off to a new life with a brand new identity. He had it all planned. The drive to La Guardia Airport would only take a couple of hours, and he'd be on a plane to an island full of beautiful women, where his money would make him a king. All he had to do was fool La Baptiste one time.

La Baptiste's street name was "Night," earned for his peculiar habit of only conducting business after dark. Few of the street-level dealers or suppliers had ever seen him at all. Those who were trusted enough to see the man's face did so after dark.

Night was part of a new wave of big city-styled crime that had migrated up the Hudson River to the Capital District from New York City, and he currently supplied most of the drugs sold there. The beauty of La Baptiste's operation was that his security was so tight, even the police had never heard of him. His drug supply operation was completely secret. Attempts made by area police agencies or the New York State Bureau of Criminal Investigation to find who was responsible for the influx of drugs were dismal failures. They caught a few street-level dealers, but they could never get one to give up their boss, despite receiving maximum sentences from area courts. No matter what, the cops could never break the silence, an unusual circumstance for law enforcement.

Deusler had been La Baptiste's courier for over a year now. Each week, he drove to New York City and exchanged a suitcase full of cash for a suitcase full of drugs. He had never set out to be a drug dealer, but a guy who barely scraped up a sociology degree from college and had a taste for cocaine needed a way to supply his habit. His wages as a social worker with Albany County certainly weren't going to do it. After he had finally landed a job, his wealthy parents cut him off, so he had to find creative ways to buy his booze and dope.

Many of Deusler's clients at the county office were involved in the area drug scene. He found his way in as well. Initially, he started dealing on the street, but he soon managed to work his way up within the organization. After all, there weren't many other college graduates on the job. He was smart enough never to rip off anyone higher in the chain. In fact, he was as well trusted as any drug dealer could ever get.

He eventually became courier for the organization. Being trusted with suitcases full of cash and drugs was good for him. La Baptiste tipped Deusler with coke each week to keep his habit going. The extra cash enabled him to live a lot better than the average social worker.

This arrangement had worked, until Deusler wanted more. Perhaps it was his parent's success in life, or maybe just pure foolishness, but Steven always wanted more. His plan allowed him to use the trust he'd earned to create a deception. Finally, the day came when La Baptiste sent him to pick up a shipment twenty times the size of the usual run, and he would be carrying a fortune in cash.

Deusler had a week to come up with a plan to switch the drugs without getting caught. He'd arrange the drugs in the case in such a way that he'd be long-gone before anyone realized they'd been had. Steven knew that the chemical test dealers used to check cocaine was color-metric. It didn't pick up the quantity of the drug, or the quality. It merely verified its presence. Like a home pregnancy test, the answer was either yes or no. He rigged the packages so the kilos on top had enough pure coke on the outside of the bundle to trigger a positive on the test, if they even bothered to check.

By the time La Baptiste figured out that he had been screwed, Deusler would be half a world away living large under a new identity. La Baptiste's own arrogance would be the key to getting away with the scam. He rarely checked shipments. Instead, he and his cronies would joke with him about what would happen if anything was missing, or if anything was wrong. They figured Deusler was too afraid of them (and truth be told, he was) to try a rip-off. Deusler would rely on La Baptiste's arrogance and his 'I'll kill you deader than hell shit' attitude. Chances are he wouldn't even check the contents of the packages. He'd just make sure the weight was right and head out.

A jet-black Mercedes pulled up behind Deusler's Honda. *Show time.* The sight of La Baptiste's car didn't help Deusler's nerves, but it was too late now, the real drugs were in a locker at the airport. He had no choice but to go through with his plan.

Steven grabbed the suitcase full of "coke" and walked back to the Mercedes. The tinted window on the driver's side slid down, revealing the golden grin of La Baptiste's lieutenant, Willie. Willie's broad, ugly face was distinguished by a crooked, flat nose and a smile punctuated by a mouthful of gold-capped teeth. "Get in the back, Stevie," Willie said, "man wants to see you."

Deusler opened the rear door and climbed into the back seat of the beautifully upholstered car. "Good evening, Mr. Deusler," the dark figure on the other side of the leather seat spoke in a broken French accent. "Shall we have a drink?"

His best bet was to play along. "Rum and coke if it's no trouble, Mr. La Baptiste."

"Oh, it is no trouble at all, Mr. Deusler," La Baptiste said.

Deusler eyed him in the dim light of the backseat bar. Armand La Baptiste was not the stereotypical drug lord, not by a long shot. He was a small man, probably no taller than five-six and of relatively slender build. Despite his diminutive size, his features were very sharp. He had deeply black skin and a narrow nose that came to a point. His lips were also thin, and he wore no facial hair. The hair on his head was cropped short. La Baptiste's clothing was impeccable. He wore a neatly tailored, dark blue Armani suit and red silk necktie. Certainly not the typical look of a drug lord.

"The view of the Capital is quite good from here, don't you think?"

"Never cared for the place myself," Deusler replied.

"A man should take the time to enjoy the finer things in life, Steven. Architecture, art, well-made automobiles, fine women. All should be appreciated. Still, art is not as important as the most treasured concepts of mankind, like honesty and integrity, don't you think? The voice was as smooth as butter, but the man wasn't here to discuss culture."

Here it came, the make the flunky sweat part of the show. "Maybe someday I'll have more time for those things."

"Very well, Mr. Deusler, enough of the pleasantries. I believe you have something for me," La Baptiste said.

"Yes, Mr. La Baptiste, here you go," Deusler sipped his drink, as he slid the briefcase across the seat.

La Baptiste opened the case and took a small leather bag containing a chemical testing kit from inside his suit jacket. He deftly slit open one of the top packages and mixed it. As he did, the color instantly turned blue. "It appears that all is in order as usual, Mr. Deusler."

Deep inside, Deusler held in a silent sigh of relief. He'd nearly panicked when La Baptiste brought out the test kit, but his plan had worked. He'd gotten away with it!

"Mr. Deusler, I have been talking to an associate of mine." The drug lord leaned forward, bringing his face close enough so that Deusler could smell his breath, smiling as he spoke. "He tells me that you stored the real shipment of merchandise in a rented locker at La Guardia Airport. This is unfortunate. Now I must decide what to do with an employee I can no longer trust."

Willie turned around and leaned over the driver's seat, grinning at him, the light from the mini bar glinting off gold teeth, as Deusler's bladder emptied all over the fine leather seat. He desperately wanted to run but couldn't move his arms and legs. La Baptiste must have drugged his drink. He was as paralyzed as a fly caught in a spider's web, and now the spider was coming.

"Fear not, Mr. Deusler," La Baptiste said, "you will continue to serve me, for a short while anyway, but now I am afraid you fulfill my more personal needs."

Deusler would have screamed if he could have opened his mouth. As the drug lord spoke, La Baptiste's eyes changed, gradually shifting from dark brown, to electric, blood red. They glowed like coals in some hellish fire.

The real horror for Deusler, though, was the drug lord's grin. As the crimson lips parted, they revealed a mouth full of hideously sharp, white, teeth.

Book I
Chapter 2
Wilmington, New York— April

Sheriff Glen Hollister sped along as fast as he dared in his Jeep Cherokee patrol vehicle. He stopped and shifted into four-wheel drive as he turned onto the icy mountain road. Driving at normal speeds was dangerous at this time of year in the heart of the Adirondacks, and Hollister was going way faster than he would have under ordinary circumstances. He tried to use the short time he had left on his ride to figure out what he would say to Bonecutter.

Sweat beaded on his forehead as he drove. Hollister was totally bald under the baseball hat that was part of his uniform. He hated the Smokey Bear hats that were standard issue in Sheriff's departments in the area. He had made getting rid of them one of his first tasks as Essex County Sheriff. Hollister was tall, over six feet, but he had let his condition slide over the years. He had a decent-sized gut hanging over his belt that his wife's good cooking did not help. Despite his size, his eyes reflected his true personality, giving off genuine warmth. A kind, levelheaded individual and an excellent sheriff, Hollister was well liked by most of the residents in the county.

Every second wasted on this drive made his predicament even worse. This was an election year, and as luck would have it, Hollister was smack dab in the middle of a hostage situation that his opponent could easily turn into political gain. His former deputy, Dennis Gallow, was running on a platform of "Hollister can't handle the complex police work of the new millennium."

The current situation was something many folks in the sleepy village of Wilmington Notch had predicted long ago. Del Scribner, the worst drunk and all-around hothead in the town, was holding his wife Charlene and their two children hostage in their run-down house. To make things worse, the biggest news channel in Upstate New York had a truck in the area covering another story and had managed to get wind of what was going on. TV-8 had already set up cameras at the scene and other channels were undoubtedly on the way.

Hollister knew his men could not handle this situation, because Scribner, in addition to being huge, was also a raving maniac when he was drinking. He'd been pounding beers down at Smitty's bar all day, because he had lost yet another job. After buying a fifth of vodka and heading home, he had decided that he and his whole family were going out in a blaze of glory. Worse yet, he owned plenty of guns and was heavily armed.

Normally, Hollister wouldn't send a bunch of his deputies into a situation that was going to certainly get somebody killed if he could find another way. He didn't needlessly risk lives, and this situation was pretty much hopeless.

The only man who could possibly put an end to this mess without getting someone blown away on the six o'clock news wasn't a deputy. He wasn't even a cop. Hollister's only chance of bringing a happy ending to the situation was Nicholas Bonecutter.

Here goes nothing. He turned into the driveway that wound up to the Bonecutter cabin. The townsfolk had not exactly been kind to Nicholas and his grandfather over the years. Being Mohawk Indian was one thing that many of the small minds in town had against the Bonecutters. Both Nicholas and his grandfather before him were feared for what everyone knew they were capable of, even though neither used his "talents" unless provoked. Hollister was relieved as he ran up the walkway to the cabin and found Nicholas in the side yard splitting wood.

Bonecutter spotted him and leaned his splitting maul against the chopping block. He was tall, a couple inches over six feet, and as solid as a rock. He did not look like a body builder. The muscles rippling under the flannel shirt were long and flat, and his physique exuded both balance and grace, in addition to obvious strength.

"Nick, I need your help," Hollister said. "I have a problem and you're the only one who can take care of it."

"What sort of problem would that be, Sheriff?" Bonecutter ran his hand over his closely cropped black hair, and wiped the sweat from his brow.

"I don't have time to explain. Del Scribner is holding his family hostage, and he's probably going to kill them."

"Sounds like a job for a cop," Bonecutter said, bending to retrieve his maul. "Since that's your department, deal with it. Besides, I really don't give a damn what happens to Scribner." He hoisted the maul and split the next log, tossing it on the woodpile.

"You shouldn't give a crap about him," Hollister said, "but I was hoping you would care about his wife and kids. He's going to kill someone this time. He's finally snapped, and every second you and I spend arguing might be the second that made it too late. Look, Nick, my deputies are good cops, but this sort of thing is way over their heads. Heck, they can't even cut the power to the house, because he takes shots at anyone going up the pole. You're the only one who can pull this off without bloodshed."

Bonecutter leaned the splitting maul against the stump and considered the matter. "If I do this, Sheriff, we do it my way. No questions. No arguments."

"Fair enough, Nick, but we need to hurry."

"Wait here." Bonecutter ran into the cabin. Two minutes later he returned carrying a longbow with five arrows strapped in a quiver, a couple of short bamboo sticks, and black military clothing.

It took Hollister twenty minutes to drive to Scribner's place, and the sun had set during the ride. "What's going on, Jim?"

"More of the same, Sheriff, but he seems to be getting worse," said the deputy in charge at the scene. He's been pounding down the vodka, and the stuff that he's screaming keeps getting crazier and crazier. He even shot out one of the roof lights on a patrol car."

"What the hell's he doing here?" Deputy Jan Benson glared at Bonecutter. Benson had no love for Nicholas and didn't mind showing it.

"Listen to me, all of you." Hollister unfolded a diagram of the house on the hood of his vehicle and stepped back. "Nick is going to do the entry into the house, and you will do exactly what he says, as soon as he says it. Anyone who isn't with the program can give me their badge right now!"

At that moment, all two hundred fifty pounds of Del Scribner burst through the front door into the spotlights trained on the seedy house. He held his youngest son Tommy by the hair and had a .357 magnum Ruger Blackhawk jammed in the boy's mouth. The hammer on the single action revolver was cocked and ready to fire.

"If you bastards doan get offa of my land, I'm gonna shoot the kid," Scribner bellowed. The men surrounding the house aimed their guns at Scribner. They could see the boy's bloody mouth wrapped around the gun barrel, and most of them would have gladly shot him.

"Hold your fire," Hollister shouted. "He may touch off the trigger on the way down."

After hearing Hollister's order, Scribner backed off into the house, pulling the terrified little boy with him. Hollister grabbed the radio mike clipped to his uniform shirt. "Unit One, what's he doing in there?"

"Looks like he's tying the kid to a chair with duct tape, Sheriff." A voice replied. Hollister showed Bonecutter the floor plan they had put together from a neighbor's description. "He's holding them in the dining room and has them tied to chairs at the dining room table," Hollister said. "My sharp shooter reports a number of guns visible on the table. You're the expert, can you get in there and stop him without any bloodshed?"

"I think so," Bonecutter said, "but what happens if I can't?"

"Nothing, just try and save his family. Do whatever you have to with him."

"Then let's get this over with."

"What to you want us to do?" Hollister asked.

"Okay, Sheriff, here's how this is going to happen..."

It took five minutes to coordinate the entry. Bonecutter donned his black clothes, including a mask that covered his face. He and Deputy Benson snuck around to the back of the house where the kitchen was located.

Bonecutter alerted the deputies through a headset radio. "In thirty seconds, we hit the house. Everyone keep away, unless I call for help." He and Benson were at an angle to the picture window on the dining room of the old house. "As soon as I tap your shoulder, I want you to blow out the window. Angle your shot so the pellets won't go near the hostages." Bonecutter unsnapped an arrow from the longbow's quiver. The arrow bore the cresting marks his grandfather taught him to make, the colors of the Bonecutter family.

"And just what are you going to do with that?"

"I'm going to take out the power cable before I go in, now get ready." Nicholas said.

Bonecutter drew the bow and took aim, "Three, two, one, now!" Bonecutter loosed the arrow, and the steel broadhead severed the sparking power cable. Then he tapped Benson's shoulder.

Benson's Ithaca pump shotgun roared as a load of .00 buckshot blew the window into a thousand shards of glass. The roar of the 12-guage hadn't stopped ringing before Nicholas dove through the hole.

Scribner jumped out of his easy chair when he saw the lights go out and watched the window blow apart. Something dark hit the floor inside the dining room window and was moving across the floor. Nicholas executed a front roll as he passed through the window frame, and came up to a standing position near Scribner. Scribner wheeled his revolver to shoot him, but all the booze slowed his reaction. Bonecutter swung the fighting stick, slamming the wrist of Scribner's gun hand.

The big man howled in agony and dropped the gun.

One of the deputies outside the house disobeyed Hollister's orders and beamed his flashlight on the two combatants, allowing Scribner to clearly see the figure clad in black standing before him. He swung his huge fist at Bonecutter, and tried to pick up one of the guns on the table.

Bonecutter, temporarily blinded by the flashlight, nearly failed to duck the punch. He quickly swung the rattan sticks in unison. The sticks hit Scribner simultaneously. One smashed the gun grabbing arm, the other cancelled the punch, smashing the collarbone on Scribner's opposite shoulder, canceling the attack.

Scribner swung again, and Bonecutter used a technique called "Aiuchi." He struck so quickly inside of Scribner's next attack that the big man never had a chance, hitting him on the side of the neck, while simultaneously smashing the previously damaged wrist.

Scribner gagged from the stick strike to his neck. Most men would have been all done, but Scribner was buoyed by the combination of booze, pure adrenalin, and the mental capacity of a block of concrete. He shot his arms out to grab the black-clad figure.

Bonecutter saw the hands coming and switched from karate to aikido, stepping to the left, and outside of the attack, shooting his right arm forward in a corkscrew motion and executed a technique that slipped around Scribner's oncoming arms and smashed against his neck, taking the huge man off his feet like a running back hitting a neck-high clothesline. As Scribner's massive bulk hit the floor, Nicholas applied a lock to Scribner's wrist joint from another art he was fluent in, Jiu-jitsu.

"You can give up," said Nicholas, "or you can have a broken arm."

Del Scribner, true to form, opted to resist. "You prick, I'll kill your ass," he screamed, as he tried to get off the floor. The sheriff's men were now in the house and there were enough flashlights to illuminate the dining room and the scene.

Bonecutter glanced over at poor little Tommy Scribner taped to a chair, crying, with a bleeding mouth and missing teeth. With the same emotion he would have used to squash a bug, he pushed downward and broke the big man's wrist just as the sheriff's men ran up to help.

Hollister burst through the front door and got to the dining room just in time to see his men pounce on Scribner and handcuff him. He had really lucked out on this one. Not only was everyone alive, Channel 8 News had filmed the whole thing. The coverage would surely usher him to an easy re-election.

Hollister walked up to Nicholas. "Nick, I couldn't have done this without you. The news team is out front, and I'd like to have you there for the big moment. Here, put on this Sheriff's jacket. If anyone asks, you 'e one of my deputies on special assignment."

"Like I told you before, Sheriff," Bonecutter said, "I'm not a cop." He turned away and walked into the dark woods behind the Scribner house on his way back to his cabin.

Book I
Chapter 3
Albany, New York—April

Hattie looked like a witch from a Shakespeare play. Her grotesquely long hair hadn't seen a comb or a brush in years. The little kids who played on the street in front of the Arbor Hill Funeral Parlor called her Mattie because of it. Mattie/Hattie was one of the many people who had been emptied out of mental institutions and onto the streets when the state cut funding during lean budget years.

Her physical features were deceiving. If you did not look too closely, you saw only the obvious—matted hair, dirty appearance—in the simplest terms, a street person. Closer examination and a little imagination revealed what had at one time been a very pretty girl who had somehow gone down the tubes.

Most adults in the neighborhood found Hattie frightening. In addition to her hair, she was known for spouting Bible quotes, or at the very least, she would give out the numbers of her favorite passages, like John 3:15. Her usual street sermon saying was, "Evil is coming. Only those who recognize the face of evil and denounce it will be spared."

Hattie knew the face of evil.

She passed by the Arbor Hill Funeral Parlor every day on her rounds, collecting the cans she traded for nickels and scrounging for food. As she looked in the window, she saw the smiling face of Willie Robinson. She froze at the sight, and when she finally collected her wits, she quickly scurried past the parlor window.

Willie laughed aloud, as he closed the white lace curtain in the front window. He made his way through the back hallway and down the stairs to the basement, the place where the real work done in the parlor was carried out.

Willie, in spite of always wearing a suit and dressing well as La Baptiste demanded, couldn't pass for a funeral home assistant, even though that was one of his current roles. In spite of good clothes and a seemingly straight-up job, he was still nothing more than a cleaned up gang member. The only businessman he could pass for would be a rap music executive. He was a criminal trying to put on a façade of sophistication; despite the suit and tie, his look fell far short of a gentleman.

The basement of the Arbor Hill Funeral Home where he lived with La Baptiste was brightly lit by plenty of fluorescent shop lights. In spite of the lighting scheme, it was still a place that gave the average person the creeps. Ignoring the fact that the basement held the workrooms where bodies were processed, or even if there were no stainless steel tables full of surgical equipment and the room's sterile white paint scheme, something still felt "wrong" about the place.

The basement had three rooms. There was a prep room, where bodies were brought in and thoroughly washed in the initial preparation for burial. Across the hall was the embalming room, where bodily fluids and wastes were removed and replaced with embalming fluid. At the end of the hall, the final room in the basement was the finishing room, where makeup and cosmetic details made the corpses look as good as they possibly could for the mourners, who would come to parade past them in the funeral chapels upstairs.

Willie Robinson was the only man who frequently dealt with Armand La Baptiste in both his roles as funeral home owner, and his hidden life as a drug lord. Willie went about his least preferred set of chores. He did the man's bidding, without question, because of what he was paid for the risks. He did what he was told, because he had the same respect a young lion has for an elder male, a respect born mainly of fear.

Robinson was the only one who truly knew who, or more accurately *what*, Night was.

Willie had started out like many youths who find their way to crime, as a street kid getting into trouble. It started with small things, stealing some gum or a comic book. When he was old enough, he joined a gang; there, his crimes and trouble escalated. He learned quickly and gained status among his peers. At thirteen, he distinguished himself from the other members of his gang by committing his first murder.

Willie stabbed another kid about the same age, because the kid had tried to molest a fellow gang member's younger sister in the trees near a playground. Willie confronted the boy in a park at night, and while he was talking to him, he whipped out a straight razor and slashed the boy's throat from ear to ear. His only thought during this murder was amazement at how much blood flew from the wound. Blood gushed everywhere. After that, he could make himself do just about anything and not be troubled by it.

The police never solved the case, and Willie got away with murder.

About a year later, a new person came to Arbor Hill, Armand La Baptiste. Night took over ownership of the funeral parlor and set about recruiting a lieutenant. Willie was eighteen years old at the time and no longer lived at home. He needed a place to stay. Night provided that and more, but not without a price.

Willie flipped on the overhead lights in the prep room where four black plastic body bags awaited him. He unzipped the first one and lifted the small corpse off the gurney and onto the stainless steel preparation table. A drain trough ran around the outside edge of the table, but very little of the boy's fluids would make their way down it.

The boy, Nestor Williams, had died of smoke inhalation in a tragic fire that claimed him and three siblings. Willie approached the grieving family and offered the funeral home's services at a discount. He put on a good show of respect for the mother's tragic loss of four children. His generous offer did not come from respect.

Nestor was fresh. He hadn't been dead long. He had the blood of a sweet, innocent four-year-old child. Willie would get a big bonus for procuring the boy and his siblings.

Willie stripped the corpse of the charred clothing and took out a long needle with tubing attached, part of a mechanical suction device morticians used to drain a body of its blood, prior to injecting embalming fluids to preserve the tissue. He lacerated an artery in the boy's armpit to conceal the cut from mourners and deftly inserted the needle.

Ordinarily, blood was disposed of according to New York State Department of Health regulations for funeral homes. Nestor's blood was far too precious to discard.

Willie set up a blood bag, pre-treated with an anticoagulant to prevent the blood from jelling. After the vacuum machine filled the first bag, he replaced it with another and continued until the boy was dry.

Willie lit a cigarette. This would be an easy couple of hour's work. The whole process would take about thirty minutes for each body. Since the children had died in a fire, all Willie had to do was embalm them. There would be no viewing hours for the corpses. Draining a body of blood didn't give a tough street hood much to be afraid of.

No, the thing that bothered Willie was where the blood was going next.

Book I
Chapter 4
Wilmington, New York— Late April

Father John Ryan scurried about, tidying up the pews of the small Adirondack church where he served as pastor. He always cleaned St. Michael's each Sunday afternoon, right after his customary dinner at the home of a parishioner. Unlike most places of worship in the Catholic faith, his was a one-man operation. In addition to his duties as pastor, he also served in several other capacities, including doing the housekeeping around the church when members of the Lady's Altar Society could not help. Such was the life of a gray-robed Franciscan Friar.

Ryan was a sturdy specimen, despite the extra twenty pounds he carried on his five-foot, four-inch frame. He had a happy face, with chubby cheeks and a bulbous nose, both of which showed his fondness for a cold beer or a cocktail with friends. Drinking was his only vice, although he was certainly not an alcoholic or even a heavy drinker. He simply enjoyed a few cocktails when the occasion arose, but always in moderation, just the way his mother had taught him. His father fell to the whiskey bug, and his mother took great pains to see that it did not happen to John or his sister.

Ryan combed his thinning hair straight back, keeping it in place for all but the heaviest winds with a good dose of hair tonic. His one unusual feature, in addition to his lack of height, was his hands. He had large, strong hands for a man of his diminutive size.

Father Ryan's persona exuded the warmth and compassion one would expect in a man of the cloth, but his was merrier and more jovial. His glowing smile and brown eyes always reflected genuine concern for members of his flock who came to him with problems. Were he not a priest, he would have made a great department store Santa Claus. He truly loved kids, and would probably have made an ideal father, had his life taken a different path.

St. Michael's was certainly no cathedral. A quaint little country chapel, it held only ten rows of pews, with an aisle up the middle, and a small altar at the front. The outside of the church was sided with rough-cut pine, painted white, with a small steeple on top. The cross on the top of the steeple was uniquely Adirondack, built of two pieces of rough-hewn mountain cedar log.

Ryan was just finishing his "pew check," making sure the correct hymnals were in the holders for next Sunday's mass, and tidying up, when Gretta walked in.

Gretta Van Nostrand, a single mother, lived with her teenage daughter Jean in a rundown house out on Quibley Road. Gretta was a heavyset woman with little money to spend on luxuries like new clothes or cosmetics. She led a simple life. The blue dress she wore came from the Salvation Army store in Plattsburg, and she had knitted the matching sweater herself. Her hair had not been touched by a professional hairdresser in many years. These were only some of the many sacrifices she had made for her daughter, and though she gave all she had for Jean, it was never enough.

Gretta had come to Father Ryan with several problems in the past year or two, and they all involved her daughter. To Ryan, it seemed that, given her age, the girl sought all of the wrong things from the world. Her mother had already caught her drinking, and Gretta had also found a stash of marijuana in Jean's dresser. Even worse than the substance abuse, Jean had become promiscuous, and it was no secret around the town. Everyone knew, including her mother. It was no surprise that Jean attracted many boys at Wilmington Notch Central School. She was a pretty girl with raven hair and big brown eyes. Her body, built with large breasts and a firm butt, drew boys like a magnet.

"Hello, Father Ryan." Tears trickled down Gretta's chin. "Can you spare some time for me?"

"Of course, Gretta," Ryan ushered her to a seat on one of the pews. "Why don't you sit down and tell me what's troubling you."

"Father, it's Jean. She's run away to New York City."

"Why would she leave home?"

"She's too wild, Father. Our little town doesn't hold enough excitement for her. I did the best I could with her. I don't know what else I could have done. I just couldn't stop her from running away."

Though Ryan had been helping Gretta grapple with her problem child for a couple of years, he was certainly no psychologist. His best guess was that Jean never thought her life was worthwhile because of the way her father had abandoned the family. Dale Van Nostrand had left with a waitress from the local diner and had never been heard from again.

Ryan's theory was that, at some level, Jean thought it was her fault. In addition to blaming herself, the girl also undoubtedly blamed her mother. Thus, Ryan reasoned, Jean headed down a self-abusive and ultimately self-destructive path in life. That way, she could punish herself and her mother at the same time.

The trouble was that no attempts made by Ryan, the school counselors, or even the best efforts of other family members to straighten the girl out had worked. Their efforts were only temporary at best, lasting only for a short time.

Jean had been building up to this for a long time, and now she had given her grand finale.

"Let's go to my office and see if we can figure things out," Ryan said. He put his arm around Gretta's shoulders and led her out the side door of the church and across the yard to the small house that served as both his office and living quarters.

Once inside, Ryan helped her into a metal folding chair and took his own seat behind the battered old metal desk. "Did Jean say where she was going in New York City, or how she intended to live once she got there?"

"Oh, Father, you know how she gets. She planned to live in a shelter for runaways, until she found a job. She said she wasn't coming back, because she hates it here."

"What kind of job can a seventeen-year-old child find in New York City?" Ryan asked.

"She said she was going into modeling; I think she saw an ad in one of those fashion magazines she always reads and figured she could do that."

"Have you heard from her at all since she left?"

"That's the terrible part," Gretta replied.

"What do you mean?"

"A man called the other day and told me my daughter was okay, because he was taking care of her now."

"Who was this man? Did he give his name or an address?"

"He didn't say his name, but he had an accent like he could speak to Canadians that come down here for the summer, you know, French sounding. He said he was taking care of her, and I should leave her alone."

"What can I do to help?"

"I don't know. I was hoping you knew someone who could find her. I want to bring her home. I'm scared, Father. I am afraid this time she has gotten herself into something terrible."

The conversation was over, because Gretta began sobbing uncontrollably.

"Let me see what I can do," Ryan said. "It'll take me a day or so. I'll call my friend Father D'Arcy at St. Cecilia's. He's near the bus station in New York City. He has connections with the police down there. Go home and try to get some rest. I'll stop by and see how you are doing this evening."

Book I
Chapter 5
Albany, New York—May

Detective Ed Woldman sat at his desk in the Albany Police headquarters. He was nearly finished with the third shift, an assignment he had pulled, largely because he'd managed to piss off Captain Reichman, yet again. He played his favorite computer game on his Dell computer. Tetris helped to pass the time, while he thought about a case. One more of the department rules he regularly broke.

Woldman was fifty years old and had less than five years until he could retire. He had a full head of black hair, graying at the temples, and a bushy set of eyebrows to match. He might have been handsome, were it not for his ruddy complexion and slightly crooked nose, which he had broken in a fight on the job when he was still a patrolman. Marginally overweight at 190 pounds on his five-foot, eight-inch frame, he was in decent shape but lacked the discipline to cut down on the pasta and beer. His mother was full-blooded Italian who had given him a love for the fresh pasta dishes responsible for his extra thirty pounds. Even though he was one of the department's old guys, he could still break down doors and do any of the physical stuff that a cop needed to do.

Woldman was not popular among his peers. He was a loner and spent little of his off-duty hours with his fellow officers. The other cops thought he was lazy. The locker room jokes were often about Woldman goofing off. Playing games on his computer did not help his reputation.

In Captain Reichman's world, there was no place for guys like him. Reichman was a by-the-book cop, although he had spent little of his time on the street, and he hated the way Woldman did business. He also thought Woldman was a show off. Reichman went out of his way to make Ed's life miserable, but try as he might, he could never break him.

To Woldman's credit, there were also those who thought he was the best thing going, namely the mayor and the City Council. Woldman was a brilliant detective who cracked the toughest cases. What the other cops did not realize, was that while he appeared to be goofing off, the gears in his brain were spinning. He constantly mulled over investigations, looking at them from new angles, finding the pieces to the puzzle that others had missed. When he hit the same roadblock everyone else did, he would not stop. He would push on and seek a new clue, until the case was solved.

Woldman had a long list of successes, including difficult murder cases. Many of his cases were very high profile. The public would scream for results, and he was the only one who came through.

In his early days as a detective, he had first proved that the death of a local celebrity's wife was no accident. He had later come up with a conviction in the case, where the district attorney had initially refused to press charges because there wasn't enough evidence, and the minimal evidence they did find was only circumstantial. Woldman just kept on digging, until he had enough, including finding records of secret bank accounts the defendant had set up with the victim's money.

As he sat guiding the dropping squares on the game, trying to rack up a new high score, he mulled over the Valdez case. Daniel Valdez had been murdered by having his head bashed in by a blunt object. The victim was found in his bed, but there was no murder weapon at the scene. Blood spatter evidence and damage to the body were indicative of overkill, certainly much more than a random act by a prowler. Worse yet, there was no clear motive for the crime, no evidence of robbery, or any indication of someone with a grudge. Valdez had been a respected school guidance counselor, with no apparent drug or gambling problems. His finances were also in good shape.

Woldman's little Tetris squares had all come together, and the screen on the computer repainted itself as he reached the next level. *Paint. That's it.* Valdez's bedroom had just been partially repainted, but where were the paint cans? *The job wasn't finished, so where did the cans go?*

Woldman turned off the computer and signed out an unmarked car from the Sergeant at the front desk. As he climbed into the green Crown Victoria, the Sergeant ran up to the driver's door.

"Woldman," the Sergeant said, "we just got a call. You have to get over to the dock by the Green Apple tour boat, we've got a floater."

"Yeah, I'll get right on that," Woldman said.

"I don't give a damn what you do," the Sergeant replied, "but I'll make a note in my desk log that I told you about it, and what time."

"Fair enough, Sarge."

An hour later, Captain Reichman stood tapping his foot next to the body the US Coast Guard patrol boat had pulled from the river and left on the dock. Reichman was a cop of average skills, far better at telling other cops what to do than doing any actual police work himself. Reichman also weighed over 250 pounds. His round, sweaty face and cheesy gray mustache matched those of the police commissioner, who happened to be his brother.

"Where the hell is that stupid asshole Woldman?" he yelled at the desk sergeant through his cell phone. He looked up and spotted Ed Woldman stepping out of a Crown Vic, carrying what appeared to be a can of paint in a clear evidence bag. Reichman hung up on the sergeant without saying a word.

"Woldman, where the fuck have you been?" Reichman bellowed. "According to the Sergeant's log, you were notified about this floater over an hour ago! I want to know exactly where you've been!"

"Following up on a hunch, Captain."

"Following up on a hunch?"

"Yes, sir, Captain, following up on a hunch."

"This time I've got you, Woldman, Reichman said. "I'm going to have your badge for this one."

"Okay, Captain, then I guess you don't want to hear about this paint can?"

"Why should I give a shit about a friggin' paint can?"

"Because it's the murder weapon in the Valdez case." Woldman turned the paint can around so Reichman could see the blood stain on the back side. "Oh, and by the way, the perpetrator was kind enough to leave his fingerprints in the blood, and the guy next door saw him throwing away the paint can around the time of the murder. Valdez's man friend, Jimmy, seems to have left the part about beating Valdez to death with the paint can out of his statement. Say, uh, didn't you interview Jimmy?"

Woldman could see that Reichman was boiling. His beefy face turned even redder, but there wasn't a damn thing he could say. The dumb ass and his pet detectives had been totally fooled by the gay boyfriend. *Gee, who would have thought that sissy was capable of bashing a man's head in, let alone being bright enough to cover it up?* As much as Reichman wanted to get rid of Woldman, the mayor and his brother, the commissioner, wouldn't hear of it, especially now.

"Just deal with this, asshole," Reichman said, pointing to the corpse in the body bag, and stormed off.

Woldman pulled on latex gloves and unzipped the bag. Judging from the stench, this one had been in the river for a long time, finally floating up as gases bloated the body. The corpse was that of a white male; skin color was one of the few things that could still be determined. The flesh was flimsy, having rotted in the relatively warm water of the Hudson River for several days at least.

"Guy was obviously not a rocket scientist." Woldman noticed a Grateful Dead T-shirt around the mid section, and a ponytail on the back of the rotting skull.

"Harvey," he called to one of the uniformed officers manning the scene, "see that this guy gets to the M.E.'s office for an autopsy, and get statements from everyone who was in on finding him or getting him out of the water."

Somebody killed you, now all I have to do is find out why, because the why always leads me to the who. Woldman carried his prize paint can to the Crown Vic and headed back to the station, right after an unapproved trip to a local diner for a leisurely breakfast.

Book I
Chapter 6
Wilmington, New York- May

Nicholas Bonecutter sat at the kitchen table of his cabin tying the flies needed for the fishing trip he had booked for the following morning. He always marveled at the magic of tying trout flies. It always made him happy to take scraps of feathers and fur, wind them on a hook with some thread, and end up with something that looked like an aquatic insect a trout would like to eat.

Tying flies relaxed him. It reminded him of George, his grandfather, and he always found solace in the memories of the happiest time of his life. Grandfather had taught him many things; tying flies was just one of them.

He needed to relax, because last night he'd had the dream.

The dream always started the same. He was back in the SEALs during the first Gulf War. It was common knowledge that the SEALs had played an integral part in the swift success in the Coalition Invasion by faking an amphibious landing, while the real counterstrike by Coalition forces took place inland as a high-speed land assault.

One of the stories that came out of the war was how a group of four SEALs had invaded an oil rig held by twenty-seven elite Iraqi soldiers. While the story was true, the way it was done was never released to the public. The Iraqis holding the oil rig were heavily armed, including surface-to-air missiles for defense from any airborne assault. They also had a fairly sophisticated radar system capable of detecting any ship activity in the area.

The SEALs trained for any contingency, including their specialty, underwater demolition and assault techniques. The one possibility the Iraqis hadn't planned for was an assault from below. In the dead of the night, the team was delivered by submarine to the waters just off the oil rig and swam the rest of the way using the German-made Draeger breathing apparatus. The aqualungs were made for stealth operations and did not leave any telltale bubbles when the diver exhaled, no trace that could betray him to an enemy sentry.

Four divers surfaced near the base of the oil rig at exactly 4:00 a.m. The first diver to climb the side of the rig was Nicholas.

In the dream, he could almost feel the barnacle encrusted steel of the oil rig with his hands, just the way it had felt that day. He was cold, something people who haven't done much scuba diving would find amazing. The air was eighty degrees that night, but the water was still cold. The SEALs were there to complete their mission, to secure the rig with no SEAL losses, using any means possible. Taking prisoners instead of neutralizing their opponents was at their discretion.

They were getting paid for results, not methodology.

Nick was the best climber in the group. His job was to scale the steel base of the oil rig and secure a black titanium mountain climber's ladder to a railing and then slip away to neutralize any sentries. Advanced intelligence indicated there would most likely be four, one posted at each corner of the rig. Once the ladder was set, he continued to climb, so he could get above the sentries.

Through his night vision goggles, he spotted three Iraqis, but was unable to locate the fourth. Studying the situation, he noticed the flaring heat signature of a glowing cigarette directly below him. The fourth sentry must have moved away from his post for some reason and was just returning. Using a silencer-equipped HK submachine gun, a favorite weapon of the SEALs, he switched the fire selector to single shot, and shot the sentry in the head, watching as he slumped forward. The second, third, and fourth sentries went down in a similar manner, dropping without causing any alarm amongst their sleeping comrades.

Phase Two of the operation was the most dangerous. Twenty troops slept in the crew quarters. Locating them was easy. An American company had built the rig, and the SEALs had studied the blueprints of the facility for hours. The four SEALs split up in pairs, to find and neutralize any enemy soldiers not in the actual crew sleeping quarters.

The plan was for the first pair to enter the control room and secure it, then move on to the galley. The second pair would start with the chief's quarters, and then move on to the lounge area. After securing all of these areas, the team would regroup, and using concussion grenades, would take out the main body of troops sleeping in the crew quarters.

Initially, things went well. There was one Iraqi sleeping in the control room next to his radio. The fact that he was asleep saved his life. All they had to do was hit him in the head with a policeman's sap and tie him up with the special plastic handcuffs they had brought along. With the control room secured, Nicholas and his shipmate Karl, a blond Californian who looked like he had just walked off the cover of a surfer magazine, advanced to the galley.

Entering something like a crew galley in the dark was always iffy. Someone might be up getting a snack or having coffee, and any number of things could make noise in a kitchen. As Karl eased the door open, all hell broke loose. The cook was up early baking bread. When he saw the door open and spotted two masked figures, he reached for his handgun. Karl shot him before he got to it. As he fell, the fat cook knocked over a rolling kitchen cart filled with dishes and glasses and made a ton of noise.

That was enough to sound a general alarm amongst the sleeping troops. In the dream, Nicholas ran forward to try and catch the cook before he hit the cart. He never made it.

Since the sneak part of the attack was over, he quickly ran down the hall to the crew quarters. Two Iraqis armed with AK-47s were already on their way out the door, but he was quicker and shot them both. The other two members of the team, already on their way to the other exit of the crew quarters, were meeting heavy resistance.

He pulled the pins on the frag grenades he carried and hit the floor, as he tossed them into the crew quarters. He and his partner ran in behind the explosions, taking advantage of the confusion, and began firing amidst the mayhem.

At the other door to the crew quarters, the second SEAL team had been driven back by the enemy soldiers. Bonecutter and his partner came up behind the Iraqis and caught them in a cross fire. When it all was over, the smell of cordite and blood filled the air. Once the area was secure and the prisoners were handcuffed, the worst injured among the Iraqis lucky enough to still be alive were tended to by Karl, the team medic.

Bonecutter and the other team began the mop-up operation, keeping in close communication over their headset radios. In the dream, he remembered going along the catwalk on the east side of the oil rig, checking open doors for additional enemy soldiers. He entered the mechanics shop. He could smell the oil and grease. As he slipped around several metal working machines, someone jumped him from behind.

He sensed the knife coming towards his chest without actually seeing it.

He had been trained for such instances and launched a judo throw to hurl his opponent over his shoulder. He remembered what he felt that day, as he executed the throw; *something's weird, this guy is too light.* In one swift motion, born of his training, he redirected the attacker's knife hand and used it to plunge the blade into the Iraqis heart.

The dream always ended the same. He stood there watching a boy in his early teens, clad in the same uniform as the rest of the Iraqis, gasping for air, as he died on the floor in a puddle of blood.

He never slept through the dream, it always woke him up, that was why he would always remember it the next day. He would find himself shaking, his bed sheets soaked with sweat. His dog Sadie would usually run over by the bed and woof, wanting him to be all right.

Killing was something he never got used to. His team had seen plenty of covert action before the Gulf War, and he had killed enemy soldiers and terrorists before, always knowing he had done the right thing. He didn't like it, but it was necessary to protect his life and, more importantly, his shipmates' lives. He would have accepted the killing on the raid, just as he accepted the other killing he had done, were it not for the boy.

His commander called him in for a meeting after the incident. His shipmates had told him that he'd had no choice, but his mind could never let it go. He did his duty and finished the Gulf War having served with honor. When he was up for re-enlistment, he left the SEALs, because he knew he might hesitate the next time he went into battle, and that was all it would take to get one of his shipmates killed. Something he would never allow.

Although his life as an Adirondack guide was much more peaceful, the dream never went away. The dream would probably never go away.

Book I
Chapter 7
Albany, New York—May

Willie Robinson knocked at the steel door to apartment 359 in the run-down Brooklyn flat that housed the New York City portion of La Baptiste's drug operation. A bolt clicked, as a steel view hole slid open, revealing the dark menacing eyes of Leshawn Johnson, the man who ran the house.

Willie waited as Johnson opened the multiple locks and removed the steel bar that secured the door from the inside. "How's biz?" Willie asked.

"Good, man, come on in."

Willie followed him into the living room and watched him settle his bulky frame into the overstuffed leather living room chair before taking a seat on the matching couch. Leshawn called out to a young white girl seated at the kitchen table, who was inhaling lines of cocaine arranged before her on a flat mirror, and told her to get a couple of malt liquors for him and his boss, Willie.

Surprisingly well-decorated and clean, the apartment was not the norm for this rundown part of the city. The area had once been a respectable neighborhood full of working class folks. Now it was a war zone, home to nothing but people who were too poor to live anywhere else, along with all of the drunks, drug users, and the dealers.

The living room, in addition to the black leather furniture, had an expensive oriental throw rug covering new hardwood flooring. Framed posters of various Caribbean Island scenes filled the walls. The decor would not have been something found in most interior decorating magazines, but it was modern and pleasant.

Leshawn shifted in the soft chair, getting comfortable while he waited for his bottle of malt. He was a big man, with arms and a chest covered in heavy musculature he'd gained while weight lifting in prison, where he'd had plenty of time for exercising with the rest of the gang affiliated prisoners he did time with. He still maintained his build with regular workouts at a local kickboxing gym. Leshawn loved the hip-hop culture and dressed like a rap star, complete with baggy pants, an oversize New York Yankees hat, worn tilted to the side, and plenty of gold around his neck. He kept his head cleanly shaven, and he had a wide, flat nose and very full lips.

Willie cocked his head towards the kitchen. "Who's the girl?"

"Name's Jean; picked her up at the bus stop."

"Make sure she don't come with no strings, man, La Baptiste don't want no attention."

"It's cool, she come from a trailer up in the mountains. Nobody know she here. Met her when she got off the bus and asked her if she want to party. She and her moms don't get along. She just wanna party and have a place to crash."

As the girl approached with the beer, Willie cut the conversation short. Leshawn didn't make stupid mistakes, but Willie would be the one to pay for any screw-up his underling made.

The girl went back to her coke. From where Willie sat, he watched her greedily inhale a nose-full of the drug. The kitchen counter behind her was the packaging and distribution center for the New York City operation. Arranged along the countertop were piles of small plastic bags, several kilos of cocaine, and a triple beam balance used for weighing out the drugs. Also in various states of packaging were a number of rocks of crack. Small glass vials were filled with the drug. Other narcotics were also being packaged for sale, including crystal meth and ecstasy.

"Ain't touched her, have you?" Willie asked.

"No man, no time to."

"Good, cause I'm gonna to take her back to Albany when I go. Give her to the man; he take care of that young thing."

"Figured it'd be like that; that's why I didn't do her. Don't want the man getting pissed at me."

"Me either, 'specially after the way he did Deusler. Man he bugged out on that dude."

"Yo, Jeannie, you wanna go to Albany? You can work for the boss man, be his girl. He give you anything you want, how's that sound?" Leshawn asked.

"That'd be cool," the girl replied with a big smile. The white powder all over her face and eyes as big as saucers made her look like a kid eating her first sugarcoated donut.

Book I
Chapter 8
New York City—May

Father Richard D'Arcy was working late into the evening in his office at St. Cecilia's. He worried about how he was going to keep the church as he went over the budget figures. The parish was fairly large, and being its administrator was a big job. The church, in addition to the spiritual services it provided, also ran several programs that brought a great deal of good to the community.

Under D'Arcy's leadership, St. Cecilia's had become a little more modern in its views. While the church's doctrine was quite clear about what behavior was unacceptable, under D'Arcy, St. Cecilia's condemned the sin and not the sinner. There were programs for unwed mothers, drug and alcohol abusers, counseling for AIDS patients, and a camp program where city kids spent a week during the summer in the Adirondacks, at a facility run by his good friend Father Ryan.

All of these programs did much good in an area of the city where prostitution, drugs, domestic abuse, and all of man's darker activities ran rampant. D'Arcy raked his hand through his thick gray hair. He was a tall man, in fairly good shape for a sixty-five-year-old, with the broad shoulders of a lumberjack. Tonight, he had the unfortunate honor of figuring what was going to be cut and what was going to stay. Being in charge had its major drawbacks, and this was one of them.

Money had become the problem with keeping everything going in a parish as large as his. Attendance at mass had fallen off in the last decade, especially with the priest sex-abuse scandal. There were also many other charities competing for the public's dollars. Some of the charities also had much more ability to promote their causes than he did.

While he pondered his dilemma, he stared at the fine mahogany woodwork installed during better times, wood that now showed its age and blemishes. He was startled when the phone rang.

"St. Cecilia's, how can I help you?"

"A good bottle of scotch would be of great help, Father," said a merry voice on the other end of the line.

"John, how are you?" It was good to recognize the always cheerful voice of his friend Father Ryan. "How are things up there in the mountains?"

"Oh the same, Rich, the drugs haven't been a huge problem but we seem to have more than our share of abusive family situations. How are things in the big city?"

"Well, we seem to have a big money crunch at the moment."

"You should come up to the mountains with me. Let one of the younger priests handle things down there, even if it is only for a break."

"Maybe I'll do that," D'Arcy said, knowing full well he would never take his friend up on his offer; there was just too much to do here.

"Rich, I need a favor."

"What is it, John?"

"We have a girl who seems to have come your way. I'd like you to see if you can find out where she is."

"What can you tell me about her? Is she in some kind of trouble?"

"Her name is Jean Van Nostrand, and she's about five feet, five inches tall. She has long dark hair, blue eyes, and was wearing a Stone Temple Pilot's T-shirt—I think it's a rock band—and blue jeans when she got on the Trailways bus to New York. The bus was scheduled to arrive yesterday around midnight."

"Give me a couple of days, John. I have a priest on staff here who knows several people at the bus station. I'll see what we can find out, and then I'll call you back."

"Thanks, Rich, I sure appreciate it. I hope you can find her. Talk to you soon."

D'Arcy hung up the phone. *Guess I'm not the only priest with problems.*

Book I
Chapter 9
Albany, New York—May

Jean Van Nostrand was having the time of her life. *Man, I am so lucky.* She had learned at an early age that her looks would get her what she wanted from men, usually dope, booze, or both. She was still groggy, having woken up at noon the day after her arrival in Albany. Her head throbbed and her mind was fuzzy from the combination of coke and malt liquor she'd consumed the night before.

She loved how things had ended up. All she had to do was show up in New York and she was set. She met Leshawn who took her to his apartment. Then she got a ride in the back of a Mercedes to Albany. She had no apprehension about going home with a stranger; at least she'd never have to go back to that dump in the Adirondacks.

Even hung over, she was a pretty seventeen-year-old who could pass for legal. With silky, straight black hair, hanging down to a firm butt, a solid body with ample breasts for a girl her size, when she walked down the street, men's heads turned.

To Jean, life was simple. It was supposed to be a party. Her wants were few. She got off on doing drugs, having sex, and drinking, and had little time or concern for anything else. She didn't worry about the future. *I'm never going to get to be an old hag like my mother. I'm going to party and die young.*

She was amazed Leshawn hadn't put a move on her. She would have had no problem having sex with him, but he kept saying some guy named Night wanted her, that he would get her anything she asked for. Now she had a room of her own, with all the booze and drugs she wanted.

"Well, Mr. Night, sounds good to me, no more Gretta and no more school," she said aloud. *I wonder what my friends will think when they find out I'm a professional partier?*

There was no way Gretta could find her trail. Hell, Leshawn had even called her mother and told her to stay out of it.

The only thing left was turning on Night, and Jean knew just how to do that. *This is going to be so fucking cool.*

Book I
Chapter 10
Albany, New York—May

Detective Ed Woldman pushed open the heavy steel doors and stepped into the morgue at the Albany Medical Center. He was there to attend the autopsy of the male body fished out of the Hudson River the previous day. Attending autopsies was one of the least favorite tasks of a police detective. Over the years, he had stood by and watched a couple dozen of these dissections, and while he could tolerate them, today's festivities would certainly be one of the worst.

"Good morning, you must be Detective Woldman," said a diminutive woman dressed in surgical scrubs.

"Yes, I am. Are you Doctor Carter?"

She curtly nodded her head. "I'll be conducting the autopsy, today; if you could go into the men's locker room and put on these scrubs and face shield, we can begin." She handed him a plastic bag containing all of the protective clothing and equipment for an autopsy to protect the wearer from bodily fluids.

Woldman donned his gear in the locker room and tried to figure out Doctor Carter. Louise Carter, like many doctors who specialize in cutting apart dead bodies, was an odd person. *She probably doesn't have much of a sex drive and lives alone with a cat, reading books and watering her house plants.* She was certainly a nerdish-looking woman. Her eyeglasses were ten years out of style, and her short haircut didn't fit any of today's looks. While she was small, she certainly did not have a body or the sort of looks that would bring out any sense of desire in most men.

Woldman struggled with the surgical outfit. His pants were barely large enough to go over his service weapon. He would never leave his sidearm unattended, and the drawstring of the pants was a tight fit over the holstered 9mm Glock 17 he carried every day.

After finally wrestling the pants on and donning the clear plastic face mask, he left the locker room and entered the autopsy chamber, where he found

Dr. Carter standing over a stainless steel tray filled with various wicked look-ing surgical instruments. The room was impeccably clean, but Woldman's nose detected the faint odors he always noticed in the autopsy chamber—alcohol and decaying flesh.

She looked up as he entered and flipped the switch on a microphone hanging from the ceiling. "Let's begin," she said, as the tape recorder preserved her every word. "Male subject, Caucasian, height five-foot-nine, weight of re-mains, one hundred, twenty pounds. Body retrieved from the Hudson River near the Port of Albany. Body has an advanced degree of saponification, as evidenced from the condition of the external tissue and low mass weight of the remains. Some unusual tissue damage is evident in the neck area, probably due to fish or crustaceans feeding on the body."

As the doctor droned on in her detached monotone voice, Woldman thought about what he was seeing. He always felt, in a way, that what they were doing here was very disrespectful to the dead person. The doctors in an au-topsy would cut the body up without any apparent hesitation, including skin-ning the persons face back to expose the skull, and then sawing it open with a small circular electric saw. The part that always got to Woldman, however, was when they started taking the organs out of the body and flopping them onto a hanging scale, like a butcher weighing out a hunk of meat.

To these doctors, it was nothing unusual, just another day's work. Hell, they would finish, wash their hands, and go eat lunch!

"Okay, making the incision to expose the internal organs," Carter said, as she made the "Y" incision, cutting from the left and right shoulders to the center of the chest, and then a long cut down to the pubic area. As her scalpel punctured the body cavity, Woldman heard the hiss of gas escaping, shortly before his nose picked up a putrid stench that made him think about puking.

Nearly an hour went by, as Woldman listened to Carter rattling on about the weight of each organ she removed from the body and the condition of each. Other than the obvious indications that the deceased certainly didn't take the best care of himself, there was no indication of how he died. None of the inter-nal organs had shown any signs of damage. Woldman was getting frustrated, until Carter took the heart out and weighed it.

"The victim's heart shows no evidence of trauma; weight is...just a min-ute, the weight is somewhat low." Carter removed the heart from the scale and dropped it in a dissection pan. She sliced the heart in half, laterally with a scalpel. "Here is something unusual, detective."

"What's that, doctor?"

"It appears that our victim has been drained of blood. I should have noticed it with some of the other organs. I didn't make the connection, until I weighed his heart. See here, there should be congealed blood in the chambers of his heart, but there is none. We'll get a better understanding, when we look at the major arteries in the brain."

She then picked up a smaller scalpel and sliced around the victim's forehead. After peeling the mushy skin back, she used a circular saw with a three-inch blade to cut the top of the man's skull off. This was the part that Woldman truly hated.

"Oh my, it looks like he has some company."

"Company?"

"Yes, look here, detective," she said, as she took a pair of forceps and pulled a wiggling baby eel from the inside of the skull.

At this point, Woldman's composure went south. He barely had time to get the nearest wastebasket before he threw up. From the corner of his eye, he saw Carter snickering at the sight of a big, tough detective losing his last meal.

After the entertainment, Carter removed the brain. It also did not weigh enough. The eel had eaten some of the flesh, but not enough to account for the low weight.

"It appears to me, detective, that this person was virtually drained of blood before he entered the river. Given the state of decay of external tissue, it is impossible to say how; the neck area looks ragged, but that could have been fish and crayfish eating the flesh, but I would say this man has definitely been murdered, although I have no idea how."

"Great, doctor, that's where I come in."

Book I
Chapter II
New York City—May

Father Diego Riverez walked into the Port Authority Bus Terminal via the 8th Avenue entrance. He pulled his New York Yankee's cap down over his bald head. The cap was his trade mark, and although it was not something that would typically be worn by a priest, his boss, Father D'Arcy, didn't mind. In fact, D'Arcy usually bought Riverez a new one each year for a birthday present. The only thing D'Arcy had ever objected to regarding the Yankees was that Riverez often said, "I can't bless George Steinbrenner," every time the team's owner did something he didn't like.

He was at the cruddy bus station on an errand for D'Arcy, to see if he could find information on a girl who had run away from her Upstate home. Riverez really liked working for Darcy and would never refuse him a favor, even if it meant going into the middle of one of New York City's least attractive places.

As Riverez entered the bus station, he scanned the lobby area for Moon. Moon was a street person who, for some strange reason, had the delusion that he was one of the Space Shuttle astronauts. His real name was Billy McDonald, and he had gone insane when his wife divorced him. On the day she told him she was leaving, he and the rest of the world sat watching the reports of the ill-fated Space Shuttle Challenger. From that day on, McDonald always talked about taking the shuttle to the moon, so much so, the rest of the people on the street gave him the name.

In reality, Moon was just one more person in need of mental health care who was forced to live on the streets because he could no longer function. He would occasionally go to St. Cecilia's Mission for food.

Riverez ran the Mission's food kitchen and was familiar with Moon and many of the other homeless who ate there. He hoped Moon or one of the others might have seen the missing girl at the bus station, or might know someone who had. A girl showing up in the city without a place to stay or any money would only end up with a pimp or worse.

Riverez found Moon sleeping along the south wall of the bus station. Riverez shook his shoulder. "Moon, wake up, I need to talk to you."

"Father, what are you doing here?" Moon said, coming to consciousness fairly quickly.

"I need to know something. Did you see a pretty girl, about seventeen years old, with a Stone Temple Pilots T-shirt come through here? She came off the Trailways bus from the Adirondacks." Riverez reached inside his jacket and produced a small school photo Father Ryan had given him. " This is her picture."

"I seen her. I seen this girl, Father. She went off with Leshawn."

"Who's Leshawn, Moon?"

"Leshawn is bad, Father, you don't want to go near Leshawn."

"I have to talk to him, Moon, where can I find him?"

"He's bad. Really, really bad, Father; we should leave him alone."

"Listen to me, I have to talk to him, can you show me where he lives?"

"I can show you, Father, just promise me you won't tell him."

"I promise, Moon, now please take me there."

Riverez and Moon set off on foot through one of the worst parts of the city to a seedy apartment building. Moon, true to his word, left in a hurry after showing Riverez where he could find Leshawn.

Riverez walked up the two flights that led to the apartment, stepping over a bum passed out on the second-story landing. The hallway smelled of vomit and urine and had not seen a new coat of paint in decades. The old woodwork and wallpaper probably dated back to the 1940s and had not been changed since. Leshawn's door was easy to find. It looked like it belonged on the wall of a fortress, built of steel, complete with a sliding peephole.

A trickle of sweat slid down Riverez's neck, as he tentatively knocked on the door. The peephole slid back, and the top half of a black man's face appeared.

"What the hell you want?" the face asked.

"I'm Father Riverez, from St. Cecilia's, and I need to speak with Leshawn."

"Nobody here by that name," the face replied, as the peep hole slid shut.

Riverez knocked on the door again. This time the door opened and a large black man, dressed in baggy jeans and a basketball jersey stepped out into the hall. "Listen, I don' care if you is a priest. I told you ain't nobody here by that name. Now get the hell out of here."

"Listen to me," Riverez said, "I need to know about a girl who came here. She had a Stone Temple Pilot's T-shirt, and Leshawn met her at the bus station."

"I told you, ain't no Leshawn, and ain't no girl," the man said.

At this point, Riverez should have known better and left. Although he had dabbled in boxing when he was a kid, at five-feet, four-inches, he was no match for a man this size, but the brave little priest would not give up. "I am not leaving until I get some answers."

The black man went into a rage, punching Riverez in the face, before shoving him down the stairs to the second floor landing, right on top of the sleeping bum.

When Riverez came to, he had dried blood all over his face from a broken nose and a cut above his eye.

He stood up and looked up the stairs, only this time, he knew better than to knock.

Book I
Chapter 12
Wilmington, New York—May

Nicholas Bonecutter awoke from yet another uneasy sleep, covered in sweat. Like most soldiers who see the horrors of war, Bonecutter's dreams never went away, no matter how many people told him he did the right thing. It was okay, though; it was time to wake up. He sat up in the rustic pine bed he had built himself and then stepped into the leather slippers Father John had bought him for Christmas and padded down the hallway.

He made a pot of coffee in his battered old percolator and let Sadie out for her morning constitutional. The old coffee pot was Grandfather's, and like most of Grandfather's things, he couldn't bear to throw it out. Although he often thought it would be nice to have a modern coffee maker and have coffee ready for him when he woke up.

Today was one of his favorite days as a guide, his semi-annual trip with Father John for salmon. Ryan loved fly fishing; although truth be told, he wasn't very good at it. They would always catch fish, though, because Nick was a much better guide than Ryan was a fisherman.

He had tied up a bunch of his own version of the Gray Ghost streamer fly, which he dubbed the Bouquet Ghost, named for the stream they usually fished. Ryan insisted on using that fly to fish the landlocked salmon run there each spring, because he had caught his first salmon with it. Ryan could have caught that salmon on any of a dozen fly patterns, but Nicholas always humored him and made sure he tied up a few. No matter how many flies Ryan lost with his sloppy casting, Nick would always have plenty available.

Sadie's bark announced Ryan's presence in the driveway.

"Good morning Adirondack Guide," Ryan said.

"Good morning, your holiness."

"How's the river looking this morning?" Ryan poured himself a cup of coffee.

"Oh I think we can find you a fish or two Father."

"Well, shouldn't we get going?"

"What's the hurry? The fish will be there." Every year the priest said the same thing. He was always in a hurry to get to the stream. What he lacked in skill he made up for in enthusiasm.

"Breakfast will be ready in a minute or two. Why don't you feed Sadie, while I cook the eggs?" When Ryan did not reply Bonecutter asked, "something wrong Father?

"We've been having some problems with one of our local teenagers."

"Who's that, Father?

"Jean Van Nostrand, Gretta's daughter. They come to church. If you showed up a little more often you'd know them."

"I told you, I pray in the woods. Besides, I did come to church last Christmas Eve."

"I'm sure the good Lord will take that into account. It appears that Gretta's daughter took off for New York City."

"Sounds like a standard runaway kid story, Father."

"Well, it's a runaway kid story that I need some help with, because my friend, Father Riverez, got himself beat up looking for her. Seems she hooked up with some bad people, and I was hoping you could go down there with me and look for her."

"Sounds like something for the cops, Father, and I'm no cop."

"No you're not, but you are a karate teacher, and an ex-Navy SEAL. You have skills that could be very handy in dealing with the people who hurt Father Riverez."

"Let's just get in the truck and go fishing."

"Okay, we'll talk some more about this on the river. Is Sadie going in the driftboat with us?"

"It's pretty hard not to take her. She likes to go in the boat."

Not another word was spoken on the half hour ride to the Bouquet River. The three companions rode in Bonecutter's old Chevy pickup, with Sadie in the middle, leaning against Ryan. All the way there, the priest rattled on about the big salmon he had caught the year before. Nick had heard the story a dozen times since spring. Every time the story was told, the fish got a little bigger.

At the river, they met with a friend of Nick's who shuttled the truck downstream to where they would take the boat out. After helping the priest hook up his life jacket, Bonecutter launched the McKenzie driftboat, and they headed downstream. It took about half an hour to drift to the first pool where they would fish.

"Okay, Father, the fish should be holding in the seam where the current meets the slack water in the pool right there. You need to cast a little upstream, towards that big rock, and let the fly drift down through that seam."

Ryan worked out enough fly line to reach the rock, and after a couple of false casts, dropped the fly into the water. His first drift was a little off the mark, and the fly didn't go through the seam. His second, third, and fourth casts were also off the mark. Nicholas was very patient with him, as he was with all his clients, and finally, Ryan landed the fly in the right spot. As the fly drifted through the seam, a ten-pound female landlocked salmon grabbed it and the fight was on.

"There's one," Ryan shouted, giggling like a schoolboy who had just found a dollar bill on the sidewalk in front of the candy store.

"Take your time, Father, the fish will come in when it's ready. If it wants to run, let it run."

Ryan frantically reeled in line, trying to gain line on the fish, as it turned and ran towards him.

"Keep the rod tip high, Father. Let that fish run when it comes by you."

"We'll get him, Nick. We'll get him."

After an exciting battle that lasted ten minutes (yet given the little priest's history of embellishing fishing stories, the battle would probably be stretched out to half an hour at some point in the future), the fish was finally brought to the net. Nicholas used a small pair of pliers to work the fly from the salmon's jaw and gently worked the fish back and forth in the water to revive it before letting it go.

"Oh, Nicholas, if my grandfather up in Heaven sees us letting this salmon go he's liable to come down here and kick me right in the ass."

"It's better to let the hen fish go. They create tomorrow's fishing. If we get a male, you can keep him for the grill."

"That salmon would have looked good on my office wall."

"We can get a fiberglass reproduction made if you want; there's no need to kill the fish. I measured her with the scale on the net before I let her go."

"Well, you're the guide. Now, getting back to that New York City problem, I really would appreciate it if you could come with me and see if we can find out where Gretta's daughter is."

"Father, we've already been through all this. I'm not a cop."

"Listen, sometimes the police can't or won't help, and this is one of those times. You're the only one I know who can help me. Now, are you coming, or do I go by myself?"

That was all it took. Bonecutter did not want to get in a fight. Ryan was a typical Irishman, as stubborn as the day was long. If he didn't go, Ryan certainly would go himself, and the thought of anything happening to his friend Father Ryan was enough to get him involved.

"Father, if we do this, I'm in charge. You do what I say, when I say it."

"Wouldn't have it any other way…after all, you're the guide," Ryan said. Then he lit up a celebratory cigar.

Book I
Chapter 13
Albany, New York—May

Aaron Tulley lay on what he figured would be his death bed. Tulley had lived his entire eighty five years in the Arbor Hill section of Albany. He was born there, went to school there, married and raised his six children there, and now he was going to die there.

Tulley had a simple life. He had never owned a car and took a bus to his job in the canon factory in nearby Watervliet. Although he never had much money, he worked hard and did an admirable job of providing for his family. While his wife and children did not live in the lap of luxury, no one ever went to bed hungry, either.

Tulley's wife Lorretta had died five years before of heart failure. His children repaid him for their upbringing by abandoning him in his Golden Years. Tulley, a man who prided himself in never taking a handout from anybody was now a ward of the taxpayers of Albany County. His house and what little money he had in the bank was taken by the county to pay for his care, when they sent him to the adult home. Everything he had worked so hard for was now gone.

Although he was bedridden, his mind was still sharp. He played chess with several of the other residents and was usually the winner of his matches. He'd only managed an eighth grade education but had a natural aptitude for strategy and thinking ahead of the game.

Like many people his age, Tulley rarely slept well. He quickly woke at the sound of the doorknob to his private room turning. The glowing hands on his old alarm clock showed the time was 2:45 a.m. He was relieved to see Tommy Jackson, the night orderly.

"Tom, what are you doing here so late?"

"Just checking on you, Mr. Tulley," Jackson replied, "Doctor says you have to take some medicine."

"What medicine? I already took my pills."

"I don't know, Mr. Tulley, I think it's for your liver problem. As soon as you take the medicine, you can go back to sleep."

"Okay, Tommy, give me the pills."

"No pills, Mr. Tulley, it's a liquid. Let me help you sit up."

Jackson handed the old man a small cup of white liquid, and waited until he swallowed it, then helped him lie back down.

"Is something wrong, Tommy? You seem like something's bothering you."

"Nah, Mr. Tulley, everything's just fine." Jackson stepped back from the bed and continued to watch his patient.

Tulley immediately knew something was very wrong. He started losing sensation in his arms and legs. "Whaaaa," was all he could say, as he began to panic, before the paralysis crept its way up to his face and neck.

At 6:00 a.m., Aaron Wendell Tulley was found dead in his bed by the morning shift nurse. The doctor on duty that morning signed his death certificate, citing natural causes due to advanced age. As a ward of the county, Tulley's body was sent to the Arbor Hill Funeral Home, whose director, Mr. La Baptiste, was kind enough to provide free service for poor folks who did not have money to pay for a funeral.

Shortly after Aaron Tulley took his last Cadillac ride, Tommy Jackson sat on the floor of his rundown apartment, shooting his "bonus" into his arm, waiting for the sweet high of the heroin he could feel coursing through his veins. Waiting for it to dim the memory of what he had done the night before to get it.

Book I
Chapter 14
Albany, New York—May

Armand La Baptiste returned to his apartment on the second floor of the Arbor Hill Funeral Home, after attending a night meeting of the Civic Association. La Baptiste was active in his community, although he always limited his role to the background of any project. He occasionally attended a meeting, but for the most part, was rarely seen by anyone outside the funeral home. Tonight's meeting was for a subcommittee discussion on establishing a new Charter School in the neighborhood. He was there to make a donation for the building. La Baptiste always made it a point to give generous donations to the local scene wherever he lived. That way, the locals would always be on his side if the authorities ever took an interest in him.

As he walked into the apartment, he loosened his tie and removed his jacket. La Baptiste wore only the finest imported silk suits. He played his part well around the city, right down to being seen driven around town by his assistant Willie, in the his jet black Mercedes. To those who lived in the neighborhood, he was the best thing that ever happened to the place, a wealthy businessman who helped out the community.

His apartment was well decorated and very neat. Expensive paintings adorned the walls, and the furniture was the finest French Provincial that money could buy. The apartment had several rooms, including a kitchen a chef would be proud of, complete with a full dining room adjacent to it, a pair of bedrooms, and a large study off the living room. Clearly, the funeral business had been good to La Baptiste.

He was glad to be home this evening, because the surprise Willie had arranged for him was waiting on the silk sheets in the master bedroom. A backwoods trailer queen had been delivered to him via the New York City operation. According to Willie, she was extremely beautiful, and best of all, her presence here was not traceable. La Baptiste had been shown a picture of the girl in advance of her arrival. She was seventeen, with long dark hair and a tight young body. Just the way he liked them.

He went into the adjoining bedroom, stripped off his clothes, and donned a silk robe. He returned to the dining room's small bar and poured a drink for himself and his guest, then carried the liquor to the elaborate master bedroom, complete with a canopied four-post bed with intricately carved headboard and chandelier.

"Hello, I am Armand La Baptiste," he said, drinks in hand, entering the bedroom. "I am your host here." The girl stirred and smiled at him. He stood there admiring the girl's body. Her legs were perfect, and she looked stunning in her new lingerie. Her eyes were dilated. Obviously, she'd been enjoying some free samples of the product.

"Hi, my name's Jean Van Nostrand."

"Wonderful. Is there anything we can get you, Jean? Anything else that you require?"

"No, everything's been great."

"Now, Jean, I know you had some difficulties at home, and this is why you left. I must advise you that, while you are now an adult and quite free here, there is one rule that you must follow."

"What's that, Mr. La Baptiste?"

"Loyalty, my young Jean. I demand the total loyalty of my friends and associates, and this will include you. My true business is a secret, as is my life. If you follow this rule and never compromise my security, you will be welcome here for as long as you wish to stay. While you are here, you shall have everything you will need or want."

"I understand, Mr. La Baptiste."

"Very good." He opened the robe. He was a small man, but had a very muscular chest, which was obviously shaved clean. "Let us get to know each other."

The girl reached up and embraced him. Her smile was hollow. Clearly, she liked sex, and the drugs would keep her spirit up for the duration of her session. She was but one more of many, but La Baptiste still smiled. Willie had done very well this time and would be justly rewarded.

La Baptiste softly kissed her neck, and licked the lobe of her ear.

The girl recoiled slightly from the coldness of his touch, before giving him a look of surrender.

"Oh, and Jean," he said, "there is one more thing that I will require."

"What's that, Mr. La Baptiste?"

"This." His brutally strong hand yanked the girl's hair, pulling her head back, nearly snapping her neck and exposing her tender throat. His face contorted into a gaze of evil lust, as he sank his fangs into her jugular vein, laughing at her pathetic struggling, as the hot blood gushed into his mouth.

Jean's eyes grew wide in horror as she struggled to get away. This was real. He was some kind of monster right out of the horror movies. Yet she couldn't get away; he was too strong. Soon her fear melted. Suddenly, the horrible thing he was doing felt wonderful. She felt an ecstasy far better than the best sex she'd ever experienced. She ceased her struggling and closed her eyes, surrendering completely, as she felt the life drain from her throat.

"Oh, Jean, we shall have such fun together, you and I," La Baptiste said, as he pulled her silk negligee off with one swift rip.

* * *

Willie Robinson worked alone in the basement of the funeral home, while his master took his pleasure with the girl. He didn't mind. He too had suffered La Baptiste's bite. Willie had no homosexual aspirations, but being bitten by the master was one of the most sensual experiences that he'd ever had. He, like others bitten by the master, was bound to him. Willie did his bidding without hesitation....without question, and so would the young slut upstairs, once she woke in the morning.

Willie thought of himself as better than the others, though. He was La Baptiste's lieutenant. He was second only to the master. He not only directed the drug operation, but also saw to the procurement and disposal of the master's food, as he was doing now.

Sure, the girl would amuse the master for awhile, but she would end up as all the others did. Shame, though, because she was too hot of a piece to be burned to ash and buried in the flower garden out back.

He hefted a body bag off the gurney and onto a table in the hidden room in the basement. The table was equipped with restraints and an attached intravenous bottle stand. He unzipped the bag. "Hello there, glad you could make it," he said to its occupant.

Aaron Tulley's seemingly sightless eyes, though unblinking, were fully functional. He thought he was having a bizarre nightmare as he looked into the light after being plunged into darkness. Tully, instead of seeing God or maybe his dead wife, saw a smiling black face and a lot of gold teeth. He would have screamed, if only he could find his voice.

Willie slid the body bag from underneath Tulley, and strapped him to the table. He skillfully inserted an intravenous needle into the vein in the back of Tulley's right hand, and started an IV drip. "Don't you worry none; we gonna take care of you here, just as good as they did at the nursing home, so don't you fret none."

Aaron Tulley was wheeled to the back of the room. His head flopped to the right, and he could see another table. His body had seemingly failed him, but his mind had not. Deep within the inner recesses of his brain, Tulley screamed a silent scream that could wake the dead. The face staring blankly at him from the next table was someone he knew. It was Joe Baird, his friend at the home who had died over a month ago.

Book I
Chapter 15
New York City—May

Nicholas and Father Ryan drove to New York City in Bonecutter's truck. The mood on the three-hour ride to the city was contentious. Nick had to cancel his guiding appointment for the day and would be out $250 dollars. Ryan, in his typical fashion, was also asking far too many questions.

"Why'd you bring that?" Ryan pointed to the bulge the Colt Model 1911 .45 caliber handgun made under Bonecutter's jacket.

"What happened to our deal, Father?"

"What deal?"

"The one that went something like, you do what I say, when I say it, without question. That deal."

"I remember."

"Listen, Father, I don't tell you how to save souls, so don't tell me how to do my thing. The handgun evens the odds. From the sound of it, we'll be dealing with some very nasty people. Most people won't beat up a priest. This guy has something to hide, most likely drugs, and he's sure to be armed. I don't want either of us meeting the big guy prematurely because I was unprepared. I'm doing you a big favor by looking for this girl. Once we cross the border into New York City, I'll be breaking the law, because my handgun permit isn't valid there. Only a resident can hold a permit. If I get caught, I'll end up in jail."

"Well, you know more about these things than I do. I'm just an old, country priest. Sometimes I forget about the stuff you know how to do."

"There are times when I would like to forget them too, Father."

Your problem is that you need to let go of the baggage, Nick. You were in a war, and you did what you had to. You were attacked by an enemy soldier, and God didn't want you to die. You had no way of knowing that soldier was a boy. Stop blaming yourself. A madman named Saddam Hussein was responsible for that boy's death, not you."

"You weren't there, Father. Unless you've been there, you'll never know what it's like. Let's talk about something else."

Bonecutter drove through the crowded Manhattan streets. He was amazed by what he saw. New York City reminded him of the cruddy cities he had visited in various third world countries. Burned out buildings, trash and garbage everywhere, not to mention the human debris—the winos and the hookers. Get off the main drag, and the place was a war zone, and this was supposed to be the nice part.

"All right, Nick, you need to turn left here, this is St. Cecelia's."

Bonecutter drove through the iron gates into the parking lot. The two walked directly to the building that housed the rectory and priests' quarters. Ryan knocked on the large oak door and was greeted by a Hispanic priest with a face full of bruises.

"Father Riverez, are you all right? I'm very sorry that I got you into this."

"I'll be okay, Father; it looks a lot worse than it is." Father D'Arcy is waiting in his office, upstairs and on the left." Riverez pointed the way.

"Father Riverez, this is Nicholas Bonecutter."

"Good to meet you, Mr. Bonecutter. This way, gentlemen."

As the three entered D'Arcy's office, it was apparent that they were not getting a red carpet welcome. It was obvious from the look on his face that D'Arcy was not happy with his buddy Father Ryan.

"Bill, how are you?" Ryan asked.

"You know me well enough to know how I am. I'm pissed off, that's how I am."

"Look, I had no way of knowing the girl took up with some rough customers. I'm very sorry that Father Riverez got hurt."

"I barely have enough priests to run this place. I can't afford to have them get tossed down a flight of stairs. To make things worse, the cops can't do a thing about it because there were no witnesses. When they went to the apartment, the people told them that the guy renting it had moved out."

"We'll take up the search from here."

"What the hell do you mean by that? Are you trying to tell me that you two are going back to that apartment and see if you can't get yourselves thrown down the stairs too, John?"

"I'm sure that won't happen, just give us the address."

"No. Not this time, you don't. I'm not letting someone else get hurt."
D'Arcy slammed himself down in his chair.

"Nick can handle situations like this, just give us the address."

D'Arcy stared at the cold, dark eyes of Nicholas Bonecutter, shrugged
and gave up. He'd spent his whole life trying to read people's faces, and in this
case, there was something in those eyes that told him his friend Ryan was right.
"Here, take it," he said, taking a small scrap of paper from his desk and handing it to Ryan, "but I'm not responsible for anything that happens."

It took Bonecutter and Ryan ten minutes to walk to the bus station and
about that much longer to reach the apartment building. Ryan was about to
step off the sidewalk to enter the building, when Bonecutter gently, but firmly
grasped his left elbow. "Smile, Father, we have to take a little walk first. Remember, do what I say."

The two walked up the street and turned to the right. At Bonecutter's
insistence they stopped at a grimy coffee shop and sat down and ordered hot
dogs.

Ryan was already growing impatient with the cloak and dagger stuff.
"Why the hell are we eating hotdogs instead of doing what we came here to
do?"

"Father, this is the last time I am going to explain things, so here goes.
We're going around the block to check the building out. In case you hadn't
noticed, a half- Indian and a priest kind of stand out in this neighborhood.
You also probably didn't notice that we're being followed. The guy sitting two
booths back was on the front steps of the apartment when we walked by. He
tailed us all the way around the block. This looks like a drug operation, and
he's the lookout for the drug dealer.

"If they're watching the place, how are we going to get in?"

"We have a saying in the SEALS: we're going in the back door."

Four hours later, after the sun had set, the two made their way back
through the rundown neighborhood to the back side of the building. Bonecutter hoisted the little priest up on top of a garbage dumpster and up the fire
escape ladder. They climbed the landing one floor below the apartment they
were interested in. As he looked up, Nicholas pointed to the lights above them
and whispered, "looks like someone's home."

The target apartment had lights on, but there was no sign of any activity.
Bonecutter put his finger to his lips and whispered, "Stay here," in the priest's

ear. He then stood on the railing of the fire escape landing and pulled himself up along the outside metal frame, instead of climbing the stairs.

As he hung by his fingers three floors above the pavement, he peeked over the next landing and saw what he was looking for in the dim light outside the apartment window. A security camera was covering the area of the landing where someone climbing or descending the fire escape would be. There was also a trip wire at the top of the landing. Bonecutter pulled himself up the railing to the security camera and gently turned it to point upward. He held his position for a couple of minutes. *Good, they aren't watching the camera. Now for the backup plan.* He hoisted himself over the railing and gently felt along the wire. It was connected to a small junction box, which most likely led to an alarm in the apartment. After disabling the trip wire, he motioned for Father Ryan to join him on the landing.

His final obstacle was the steel mesh grating over the apartment window. He peered in the window to make sure no one was near and took a tiny hand-held cutting torch from his pocket. His task was made easier by the fact that the grating and its frame were connected to the building by only four bolts. He cut each of them as Ryan held the grating. The window on the apartment wasn't even locked, and they simply slipped it open and quietly climbed inside.

The room they had entered was a bedroom; but it was clear to Bonecutter that it was a prop. Nobody's bedroom looked that neat. There were always clothes, or an ashtray, or some other sign of use. This bedroom was clearly just in case anyone ever looked in the window. Once he entered into the apartment, he stood and listened for a full minute before taking another step. It was pretty clear from the sounds coming from the other side of the door, where the occupants of the apartment were, and what they were doing. He could easily hear a symphony of grunts and groans from what could best be described as a raucous sex session in the back room.

"Stay here," Bonecutter whispered, as he gently eased open the bedroom door. He crept along the carpeted hall in a crouch, the .45 pointed ahead of him, which now had a very illegal silencer attached to it. As he made his way down the hall, he saw a flickering light coming from what he guessed was a candle.

The couple was on the couch, in the middle of the room, and he silently crept his way to the back of the sofa.

"Oh, Leshawn, give it to me, baby," the woman groaned. The large black man was apparently deep in concentration on the task at hand, because all he could manage in reply was a grunt as he thrust his hips, entering her even more deeply. Just as he was making his next thrust, Bonecutter smashed the butt of his pistol into the base of his skull, knocking him cold, and then shoved his gloved hand over the mouth of the sixteen year-old Chinese girl under him.

"Do not make a sound." He shoved the man off the girl and onto the floor. He took out a set of plastic handcuffs and tied the girl's hands behind her back and slapped a strip of duct tape over her mouth. Then he used another set of plastic cuffs and bound the man's hands and feet together.

After sweeping through the rest of the apartment, he went back to the bedroom. He reached in his pocket and produced a ski mask, handing it to Ryan. "Father," he whispered, "get this mask on and don't call me by name or say anything, just stand there. Oh, and here, hold the gun like you know what you are doing. I want him to have no idea who we are, or what we want."

"What are you going to do?" Ryan asked.

"Search the place and find out what this guy's hiding."

After twenty minutes of searching, Bonecutter came back with several bags filled with packets of a substance that looked like powdered sugar, as well as several vials, some other drug paraphernalia, three handguns, and a wicked looking 12 gauge Winchester pump shotgun rigged with a folding stock and a magazine extender. He also found a safe, well hidden in the closet, and using an electronic device that could detect the click of the lock's tumblers, he unloaded around $300,000 in cash from it.

Ryan was relieved when Nick returned from the back rooms of the apartment. He had never fired a gun and wasn't comfortable being around two buck naked people trussed up like Thanksgiving turkeys.

Bonecutter dumped a bucket of ice water on the man's genitals, rudely waking him from the nap he'd been given. The man looked wildly at Nicholas and would have screamed at him, were it not for the duct tape gag on his mouth. In spite of the cuffs, the guy leaned forward to attack Bonecutter but stopped when the muzzle of the .45 was pressed into his forehead. Bonecutter pushed the silencer against the skin so hard it left a mark.

"It's simple, if you want to live, you do what I say," Nick said to the man. "I'm going to take the tape off, and if you know what's good for you, you're not going to make any noise." Then he ripped the tape off the black man's mouth.

"Who the hell are you?" the black man asked. "You ain't no cop, so what the fuck you want?"

"I ask the questions, you give the answers," Bonecutter replied.

"I ain't gonna tell you nothing!"

"I figured that was what you would say, Leshawn."

"How'd you know my name?"

"Like I said, Leshawn, I'll ask the questions. I know a lot of things about you, including the fact that your father's name is Frank, your mother's name is Aretha, just like Aretha Franklin. You've been in and out of jail for many years. Now, Leshawn, do you own a computer?"

"Man, if you here to steal a computer, you in the wrong place."

"That's too bad, because they can do wonderful things, but like anything else in the wrong hands, they can cause a man a lot of trouble."

"Look you sonofabitch, you didn't come here to talk about no computers, what's your game?"

"Well, my man it's like this. I need to know something. If you tell me what I want to know, we're just going to leave. If you don't, I have a little computer geek friend who is going to turn your life upside down."

At this point, Leshawn started laughing, "What the hell can you and some fool with a computer do to me?"

"Dude, you aren't the brains of this drug operation. When I leave, all of this stuff goes with me. And guess what? My little computer buddy is going to create an offshore account for about $200,000 grand in your name. He's also going to book an airline flight for you and your honey, here, and leave an electronic trail that your boss will easily follow right to you. Is your boss an understanding guy?"

Leshawn went from amused to terror stricken in a second. All he could think of was what La Baptiste had done to Deusler. The man didn't put up with big mistakes; mess with him and you paid, and paid large. He was dead either way. If this guy took the dope and set up the bank account and plane ticket, he was dead. If he took off and ran, he was dead. Leshawn knew the only thing he could do was try and cut a deal. "What you wanna know?" he asked.

"A girl came through here about a week ago. Her name is Jean, and I want to know where she is."

"She in Albany, at the Man's place."

"Where in Albany?"

"Arbor Hill Funeral Home, but you'd be smart to let it go and stay away from there."

"Thanks, Leshawn, I'm glad we could do business. By the way, if you call him and tell him we're coming, you won't live very long. I have many friends and have left word with them about you. If anything like that happens, you will die within a week. Besides, you're smart enough to know that if I don't get your boss, he's gonna get you." With that, Bonecutter and the astounded priest left the apartment the way that they had come in.

Book I
Chapter 16
Albany, New York—May

The ride up the state thruway from New York City to Albany turned out to be the toughest the two lifelong companions had taken in their quest to find Jean Van Nostrand. Most of the disagreement was over what Nick had done back in New York.

"Look, Father John, you dragged me into this."

"That's true, but I had no idea we were going to kidnap people, and point guns at them. Where the hell did you learn to do all of that stuff? I thought you were in the Navy. We just committed a crime, or several!"

"Father, you know damn well I was a Navy SEAL."

"What do Navy SEALS have to do with the things that we just did? Soldiers don't break into people's apartments," Ryan said.

"Father, I can't tell you exactly what I did. I can only talk about the things that are now common knowledge. During the 1980s, our government recognized that terrorists were a major threat to this country, and an elite unit of Navy SEALS was trained in counter-terrorism interdiction."

"But terrorists take over airplanes and hijack ships."

"No, Father, terrorists do a lot more than that. We trained to board hijacked cruise ships, to sneak onto captured offshore oil rigs, to hunt down stolen nuclear material, and many other things that didn't make the papers at the time, and, oh yeah, we were also trained to go after large-scale drug czars."

"Why would the Navy go after drugs?"

"Because many terrorist organizations and foreign governments have tried to destroy the United States from within, by dumping tons of cheap cocaine and heroin on us."

"But the Navy can't operate in the United States on something like that, can they?"

"No, they can't. There's a section of the Constitution that forbids it, but we did go into other countries and hit some major drug operations that the terrorists were involved with," Bonecutter said.

"So that's how you knew what to look for in the apartment."

"That and more, Father, a whole lot more."

"What do you mean...more?"

"I knew how to get that guy to talk and tell us where the girl is, without hurting him. A guy like that has only one major fear, and it overrides all of the other smaller fears, like me shooting him for instance. They're scared to death of crossing their bosses because the drug trade is ruthless. Using his fear was the only way we'd ever find Jean without tipping off the next guy up the ladder."

"I just wish you'd told me what you were doing. I thought you were going to shoot that guy."

"Father, we had a deal. You do what I say, and not ask questions. If I'd told you what I was going to do, you wouldn't have gone along with it.

"What the hell else did you learn in the Navy?" Ryan asked.

"That's classified information, Father; besides, I'm not in the Navy anymore, I'm a fishing guide."

"Well, you're not a very good one. That last salmon only weighed nine pounds," the diminutive priest said with a twinkle in his eye.

"That was a nice fish, besides which, the one you lost was bigger."

"Well, I didn't have good instructions from my guide!"

With that, the two rode the rest of the way to Albany in silence, having reached an unspoken understanding about what they had done, and more importantly, what they were about to do.

Book I
Chapter 17
Albany, New York—May

Detective Ed Woldman had a mystery on his hands. The autopsy proved that he had a murder victim. Dental identification of the body matched a missing person report for a social worker named Stephen Deusler. Woldman started really digging deep, trying to find out who the victim was and what he was all about.

In essence, Deusler was a loser. The son of a pair of wealthy downstate lawyers, Deusler had barely managed to squeak through college with a sociology degree, and then he had become one of thousands of nameless, faceless bureaucrats in the City of Albany. Deusler didn't have a criminal record or any major run-ins with the law, so tracking his past in that manner proved fruitless.

Woldman, unlike many of his peers, was a very patient investigator. He knew he could eventually get the truth out of a situation. Woldman went to Deusler's apartment, and more pieces of the picture emerged. He had found Deusler's college yearbook. In the book, it was obvious from the number of references Deusler's buddies made to partying or getting high that the guy liked his dope. The guy was no stranger to a variety of drugs.

Woldman knew that if Deusler was into drugs, there must be some sort of stash in the apartment. Deusler was quite clever, compared to most dopers who hid their stuff in their homes. Woldman eventually found what he was looking for on a bookshelf. One book title didn't fit in with the others. The book, ironically titled *Powers of the Mind*, had been cleverly hollowed out, and contained a small vial of what later proved to be cocaine, as well as a small mirror, a razor blade, and some other drug paraphernalia.

Okay, now we are getting somewhere. This dude liked his coke, and coke is too expensive for a social worker to make a regular habit out of. Woldman had seen enough cocaine during his experiences as a police officer. He knew how it wormed itself into a user's life and eventually destroyed it. The stuff was highly addictive, and most people eventually developed a habit they could no longer afford. Ironically, the best buzz these people ever got from the drug was the first time they used it. They ended up spending thousands of dollars and destroying their lives trying to recreate that initial euphoria.

After leaving the apartment, Woldman went to the Department of Social Services where Deusler worked. Once there, he was introduced to Janise Hattalia, Deusler's supervisor. Hattalia was a tough nut to crack and wouldn't give up information easily. She eventually said that Deusler's job record was nothing to write home about. Every one of his evaluations was satisfactory, but the comments his superiors had used conveyed no sense of great admiration for his work performance.

Hattalia, in her own way, made it clear that she didn't like Deusler at all, but she would not elaborate. She was a typical bureaucrat, instinctively protecting her agency, rather than spilling the beans. Woldman poked and probed at the wall she had quickly erected when he started asking questions, but he didn't get very far. She gave one word answers without any elaboration, but she obviously knew something.

He then asked to see Deusler's time and attendance records. Finally, he had what he was looking for. Deusler frequently took time off, too much time off. He was usually gone from his job on a Thursday or a Friday, nearly every week. "Tell me, Ms. Hattalia, did Deusler ever tell anyone where he went when he took these days off?"

"No, Detective, he wasn't specific. He told us he needed medical treatment and had to go to New York City several times a month to get it.

"Did he mention what the specific medical problem was?"

"No, he never told us why he had to be treated, and it's our policy not to ask. We would never refuse to allow an employee to use sick leave for a treatment program."

Woldman wondered how many employees had to take frequent eighteen-hole treatments at their favorite country club during the summer. He was very familiar with the work ethic of some civil servants. Next, he asked Hattalia to provide him with Deusler's personal financial records. Deusler had named his parents prime beneficiaries on his retirement system death benefit. At least the bum's parents wouldn't have to blow their own money to get him planted.

The rest of the financial records were also interesting. For a coke head, Deusler was prudent in saving for his retirement. He had money going into a 401K, and his investment was doing well. He had never borrowed against the account, either. He also had money going into the Civil Servants Credit Union each week.

Woldman then searched through Deusler's desk. The guy was basically a teenager who had never grown up. He had cartoon character coffee mugs, posters of the Grateful Dead and other rock bands. Hell, he even had a Gameboy in the top drawer that he must have played when things got slow.

Inside a file cabinet in his cubicle were the case files that Deusler was working on. Woldman took down the names and addresses of all the people Deusler was managing. Deusler's clients were mainly poor whites, living in crappy apartments, scattered throughout the city. He did not deal with people from the poor black neighborhoods.

Wait a minute.

Woldman yanked the top drawer open again, and looked at the matchbooks sitting in the pencil tray. There were several from the Arbor Hill Funeral Parlor.

Why's this guy going there?

It would make sense if he had clients in that section of the city and had to go to funerals at the home, but that wasn't the case.

Woldman pocketed the matchbook and left the office. His next stop was at Deusler's doctor's office. He used his badge to get past the receptionist and in to see the doctor. Deusler had been there several times recently, once or twice for simple stuff like the flu, but Deusler's most frequent medical problem was a persistent bloody nose that never went away. The doctor thought maybe Deusler picked it too much.

"Well, Doc, that was probably it, but he won't have to worry about it where he is now." He thanked the doctor and left.

Woldman spent the next couple of days running down the list of Deusler's social service clients. Most wouldn't say very much, but a couple hinted that they knew Deusler did drugs. One other client hinted that he saw Deusler selling drugs, as recently as a couple of years ago, although she thought he was no longer dealing.

Finally, Woldman hit a gold mine of information in the form of a drugged-out waste product named Frank Lavotti.

According to Deusler's file, Lavotti lived, breathed, and existed for only one purpose—to smoke pot. When Woldman knocked at the door, he could smell the weed on the guy's clothes.

The file said Lavotti had once been a promising reporter, but the years of heavy dope smoking had taken their toll. Today, he couldn't function in society well enough to keep a job. He was on welfare and had managed to find a doctor who was willing to put it in writing that he had a mental disability and couldn't work. Lavotti, even though he lived in a dump of an apartment and basically owned nothing, thought he had it made. He did what he wanted to all day, and the government gave him enough money to keep a roof over his head.

The one glitch in Lavotti's perfect world was that he needed his stuff, and that was the key to getting him to talk. Woldman knew a doper when he saw one and knew the guy had something to hide. Without warning, he pushed Lavotti square on his ass at the apartment doorway and entered the dingy, one bedroom apartment.

"Nice place you have here, Frank." He gazed at the filthy walls and furniture that wasn't fit for a thrift store.

"Look man, you gotta have a warrant to come in here. I'm gonna file charges. What's your badge number?"

Woldman took his badge case out of the inside pocket of his sport coat, and as Lavotti stood up, he took the badge, which he was holding in the palm of his hand, and smashed Lavotti in the face with it so hard that he ended up on his ass again.

"Look, Frank, let's get the rules straight, shall we? I ask the questions, and you give the answers. That way, I don't have to search your apartment for the dope you're probably growing here, or for your stash. Question number one, do you know a guy named Stephen Deusler?"

"Yeah, I know him; he's my social worker."

"That's very good, Frank, but he *was* your social worker, now he's a corpse. Question number two, was Deusler into drugs, and Frank, before you answer, he won't get mad if you tell me the truth, because he's six feet underground at the moment."

"He did some blow."

"Ah, very good, Frank. Now, question number three, how do you suppose that a guy like Deusler got enough money for an expensive habit like that?"

"Uh, I don't know; I guess maybe he must have been dealin' some."

"Excellent, Frank, now we're onto the bonus round; answer this one right, and maybe I won't beat the shit out of you and take you downtown. The

$64,000 question is, who did Deusler deal for? Maybe somebody at the Arbor Hill Funeral home?"

"I don't know, man, honest, I don't know." Sweat instantly broke out on his forehead, and the quick shift of his bloodshot eyes was all Woldman needed to see. Even a rookie detective would have known he was lying. "Thanks, Frank, you've told me all I need to know."

"I didn't tell you nothing man, NOTHIN'!"

After Woldman walked out the door, Frank Lavotti sat down on the floor and cried for the first time since he was a child. He knew he wasn't going to be alive next week.

Book I
Chapter 18
Albany, New York—May

Armand La Baptiste and Willie sat at the dining room table in the lavishly decorated apartment over the Arbor Hill Funeral home. The dining room featured an antique grand buffet table along the east wall. A delicate French china cabinet and matching Louis XIV table and chair set rounded out the furniture in the room, where he and Willie were discussing business.

Willie served La Baptiste a glass of his favorite drink from a crystal decanter, and handed him his newspapers. La Baptiste flipped through the pages of the *New York Times*, *Wall Street Journal*, and the *Washington Post*, as he discussed the preparations for their latest venture, a major drug delivery to one of the old warehouses he had bought along the Hudson River. As he turned to page ten of the *Times*, he sat upright and turned the paper around to show Willie the picture. "Look, they have found the remnants of my Mexican Operation."

The article's headline read *Dig for Bodies Continues*. The Associated Press piece detailed a joint U.S./Mexican police venture to dig for the bodies of up to 100 missing persons, believed to be on a ranch in Ciudad Juarez. The DEA, FBI, and Mexican authorities had descended on the ranch by the dozens, digging everywhere. The excavation at the Ranch de la Campana, just across the river from El Paso, Texas, had yielded five bodies so far, but many more were believed to be there.

"Well, they shall find some of the throwaways, but never will they trace it to us, correct?"

"No, Mr. La Baptiste, I followed all of your instructions and took care of the place just like you said, when you sent me there. They may identify some of the stiffs, but I let the wild dogs and buzzards chew on 'em before I put them in the hole. Paperwork on the ranch won't come back to you. Left a trail to a low-level dealer in Mexico, just in case the cops get enough to start tracking someone down. The Juarez gang will be holding the bag if that happens,"

Willie said, referring to the Juarez drug smuggling operation run by Amado Carillo Fuentes, through various front men.

"Very good, Willie. As usual you have been most efficient in keeping my secrets. Pity about Senior Fuentes dying of blood loss during his heart surgery." A sly grin spread across his face. "Now, let us get on to new business. Will the shipment arrive at the warehouse on time tomorrow evening?"

"Yes, Mr. La Baptiste; the boat will leave New York harbor tomorrow morning on time."

"Good. Let's plan on having a little party when it arrives. Have some of our higher level distributors there, and I shall bring my new friend Jean along."

"Mr. La Baptiste, why are we gonna throw a party for the dealers? I thought you wanted to keep a low profile around town?"

"Willie, it is good that you think about security as much as you do. We have had an excellent working relationship over the years, profitable for us both, but you do not always get all of the information we need. I have received word that one of our best customers has sent some trouble our way, trouble in the form of a Detective Woldman."

"Who did it, Boss? I'll take care of it. I can whack him and bury his ass. I'll be back here by morning."

"All in due time, Willie; you must learn to be more patient, and you must also learn how to be a better businessman."

"How so, Mr. La Baptiste?"

"To run a successful business, one must turn problems around to one's advantage. Thus, even the greatest losses can be used in some way. The person who brought us this trouble will pay, but we will use him as an example. Our friend Mr. Deusler provided us with an excellent reinforcement of our security policies. The dealers will never talk to the police, or anyone else for that matter, but even that was not enough. You see, our customers also need an example as well. We have a loyal patron named Mr. Lavotti who enjoys our fine marijuana products. He shall be that example. Please see to it that you find him and personally invite him to our party."

"What about Woldman?"

"According to my sources, he can't be bought. I will use other means to secure his cooperation; now, please see that Mr. Lavotti is invited."

* * *

Outside the Arbor Hill Funeral Home, a bum sat on a park bench, drinking from a bottle wrapped in a brown paper bag. To passersby, he looked like many of the city's homeless. He wore a shabby Army surplus overcoat and matching trousers, both of which were torn and dirty. His hair and beard were unkempt, and his look was reminiscent of Charles Manson. He sat upright on his bench as a Catholic priest approached to check on his condition.

"How are you, my son?" asked the priest.

"Quite well, Father, would you care for a hit of Muscatel?"

"No thank you," the priest answered. "You know, my son, God does not mean for his children to live as you are."

" Okay, Father John, cut the crap. No one can hear us."

"I still don't see why we have to do all the cloak and dagger stuff, Nick."

"It's real simple. Look around you and tell me what you see."

"Well, most of the people on the street are black, if that is what you mean."

"That's exactly what I mean. It's pretty tough for two well-dressed white guys not to stand out in a black neighborhood. This is the only way I could think of to watch the funeral home without us standing out like two sore thumbs."

"Well, what have you found out?"

"Nothing much, although I had a lovely conversation with another of my people who calls herself Hattie. She has a wonderful hairstyle going for herself by the way."

"What did she say?"

"She said the owner of the funeral home, a Mr. La Baptiste is evil, and that he steals souls. Sure she probably has some serious mental problems, but I'm guessing that part of what she's saying is true. Chances are, she was trying to tell me that this guy is the local drug lord, which fits the pattern of what Jean VanNostrand's major interests are."

"That's no big surprise, so what do we do now?"

"We wait."

"What are we waiting for? Why don't we just do what we did in New York City; let's just go get her and head home."

"Look Father, I'm not going to tell you again, we do this my way. A guy named Sun Tsu told the world all about how to fight centuries ago, and we're going to keep with his philosophy on this one."

"What sort of Japanese wisdom are you talking about?"

"Sun Tsu was Chinese, Father, and what he said was, "wise is he who knows when to fight, and when not to fight, for he will always win.'"

"I don't get it."

"I know you don't get it. In this case, I mean that walking in there now could get us both killed. This is the man our friend in the New York City apartment was scared to death of. Could be for a number of reasons. His boss might be a psychotic who kills on a whim, but probably not, because in spite of what you see in the movies, people like that aren't capable of running a successful drug ring. This guy is smart, and he undoubtedly has better security than the NYC apartment. I need to find the right moment, and I also need to see how many people he has protecting him."

"How much longer are you going to watch him?"

"For as long as it takes. Now, why don't you go back to St. Mary's and go to sleep. Come and check on me in the morning."

"Okay, James Bond, I'll see you tomorrow."

* * *

Across the street from the priest and the bum talking in the park, Detective Ed Woldman stared at the funeral home through a night vision scope from the inside of a parked National Grid power company van a friend had loaned him. He had been watching the home for most of the day, calling in various favors to get into trucks that would not be out of place in the neighborhood.

So far, he had learned absolutely nothing, but Woldman was a patient man. He knew his source well and had no doubt that something would turn up very soon.

Book I
Chapter 19
Albany, New York—May

Jean Van Nostrand felt sick, nauseated almost to the point of vomiting, but it never came. She had felt like this ever since waking up in La Baptist's bed. Jean was no stranger to a hangover after a hard night of partying, but this was something different. She was weak, shocked at how pale she looked in the ornate mirror on top of the curly maple dresser.

She walked over to the window, but when the rays of the sun struck her skin, she recoiled like she had been splattered with acid. She could not believe how hot the sun's rays were today. The sunlight passing through the window glass seemed so harsh. It made her eyes hurt, made her skin feel like she was an ant caught under some kid's magnifying glass. She only briefly saw the street below, catching a glimpse of the homeless people in the park. Quickly, she shut the curtain, but the sunlight still came in, making her feel even sicker. Finally, she took the comforter off the bed and blocked the light from the window completely.

For the first time since she left the trailer home where she lived with her mother, she thought of home. While she had none of the things she wanted and the place was a dump, maybe it really wasn't that bad. Her mother made good food, and she had tried to take care of her. *If my old lady hadn't bitched about me trying to have some fun, maybe I could have stayed. It's Gretta's fault.*

Things were different now, though. Deep down inside, she felt something was weird about La Baptiste, but he was giving her the royal treatment. He had bought her new clothes, and she had whatever booze or drugs she wanted. It wasn't the same as having a family, but maybe it would be okay. The only problem was that he was a little rough in bed, and she had a noticeable bite mark on her neck to prove it.

La Baptiste also seemed to have something other than all the hush-hush stuff about his business going on.

The oddest thing of all was the way she felt about La Baptiste, a man she had just met. When she was thirteen she had met her first boyfriend, a young man whom she was completely infatuated with. The boy was almost twenty and only used her for sex. After she got over the heartbreak, she vowed never to care about boys, or men, either, for that matter. They only existed to buy her drugs and booze. As far as sex went, it was only just for her fun.

This is weird. Since meeting La Baptiste, she could think only of him. It didn't feel like her first crush, though. She felt like La Baptiste had somehow done something to her, almost a physical thing, and it was what was making her feel this way. She had never believed in love. Love was the reason her father had left. Love was the reason Gretta cried herself to sleep at night in that crappy trailer. No, she didn't buy into love, but she couldn't shake her yearning for La Baptiste. Jean knew that she would do anything for La Baptiste. Anything.

* * *

Across the street in an apartment overlooking the funeral home, Detective Ed Woldman continued his vigil. He had been watching the place for over twenty-four hours, now. Thus far, there was no indication that it was anything other than a funeral home. Typically, a crack house or an apartment where someone was dealing drugs would have skanky people coming and going at all hours. There was a funeral at the home earlier that day, but other than that, there was nothing unusual going on.

An after-hours delivery of a body came in the home's hearse. Woldman had watched the hearse driver unload a gurney, whose occupant was covered in a sheet. "Poor bastard," Woldman thought, as an attendant wheeled the corpse in through the delivery entrance at the rear. What struck Woldman as odd was the way the man was looking around, almost like he was doing something he shouldn't have been, as he wheeled the body in the home. Woldman could see a hand poking from under the sheet, and there was no way that there was anything other than a body being wheeled in.

As Woldman watched the sunset through the filthy window of the apartment, he noticed lights coming on in the upstairs apartment. There was a flurry of activity, as lights went on and off in various rooms. Through his binoculars, he saw a young Caucasian girl and a sharply dressed black man scurrying about the apartment. Apparently, they were going out. Woldman could see the girl being hurried along by the black man as she dressed. Shortly afterward, the upstairs lights went out and the hearse driver exited the funeral home and walked back towards the garage. He returned in a jet black Mercedes and pulled up to the front.

Woldman was watching the driver of the Mercedes through the binoculars, when he noticed a bum staggering up the sidewalk toward the car. The bum appeared to be quite drunk and lost his balance, falling off the curb into the passenger side quarter panel of the car. From his perch in the apartment across the park, Woldman saw the car's driver have a heated exchange with the bum, throwing him to the ground and running him off as the well dressed black man and young girl from the apartment got in the car.

As the expensive sedan drove off, Woldman turned the binoculars on the bum, who suddenly appeared to have regained his balance. The guy was in pretty good shape for a homeless person. The bum threw down his brown paper-wrapped bottle and waved to someone up the street. An old Chevy 4X4 truck pulled alongside the bum, driven by what appeared to be a Catholic priest. The bum got in and the vehicle drove away.

Woldman sat there for a second in shock. *Who the hell are these guys?* He ran out the back of the apartment building to his car. He screeched around the corner, just in time to see where the Chevy went. *Must be DEA or FBI. Damn feds never tell us what they're up to.* He had long thought that, one day, his department would get mixed up in a Federal undercover investigation, and that cops would be shooting at other cops by accident, because no one knew what the hell was going on.

* * *

Father Ryan smoothly accelerated the truck and pulled in the right lane a couple cars behind the black Mercedes, as it threaded its way through Arbor Hill to Route 787, and then exited the ramp for the Port of Albany and onto Route 9W. The Mercedes turned left off Route 9W down a dirt road leading to an old warehouse, along the Hudson River, next to an abandoned oil terminal.

"Nick, it looks like they 'e turning down that dirt road."

"Keep going straight, Father, just drive right on by and don't slow down," Bonecutter replied, as he watched the Mercedes with a night vision monocular.

During his surveillance of the funeral home, Bonecutter had seen Jean's face briefly appear in the third-floor window of La Baptiste's apartment. As the Mercedes pulled up to the warehouse's dimly lit entrance, he clearly saw her and a black man exit the rear of the vehicle. The girl was there, all right.

Now, the question was, how were they going to get her? He and Father John had already agreed that they were going to take the girl home to her mother, one way or another. The plan was to get her away from her new "friends" long enough for Father John to have a talk with her and try to convince her to go home. If not, she was going anyway, after what Bonecutter had seen of her new acquaintances.

Bonecutter needed to know what was going on in the warehouse. He left Father Ryan in the truck and walked through the woods, along the old dirt access road to the back of the warehouse.

He spotted a drain pipe on the side of the building that he could climb to reach the roof. If he could slip inside without getting caught, maybe he could grab the girl and get back to the truck with her, before anyone could follow. Before he scaled the side of the building, he snuck back to the front, where the black Mercedes was parked and deflated all of the tires.

The climb up to the roof took less than a minute. The old drainage pipe was securely bolted to the northwest corner of the building, and it was an easy climb up. Climbing and scaling buildings in the dark was something his unit had practiced, as part of their counter-terrorism training. Some of the guys even used their skills to sneak back inside their apartments so their girlfriends wouldn't catch them coming home late from the bar.

On the roof, he quietly walked along, until he found what he was looking for—a skylight. Old warehouses usually had skylights to light the interior.

From his perch next to the skylight, he had a pretty good view of what was going on below. It appeared to be a party. A number of tables and chairs had been crudely decorated, like they were having a high school dance, with crepe paper and balloons. There was a table of food and a bar of sorts, complete with cases of cold beer in an ice tub. The thing that struck Bonecutter about the scene was that the guests below looked like they'd been emptied out of the men's and women's wings of a county jail and dressed up for the evening. He could clearly see the men who had left the funeral home in the Mercedes, and he quickly spotted Jean Van Nostrand. All he could do now was watch and see what happened.

* * *

From his parking place a few hundred yards behind the Chevy truck, Detective Woldman watched through a night vision scope, as the fake bum deflated the tires on the Mercedes. He lost sight of him for a while, picking him up again on the roof. *Who the hell are these guys? Obviously, something is about to happen, but what the hell are they up to?* He decided they were not with any police agency. Real cops wouldn't make moves like the ones he had just seen. Police officers never went into a situation without plenty of backup. He could also clearly see that the guy dressed as a priest was too old to be a cop, and he didn't look like the drug type; he looked like an old priest.

Woldman was in a real quandary. He couldn't call for backup, because Reichman would find out what he was up to. All he could do was sit and watch, and hopefully nothing bad would happen.

* * *

Inside the party, twenty of La Baptiste's higher-echelon dealers were availing themselves of everything their boss had to offer. Over at one table, several people were busy inhaling lines of coke off a mirror. Others drank free beer and malt liquor, or hit the bar and mixed themselves a drink. The stereo set up on the table was tuned to the local rap music channel, but wasn't turned up too loud, because everyone knew the boss didn't like a lot of noise.

La Baptiste sat at the head table, sipping some of the special drink that Willie had brought along for him, while he watched Jean over at the table full of coke, taking her turn at the lines of dope. Willie, smartly attired in a black Armani suit said, "Boss, when you gonna get rid of her?"

"Soon, Willie, soon, but for now I find her amusing, so she shall not join Mr. Lavotti this evening," La Baptiste sipped the red liquid and grinned his toothy grin. "Speaking of which, have all the preparations been made?"

"Yeah, Boss, we did it up just like you said."

"Good, we shall bring the guest of honor out in an hour or so, after everyone has had time to enjoy themselves."

* * *

Bonecutter was getting a little cramped from sitting along the edge of the skylight. He had been there for about an hour observing the party below. Avoiding detection was fairly easy, as humans rarely look up for danger. A couple of the party goers had glanced towards the skylight, but he was keeping a low profile. Only his eyes and the dark hair on the top of his head would have been visible. Besides, the light was coming from inside the building; there were no lights on the roof, and it was an overcast night.

As he watched, he could see that the party goers were getting drunk, or stoned, or both. All, that is, except for the two black men who had left the funeral home. They were drinking, but were not using drugs or going through the booze the other party goers were. From his perch, he could see the man who appeared to be the host of the occasion clap his hands together and call everyone to attention. *What's he up to?*

* * *

La Baptiste clapped his hands, and in a booming voice, called for everyone's silence. "Gentlemen, we must now talk business," he said. "Your dates should leave now; this is for members of our group only. Jean, you will stay."

The women got up and left the room in twos and threes, exiting the side door of the building, and getting into cabs there waiting to take them home.

"Now, gentlemen, we must talk. One of the most important things in our business is security, and in our particular trade, security can only come through secrecy. I have always emphasized this point to you, have I not?" Several of the men at the tables nodded in response.

"Good, good, then we understand each other. It has come to my attention, however, that one of our customers has betrayed us to a police detective named Woldman, a man who now seeks to penetrate our organization; so, without further delay, let me introduce Mr. Lavotti, our guest of honor for this evening."

At the announcement, Willie wheeled in a man strapped to the wooden surface of an orange metal cart, like the ones lumber stores use for wheeling around sheets of plywood. The man's face had a couple of bruises, but other than that, he was in good condition. While he was not physically damaged, his eyes were bulging from their sockets in total terror.

"Mr. Lavotti, I'm glad you could make it to our party. I have been informed of what you told detective Woldman, and now, I am afraid that you shall have to serve as an example to those who would betray my associates and me. I shall not bore you with any more talk. Let us begin," La Baptiste said, as Willie handed him a machete.

"Gentlemen, in my country, we ruled with the machete. Our enemies feared these blades and what they would do to them." La Baptiste swung the blade and hacked off several of Lavotti's fingers. His screams filled the warehouse.

La Baptiste grinned at the terrorized man, and licked the blood from the blade, his trademark from his military days in Haiti. Lavotti instinctively made a fist with his other hand, and La Baptiste again swung the blade, hacking the entire hand from the wrist. Then he took plastic cable ties and bound the stumps left by the wounds he'd made, and said, "don't worry Mr. Lavotti, we can't have you bleeding to death before the fun is over, now, can we?"

The other men in the room were all hardened criminals; many of them had committed murders; most had been in prison. To a man, however, they were horrified, yet none dared to say a word. La Baptist's machete swung again, and Lavotti's other hand fell to the floor. Again, he used a cable tie as a tourniquet to bind the wound. Lavotti had passed out from shock. La Baptiste slapped him until he woke up again.

From his perch near the skylight, Bonecutter had seen enough. He was no cop, but his training and his own sense of what was right would not let him walk away and do what the average person would do, simply call the police. He slid back down the drain pipe and broke in a side door on the back of the building with his .45 drawn and pointed ahead of him.

As he entered the room, most of the party goers barely noticed him. They were transfixed on the macabre spectacle before them. Only when he walked up to La Baptiste, did most of them notice.

"Drop it, and back away from him!" Bonecutter shouted.

La Baptiste only laughed at the sight of the man before him. "My friend, I don't know where you came from, but now it seems you will also be part of tonight's lesson." With that, La Baptiste leaped forward with the machete.

As the man with the blade moved, Bonecutter tracked him with the .45. *This guy is fast, but not fast enough.* Nicholas shot his attacker twice in the chest, and once in the head, using the "double taps" technique he learned in the SEALS. The head shot ensured that the attacker would be lethally hit, even if he was wearing body armor.

The .45 going off echoed like a canon in the metal warehouse. Bonecutter turned to the crowd of party goers, and pointed the gun at Willie. "You. Take the machete and cut the poor bastard loose, NOW!"

Willie would have killed the man in front of him if he could have. La Baptiste told everyone no guns were allowed at the party. Slowly, he picked the bloody machete off the floor and cut Lavotti loose.

Bonecutter held the crowd at bay with the .45. They had no doubt he would use it and kept their distance. As he pointed the gun from face to face, he suddenly noticed that no one was looking at him. They were looking at the guy on the floor he had shot. He heaved Lavotti over his left shoulder and turned to see what everyone was gawking at.

Everyone in the room stood and stared at what was happening on the floor. The chunks of brain and blood that the .45 caliber hollow point round had blown out of the back of the man's skull were somehow crawling toward each other and recombining, like drops of mercury oozing along a smooth surface, leaving little bloody trails as they went. The parts crawled back into La Baptiste's skull, pulling the hunks of bone behind them, closing the wound as if it had never been.

One of the drug dealers screamed like a little school boy, as the dead man's eyes opened. La Baptiste sat upright and grinned.

Bonecutter had seen enough. Carrying Lavotti over his shoulder, he grabbed Jean Van Nostrand by the arm and, together, they ran to the door, well ahead of the rest of the party guests who were close behind. As he hit the parking lot, he was relieved to see Father Ryan waiting with the truck. He threw Lavotti in the back, and pushed Jean next to the little priest. "Get us out of here, Father. Go, go, go!"

Ryan shifted the truck into drive and slammed his foot on the accelerator. Bonecutter looked back and saw the side door fly off of its hinges, as the dead man burst into the parking lot.

"Go, Father, he's gaining on us!" Bonecutter yelled, looking out the back window in disbelief as the dead man ran, closing the gap on a truck that was moving over forty miles per hour down the old warehouse road. He leaned out the window and emptied the rest of the .45's clip at La Baptiste. One round hit the dead man in the knee and spun him off his feet.

Ryan managed to get the truck onto the main road and ripped down the highway at eighty miles an hour for several miles before he finally calmed down.

"What the hell is that thing? What is he? I killed that guy, I killed that son of a bitch, and he got up and ran after us. What the hell is he?"

Ryan's face went white, for he knew all too well what had run from the warehouse after them. Worst of all, he knew this was far from over.

Book II
Beginning

Book II
Chapter I
Wilmington, New York- 1969

The air brakes on the silver Greyhound bus hissed, as it ground to a stop in front of the Wilmington Town Hall. The driver, Tom Smith, opened the door with a great sigh of relief. He was glad to be rid of the last passenger on his route from New York City through the small towns in the northern portion of the Adirondacks. Smith watched in the rearview mirror as a single soldier made his way up the isle.

Smith was uncomfortable having a soldier on the bus after all he'd heard on the news. Smith was very disturbed over the Vietnam War. His mind was haunted by all of the horrid images transmitted to American living rooms each night on the evening news. "Probably on dope," he muttered under his breath.

Smith opened the luggage compartment and handed the soldier his green duffle bag. "Thanks," the soldier said as he grabbed the bag. The soldier put on his green beret and walked off with his gear. Smith managed to fake a smile and quickly boarded the bus and drove off.

The Green Beret watched the bus leave and walked down Main Street to Smitty's bar. He wasn't going there to drink. He needed to call for a ride home—a home he hadn't seen in the two years he'd spent in the jungle.

Some of the people on the sidewalk tried to get out of his way. Others merely looked away as they passed. A young girl dressed in a pair of ratty-looking jeans and a tank top, with several strands of love beads hanging around her neck, glared at him through a tacky pair of granny-style sun glasses with a look of abject hatred.

The soldier opened the door to Smitty's and stepped into the smoke-filled interior. He supposed he should buy something and walked up to the bar and ordered a beer. All conversation in the bar ceased, as soon as the beer glass hit the bar's well-worn surface.

"Well, what do we have here?" asked Ralph Stewart, a local merchant and all-around hothead. "Looks like the Chief is back, and in a uniform no less. Well, Chief, I guess those stories are true. You did run off and get into the army. Here we thought you just up and run, and now here you are in the flesh."

"I need a ride home," the soldier said to the bartender, ignoring Stewart. "I was hoping I could use the phone or find someone who was going out towards my house."

"Chief, you shouldn't have come back here," Stewart said. "You were lucky one of those little gooks didn't kill you, but we sure as hell ain't gonna put up with your kind here."

"Leave it alone," the soldier said.

"Yeah, Ralph, we don't need no trouble here," the bartender said.

"Well, as soon as he leaves, there won't be no trouble," Stewart reached out and grabbed the green hat off the soldier's head and threw it on the floor.

The soldier said nothing and bent over to pick up the beret. As he did so, Stewart tried to kick him in the face.

What happened next only took a second. The soldier blocked the kick and hooked the attacking leg, trapping it with his left arm, as he simultaneously punched Stewart in the groin. He stood and lashed out with his highly polished combat boot, dislocating the man's remaining leg at the knee.

One of Stewart's buddies came at the soldier with a pool cue. The cue whistled through the air in an arc towards the soldier's head. The soldier caught both the cue and the arms that swung it, using them to throw his attacker headfirst into the jukebox. The man got one heck of a cut, as his face smashed through the glass exterior of the jukebox. Fortunately for him, the sight of his own blood made him forgot all about fighting the soldier anymore.

A couple of minutes after the fight was over, Sheriff Glen Hollister, Sr., and two deputies burst through the door. "Well, Bonecutter, they said you were back, but I didn't believe it," Sheriff Hollister said. "Of course, I have to arrest you for breaking up the bar, and from the looks of these two dumb asses, you did one heck of a job doing it."

So went the "hero's welcome" George Bonecutter received from his home town.

Three hours later, Father John Ryan visited him in his cell at the Essex County Jail.

"I'm surprised to see you, Father Ryan. It isn't often a Catholic priest visits an Indian in jail."

"The Lord doesn't worry about who a man is when he's needed, George. Besides I've got something much more important to discuss than you being in jail."

"What's that?"

"It's about your daughter. She needs you right now."

"What's wrong with my daughter?"

"Someone at the county home must have done something with her. She's pregnant."

"Who did it, Father? Who the hell did this to my daughter?"

"The nursing home investigated, but they never found out who did it, and that's not important right now. Your daughter is giving birth. The doctors sent me for you. We have to go right now. She needs you, George, and we have to go right now before it is too late."

"Father, what's wrong? What's going on?"

"She's having a difficult birth. I was on my way back to the hospital when I heard about the ruckus at the bar, and that you were home. Now, we really must be going!"

"How am I going to get out of here?"

"I talked to the Sheriff, and he's dropped the charges. Let's go."

During the half-hour ride to the hospital, not another word was exchanged. George Bonecutter had been married for all of three years, when a drunk ran his wife and two-year-old daughter off the road. His wife had died, and his daughter's injuries left her with almost no brain function. She'd spent almost fifteen years confined to a bed at the county home.

Bonecutter went berserk when the judge gave the drunk a five-hundred-dollar fine and let him go. He leapt over the table in town court and nearly killed the man, before the Sheriff's deputies pulled him off and put him in handcuffs. The judge gave him a choice, jail or the army. His daughter was left to the county, and he went away to the Korean War, hoping to never return.

In the Korean War, he had to face the prejudice that was always a part of his life. In boot camp, some of the men called him Injun or Chief. Yes, he was an American Indian, but war was a different world. He quickly earned the respect of his fellow soldiers, and many times he saved the lives of his comrades in arms. War was a great evener, and the prejudice he faced in basic training quickly passed when the bullets were flying.

After a while, the army became his home. When he and his pals got R&R, he was just one of the guys, something that had never happened in his Upstate New York home.

The war ended, and instead of returning home when his second tour of duty was over, he decided to stay in the military, where he volunteered for Special Forces training. The military, and the Special Forces training of the Green Beret's, were the only place Bonecutter ever had a chance to excel.

It wasn't long before America started sending military advisors, and then fighting forces, to a little Southeast Asian nation called Vietnam.

During his second tour of duty in Vietnam, Bonecutter went on a mission with a small group of elite soldiers from the South Vietnamese Army. Their objective was to break down a supply line used by the North Vietnamese Army and Viet Cong. During the course of the mission, they found a set of tunnels the enemy was using to hide ammunition and other supplies essential to their war effort.

George volunteered to enter the tunnels. As he moved through the underground hiding spot, he discovered it was unguarded by Charlie, but it did contain six hookers kept there to keep the Viet Cong troops happy.

Even though the Americans were supposedly in charge of the mission, a cocky South Vietnamese Lieutenant stepped forward, unclipped a dagger attached to his shoulder straps, and sliced one of the prostitutes wide open, stem to stern. The psycho ordered the other girls to talk, while they watched their companion try to hold her guts in.

George Bonecutter, veteran of the Korean War and almost two tours in Nam, snapped. He grabbed the South Vietnamese Lieutenant by the wrist that held the knife and broke the man's arm. Then he hit him so hard that it knocked out most of the guy's teeth. It took the other five Special Forces troops to pull him off the Lieutenant. The dying hooker was the same age as the daughter he had left behind at home. Even though part of him thought he had seen enough of war, deep in his heart, he knew it was time to go home.

George, in his grief over the loss of his wife and the horrific damage to his daughter, had escaped from his life, until now.

Father Ryan grabbed Bonecutter by the elbow and hurried him along the hospital corridor. They were met by a doctor and nurse, who made him dress in a surgical gown and mask before they took him into the delivery room.

George Bonecutter arrived just in time to witness his grandson's birth, and his daughter's death. He never had the chance to tell her anything. He only had time to look her in the eye as she passed on. He spent the rest of his life hoping that, in the moment their eyes made contact, his daughter knew how sorry he was and knew he had come home to make things right.

Tears spilled from his battle-hardened eyes. He had seen many deaths, including his wife's, and had never cried, yet this time he cried like a baby. When he finally got himself back together, he knew he was a failure as a father, but he would never fail his family again.

Book II
Chapter 2
Port-au-Prince, Haiti —1956

The formation of a country is often a bloody process, but few countries have ever endured Haiti's constant horror. Founded in a slave rebellion, the government changed hands many times, and each time it did, more blood was spilled.

In December, Haitian President Paul E. Magloire, taking his wife, a few close associates, and whatever possessions they could carry, boarded a DC-3 and flew into exile, while he still had a pulse. His was not the first Haitian political leader who valued his life enough to escape into exile, and he would not be the last.

Magloire's departure created a vacuum at the top of the government. From this void, four figures emerged as serious contenders for the office of President: a finance minister, a wealthy plantation owner, a well-known rabble rouser and counterculture leader, and a diminutive little doctor named Duvalier.

Haiti plunged into rioting and chaos, as soon as the Magloire's DC-3 left the runway. For the next nine months, a succession of failed attempts to establish order and the rule of law took place. A new government rose and fell at a rate of about one per month. Each time, riots, murder, and chaos tore the fledgling government apart. What no one knew until much later was that one person was the source of all of this strife.

On April 2, 1957, two Haitian police officers died when they stumbled across a bomb factory. Interim President Sylvain was forced to resign and was immediately placed under house arrest when it was "discovered" he had known about the bomb factory all along and was planning to kill three of the four top presidential contenders. What someone should have asked at the time was why one candidate, Dr. Francois Duvalier, was left off the hit list?

Later, it was learned some of the people involved in the bomb factory had links to the mild-mannered little doctor. The months of chaos following

Magloire's departure did serve one purpose—the purpose they were designed for. The bloodshed whittled the four presidential contenders down to two. Duvalier and Louis Dejoie were the last of the prospective presidents.

Finally, an election was held, which Duvalier won easily. He did so well, in fact, that a little town called La Gonave, where he hadn't even bothered to campaign, delivered him 18,000 votes, which was pretty good, considering that the town only had a few hundred residents.

Thus began a reign of terror lasting from 1957 until 1971. Duvalier was far more than he appeared to be in his meetings with American journalists. The scrawny little man ruled the country with an iron hand.

"Je *Suis le Drapeau Haitien, un et indivisible*" (the Haitian Flag and I are one and indivisible) the diminutive dictator proclaimed. There was no doubt, after he took power, that Francois Duvalier, was indeed, the state.

Taking power and keeping it for any length of time in a country like Haiti are two different things. Duvalier, though a relatively inept doctor, was highly competent when it came to knowing his country and its ways. To the world, he seemed to be a professional man who exhibited relatively modest tastes and mild manners. But looks were deceiving.

To have power in Haiti, and more importantly, to keep it, required the full support of the military. If the generals didn't care for a leader, that leader did not last very long. Long before Duvalier ever considered trying to ascend to the presidency, he solved the mystery of how to rule the country. Duvalier was certainly not a military man. He had never been a soldier, and he viewed the army as a bunch of fools in matching clothes. He was, however, a student of the history and culture of his own people. Haiti was a country that was said to be eighty percent Roman Catholic, and one hundred percent Voodoo. The Voodoo culture had always been be a part of Haiti, and Duvalier, instead of downplaying this to "modernize" his country's society, used it to gain power.

To the Voodoo practitioner, the most powerful of the loa, or Voodoo gods, was Baron Samadi. Duvalier was a Voodoo adept, at least at the level of houngan, or Voodoo priest. It was no coincidence that the little doctor always dressed in clothing that was similar to the way the Baron himself dressed, and had characteristically unblinking eyes, behind a heavy pair of glasses. Duvalier did much to convince those around him that, while he was a little man, he had great supernatural powers. Initially, the higher ranking army officers were paid off to go along with his presidency. After he had established himself, he quickly changed that policy.

At the first meeting of his cabinet, he exhibited his power. Duvalier looked about the room and began his speech. "My Presidency has shown the will of the people. The people can see my vision for our country. They have shown me loyalty, and their loyalty will be repaid. Together, we shall make this country a paradise and bring wealth and happiness to all. The loyalty they have shown me is what will make this possible.

"As the people have shown me loyalty, so must those who work with me to achieve these lofty goals. This is the only way that we can succeed. Already, it has come to my attention that one of you seeks to destroy that which the people have chosen, and this will not be."

The statement was a prearranged signal. Duvalier's right hand man, Clement Barbot, a thug capable of any misdeed, pushed a button, which activated a spring-loaded syringe, rigged to punch up through the upholstery of the chair in which an unenthusiastic army colonel sat. The syringe delivered its dose of a toxin derived from the blowfish. The toxin was the best-kept secret of Voodoo priests. As the man's eyes began to glass over, and the color drained from his face, Duvalier smiled. "Like this man who has chosen to die of fright, rather than continue his traitorous ways, no one shall stand against the legitimate will of the people." Barbot snapped his fingers and two men came in and carried the lifeless body from the room.

For the rest of those assembled, the message was quite clear. While Duvalier did not seem like much, looks were deceiving. Going against him would be impossible. Everyone at the table was paralyzed with fear at how Duvalier had seemingly killed a man by will alone.

"Now that all of you, my loyal cabinet, have been rid of a traitor, you may go and carry out my policies and the will of the people."

As the room cleared, Barbot, a dark-skinned man with thin lips and fierce eyes, only just a little taller than Duvalier, stepped over toward the little dictator. "Mr. President, what shall I do with the Colonel?"

"Send him to our place in the country and have your men give him the best of care, Clemont. Now leave me, I have more work to do."

As the little president sat down at the ornate French desk, he took the .38 caliber revolver he always carried out of its shoulder holster and placed it on the desk next to the European styled white phone. *Now for the difficult part.*

For the next several days he initiated a scheme to establish total control over the military and the rest of the country. Duvalier should have been a historian instead of a doctor, for that was his true calling in life. In addition to studying the history of his country, he'd studied the past of other countries as well.

Like all history buffs, he had his specialty area. His was analyzing the ways of other great men of the past, great men like Adolf Hitler and Joseph Stalin, men who, like himself, believed they were ultimately chosen to rule, and only a traitor would stand against them.

Duvalier knew the apparent death of the Colonel would buy him some time, but it would only work on those who were in the room. He, like Hitler and Stalin, needed a way to control real soldiers in such a way that they would never dare to go against him. Hitler had his "Brown Shirts" and then the SS, Stalin had his secret police and his KGB. Duvalier would have his own group as well.

In the next several weeks, under the supervision of Clemont Barbot, Duvalier formed his own version of a "government within a government." Under Barbot, the *Tonton Macoutes* was formed, the literal translation in Creole meaning "boogymen." Boogymen they were. They had free license to rape, torture, murder, or extort as they saw fit.

One of the dictator's powers was his ability to foresee the future, largely though a series of paid informants he had established years before. He knew in advance that on July 28, 1958, a ragtag group of mercenaries led by a couple of ex-sheriff's deputies from Florida had landed in Haiti and would attempt to overthrow the government. Duvalier told the army nothing of the invasion, and the mercenaries actually succeeded in marching to the capital and capturing a barracks of soldiers at the casernes. The mercenaries' goal was to capture the weapons storeroom and use the weapons to supply a group of rebels, who would join them in the casernes at their signal.

When they broke open the doors to the weapons room, however, they discovered to their horror, all of the automatic guns, ammunition, and grenades had been removed by Duvalier who had secretly locked them in the basement of his palace.

The Haitian military proved itself unworthy of the title. The soldiers panicked and failed to deter the handful of soldiers of fortune. Soldiers actually cowered and shouted at every burst of fire from inside the barracks.

Of course, Duvalier had long planned to use the invasion to his advantage. He personally led a group of hand-picked soldiers in a counterattack and overwhelmed the attackers easily with automatic weapons and grenades. All of the invaders were shot, beaten to a pulp, dismembered, and put on public display.

The failure of the military to stem the ill-fated invasion was all Duvalier needed to implement the next phase of his plan. The day after the invaders were routed, Duvalier called Barbot to his office.

"Clemont, we have proven that the military, as it exists, is useless. The Tonton Macoutes will rule the military and use them as we see fit. The problem is that, eventually, even our Macoutes will generate a traitor. Power inevitably corrupts; thus, the older the soldier, the more easily he is turned to mischief. We must therefore pick the apple right from the tree before it becomes rotten."

"What do you mean, Mr. President?"

"I want you to establish a training camp for young Macoutes. You shall go to the high schools and recruit the smartest young men. They shall become the backbone of this country."

"I understand, Mr. President, and if I may be so bold, I would like to volunteer my nephew. His name is Armand La Baptiste, a bright young man who would make a very good member of the Macoutes."

Book II
Chapter 3
Wilmington, New York— 1975

Nicholas Bonecutter, dressed in his brand new yellow and white checked shirt, was on his way to school for the very first time. Grandfather walked with him. He was not afraid and crying like some of the other kids making their way to their first day of school; he was more in wonder of it all.

The day passed without incident. Small children do not have prejudices, and the little kids in his kindergarten class weren't aware that they shouldn't like a half-Indian like Nicholas. He even had friends for the first week or so.

All of that changed at the end of the second week of school, when he drew the attention of a third-grader named Delbert Scribner. Del was the sole child of a pair of alcoholic parents who only stopped verbally abusing each other long enough to share some of the joy with their son.

Del's old man had no use for most people, let alone anyone who was different. Thus, young Del automatically recognized Nicholas for what he was, and made sure his life was miserable every chance he got.

"Hey, Injun," Del taunted, "where do you think you're goin?" He jumped in front of Nicholas at the end of the day, out in the yard in front of the old brick schoolhouse.

"Leave me alone; I didn't do anything to you."

"I don't like you, Injun, I don't like you at all, and I don't like your kind. Smelly Injun bastards shouldn't be able to go to school with white folks."

"I said leave me alone." Nicholas tried to walk past him.

Scribner, in addition to being older, was much bigger. He took advantage of his size and pushed the kindergartner right into the mud. Nicholas leapt up, his only instinct was to fight. He swung a wild right at Scribner's jaw, but missed, catching Del on the shoulder.

Del quickly punched back and landed a fist square on Nicholas' nose.

Nick, not quite knowing what else to do, reacted like a typical small kid. He cried his eyes out.

Scribner kicked more mud in his face, laughing, as he turned and walked home before one of the teachers showed up and he got in trouble.

Nicholas took his time walking home. He tried to clean himself up as best he could, but there was no way he could hide the muddy clothes. Grandfather would know and would be ashamed of him.

When he got to the cabin, Nick decided to just get it over with. Grandfather didn't have any guiding customers today. He would be there working on his gear, or tying flies for the fishing trip he had booked tomorrow.

"How was school today?"

"Not very good, Grandpa."

"I can see that. How about telling me what happened?"

"You'll be mad at me." Tears slid down his cheeks as he spoke, in spite of his best effort to keep them inside.

"A man has to tell the truth. Even when it hurts, a man has to be honest with himself and the people around him."

"Well, I sort of got in a fight at school. A third grader named Del Scribner called me a smelly Indian and pushed me in the mud. I tried to hit him back, but he punched me first."

"You can't worry when somebody calls you a name, son," Grandfather said. "This boy Del is just stupid. He's never learned any better. You can't let somebody hurt you, so I don't blame you for taking a poke at him."

"But Del's bigger than me."

"Bigger, yes. Better, no. Tomorrow's Saturday. If you help me on my guiding trip to Palmer Pond, I'll teach you how to defend yourself from the likes of Del."

When Saturday came, Nicholas got up early and got the wood stove going so the client would have a hot cup of coffee waiting when he arrived at the cabin. Grandfather's client was a doctor from Albany who fished the ponds with him every year. Dr. Bough was a gray-haired man with a thin mustache and a beaming smile. He loved the woods and was glad to be away from his patients for awhile. Dr. Bough was a tad overweight, but he could follow along the trail well and kept up with grandfather.

When they reached the pond, Dr. Bough busied himself stringing up his fly rod as grandfather got the canoe ready. The trout were beginning to rise on the glassy surface as the two men shoved the canoe off from shore, ripples from the vessel moving in every direction. Nicholas' job for the day was to gather firewood and make sure a fire was ready at noon, when the men came in for lunch.

Grandfather sat in the back, paddling the cedar strip canoe, while Dr. Bough cast to rising brook trout. Nick watched the old doctor fish for a while and then set about doing his job.

Gathering firewood for lunch was a difficult task for a six-year-old. It was even harder, because this pond received a decent amount of fishermen, and there wasn't a lot of dead wood near the edge of the water. It took him a couple of hours to gather enough for the lunchtime fire. He dropped off the last armload of big sticks and walked down to the shore just in time to meet Grandfather and the doctor.

After they finished their lunch, Nicholas cleaned up and packed the dishes in Grandfather's pack basket. Grandfather and his client exchanged a glance and Grandfather said, "Doctor Bough is going to take a nap, and he's already caught his limit, so how would you like to catch a brook trout?"

"Boy, would I," the boy replied, his eyes as big a saucers.

Grandfather put him in the front of the canoe. He already knew how to cast a fly rod, but he'd never had the chance to try fishing with one. This was the first time Grandfather had ever taken him along on one of his guiding trips.

The elder Bonecutter paddled the canoe out to the middle of the pond, where the trout were still rising to a heavy hatch of mayflies. He tied a large dry fly to the leader and handed the rod to his grandson. Nicky was a little nervous, but he'd had plenty of practice with Grandfather in the yard. He could drop a fly on most any target his Grandpa picked out.

A large ring appeared as a hungry brook trout gobbled up a mayfly struggling to free itself from its nymphal shuck. He cast the fly into the middle of it. Nothing happened. Another fish sipped an insect off the surface, and Nicholas cast the fly into the ring with the same result.

"Nicky, try to see which way the fish is moving and cast out ahead of it." Grandfather gave the canoe another silent thrust with the paddle, propelling it towards more feeding trout.

Nicholas looked ahead, spotting another fish rise once, and then rise again a little to the left. He cast the fly out in front of it. The fish startled him a little bit when it inhaled the insect imitation (expertly tied by his Grandfather) beneath the surface. He set the hook, and the rod bowed as a two-pound Adirondack brook trout took off, peeling line from the reel. He kept up the pressure on the trout, letting it run when it wanted to. Somehow, the fragile leader held, and he brought the trout to Grandfather's net.

Grandfather's sun-worn face beamed with pride, as he lifted the net from the water and congratulated the boy on a good piece of fly fishing. He took out a pair of surgical pliers and removed the hook, holding the fish up so that Nick could see it before he released it back into the pond.

Nick couldn't stop smiling. He revered his Grandfather, and he'd finally had the chance to try one of the things Grandfather loved to do, proving he too could do it. He had never been prouder in his life and both would always remember this moment.

After Nicholas and his grandfather returned home and bade farewell to Dr. Bough, Grandfather took him into the back yard.

"Nicky, there are a lot of things that I hoped to teach you in life, but this is one I didn't want to show you so soon. This boy who beat you up, you say he's bigger than you?"

"He's way too big for me, Grandpa. I'll never be able to stop him from pushing me around."

"As long as that is what you believe, he will always win. I can teach you how to fight, but it will take time, a lot of time, but you will win one day, and when you do, he'll never pick on you again. If you train hard and practice what I teach you, you'll best him. You'll have to put up with him, until I tell you that you're ready, and you have to promise me you won't fight back until I tell you. If you do what I ask, I'll show you how to fight, just like I showed you how to fish."

"I promise, Grandpa."

His training started out with basic martial arts, the same way George had learned them in the Special Forces. Basic punching and kicking were part of the boy's daily routine. He also learned how to block a variety of incoming attacks.

Grandfather worked with him every day, and the boy kept his bargain. He still had to put up with being pushed or punched by Del, but he was less afraid each time, as he toughened up, and he didn't cry when he got hit. He knew the day was soon coming when it would be all over for Del.

The months passed, and the school year was almost over. It was a warm Saturday in the beginning of June, and George Bonecutter and his grandson went to town to pick up some groceries. George had no guiding lined up that day, and it was one of those rare occasions when the two had all day and nothing to do.

They were crossing the street in front of Romano's, a small family-owned grocery in the middle of town, when they came across Del Scribner and his son Del Junior.

"Well, if it ain't the Indian chief and his grandbrat," the elder Scribner said. You know George, folks are talking like you were some kind of war hero. Hell, I always figured you for one more yellow Injun. "

"Figure whatever you like, Del,"

"You're lucky your old grandfather is with you, Injun," Del Junior weighed in, doing his best to prove the apple didn't fall too far from the tree.

"Well, if you two kids want to run off and play, go ahead," Grandfather said, as Nicholas looked back at him in bewilderment. "It's a great day, Nick, in fact, today's the day. You and Del run along and play a while."

"You've got to be kidding me, Chief? You know Junior here is going to beat the snot out of your grandkid," Scribner snorted.

"I don't think so."

"Go ahead, Del, show Grandpa here what you think of his half-breed grandson." Scribner Senior stepped forward and pointed to Nicholas.

With that, Del Junior charged forward to push Nicholas down, just as he'd done a dozen times. Scared and nervous, Nicholas did what he'd been taught over the past several months. He deftly sidestepped the attack and simultaneously swept young Del's left leg from under him.

Young Del landed face first in the sod. He stood up and spit out a few blades of grass, totally enraged at what the Injun had done. He ducked low and charged again, like a defensive lineman trying to sack a quarterback.

Nicholas grabbed Del by the shoulders and used a judo throw to launch him onto his back. Young Del let out a loud grunt as he landed, all of the air leaving his body. He was almost crying as he rolled over. Nick could tell Del was getting frustrated, because now, it wasn't so easy to push him around. Del's face went red with rage.

This time, Del took a swing at him. Nick ducked the punch and struck out with a right hook to the lower rib cage. This time Del did cry.

"Get off your ass and bat that damn Indian!" his father bellowed at the boy.

Young Del was finished. He started throwing up from the shot to the ribs and rolled over onto his knees and cried.

"You want to cry, you little bastard! I'll give you something to cry about." Del's father grabbed his son by the hair and yanked him to his feet. He was about to slap the boy across the face when he felt his wrist stop, as if it was chained to a tree.

"I think you've taught him enough for today, Del," the elder Bonecutter said. "If you really want to do him some good, you should teach him to have more respect for others and not to act like such a little jerk."

"Nobody's going to tell me how to handle my kid, you fucking Indian prick!" Scribner launched his fist at George's face. Bonecutter blocked it with his forearm and snapped his arm taut, smashing his palm into Scribner's face, a vicious strike, which produced the desired result. There was a loud snap as the elder Scribner's nose broke.

"Come on, Nick, it's time to go."

Nicholas was riding high on the way home. He had never felt prouder of himself. "Boy, we really beat 'em, Grandpa. If Del ever comes after me again, I'm gonna really teach him a lesson."

George grabbed the boy's shoulder and said, "listen to me! There is no honor in hurting someone. It's nothing to be proud of. You have to fight if you are attacked, but only enough to win, then it ends. The best way to fight is not at all. Don't ever think you are going to win all the time, either. There's always someone bigger and badder out there. I guess it's time I taught you how to think, as well as how to fight. Did they ever teach you about China in that school of yours?"

"A little, Grandpa."

"Well, I want you go to the library and learn what a Chinese philosopher named Sun Tsu said about fighting. Then we'll talk some more."

Book II
Chapter 4
Fort Dimanche, Haiti—1957

Armand La Baptiste didn't know what to make of his new surroundings. Uncle Clemont told him he would be perfect for a new group being formed. Clemont said, "Armand, we need you to be part of the Tonton Macoutes. You will help us rule our country."

La Baptiste knew only one thing. This was the day he always knew would come.

He was a small boy, not particularly athletic, often the target of ridicule. Schoolyards in Haiti were no different from any schoolyard elsewhere in the world. The constant when it comes to children is that, in every country, regardless of how wealthy or civilized it is, schools follow the law of the jungle. In a schoolyard, the strong prey upon the weak. This was certainly the case in La Baptiste's high school.

In spite of his size, La Baptiste was an intense looking boy. He had the fierce eyes of his Uncle Clemont and the other facial features found on that side of his family, including a sharp, chiseled nose and narrow chin. It was easy for the other kids to push him around due to his size. He was a skinny kid who, as a high school senior, barely weighed over a hundred pounds.

Whether the result of the constant bullying or the constant daydreaming, where he lost himself for hours at a time, La Baptiste always knew he was going to be something big. He fantasized about it constantly. No matter what the fantasy's form, whether he was a great general, or maybe a king, one thing was for sure; someday, the life and death of others would depend on his will.

Those who knew Armand, his teachers and schoolmates, would have scoffed at his vision had he ever expressed it. His academics were good, but not great. There were no other activities he excelled at. No one, his father included, would ever guess he would be anything more than a meager shop keeper or government employee.

La Baptiste's home life was difficult. His mother had died when he was young. He had no mother's kindness to comfort him when things went wrong. His father was a cold, distant man. Papa had a certain pride in his family name, but he treated the boy like a stranger in his own home.

Worse yet, his father always pushed the boy, never satisfied with any small success. If Armand got an A in math, his father demanded to know why he did not get an A-plus. If he won second place in something, Papa wanted to know why he didn't get first.

His father did not support him in any way, other than keeping a roof over his head. Perhaps, in part, Papa was angry because his wife had died and left him alone to raise the boy. Whatever the psychology of the situation was, the boy soon learned he had nowhere to turn when things were difficult.

When Armand got pushed around and told his father, Papa would look him right in the eye and tell him it was own fault. No matter what he did, it was never right. Consequently, Armand, without friends or family to turn to, withdrew into himself. He got by with patience, always waiting for the day when his time would finally come, the day when he could get even.

His father protested when Uncle Clemont took him to the camp, but Uncle made it very clear that Papa La Baptiste was no longer in charge of the boy.

As soon as Armand arrived at the camp, the indoctrination began. The training facility was designed to emulate a military school. In reality, there was little resemblance to a real academy. This was a school for terrorists, and honor was not in the curriculum.

The cadets endured hard physical training, with the education portion of the program geared towards learning the dictates of Duvalier. The young Macoutes learned his vision for the country, studying his speeches at length.

A great change took place in La Baptiste, after only a few weeks at the school. For the first time, even though he was scrawny, he fit in because of his intellect. The school was laid out with a series of small barracks, positioned around a central parade field. Each of the barracks housed eight cadets. Soon after arriving, La Baptiste discovered he had an ability to manipulate those around him.

At first, he showed his fellow cadets he could trick the Sergeant in charge of their group. He taught the others ways of getting around the constant inspections, by inventing all kinds of little shortcuts.

The cadets at the camp also learned other, far darker skills. One day, after they had mastered some basic combat training, their instructor took them on a bus to a classroom in the basement of Fort Dimanche. They took their seats, as the instructor of a new course entered the room. This class dealt with interrogation skills.

The instructor for the day, an army Captain, told them it was necessary to protect the legitimate government of the People of Haiti using any means. Dissidents, those who would challenge the will of the people, must be rooted out.

As seventeen year-old La Baptiste and the other young men looked on, a naked man strapped to a hospital gurney was wheeled into the room. The man's eyes were open wide with terror. Two burly guards hoisted the man from the gurney and shackled his wrists to a chain hanging from the ceiling.

The instructor told them the man was a newspaper editor who had challenged the rule of the country's most noble president.

"When you are dealing with men, it is best to get right to business. As you can see, we strip him to make the interrogation process easier. Men are interesting, in that they all have something that they seek to protect. We shall use this to make our friend here tell us what we wish to know!"

As his assistants held the man still, he attached two large clamps, like those used on jumper cables to the man's scrotum. The clamps were attached to wires, leading to a box with a dial on the front.

"Now, journalist, who else is involved in your plot to overthrow our President?"

The newspaper editor said nothing, and only a whimper came from his throat.

"Very well." The Captain turned the dial on the box. Screams from the tortured man filled the room. Some of the cadets squirmed in their chairs. La Baptiste slid forward to get a better view.

"Again, who are you working with?"

The newspaper editor's eyes filled with tears. "Please, I am working with no one. I wrote a simple editorial."

"I see." The instructor turned the dial up and down again and again. The man writhed in agony, twitching so badly it seemed he would break the shackles or pull the chain from the ceiling.

As the instructor turned the dial back to zero, the man again screamed, "I…have done nothing wrong. There is no one else. I merely wrote an editorial. Why are you doing this to me?"

Again and again, the dial was turned, each time a little higher, until the man finally convulsed, smoke rose from his pubic hair. The two guards unchained the corpse and threw it back on the gurney.

"Now, students, we have learned our friend was merely using his skills as a journalist to attack our beloved President. Yet he attacked, nonetheless. Words are just as dangerous as bullets. Fortunately, he is not part of a larger plot to upset the will of the people."

As the course progressed, La Baptiste learned he had a true talent. Each of the "students" had to take a practical examination. Each, in turn, got to try out what they had learned on a defenseless human being. Though they all performed to a certain level, none had the finesse for cruelty the seventeen-year-old La Baptiste had.

La Baptiste's final exam was a man who owned a shop in Port Au Prince. This particular store owner was secretly trying to organize other shop owners to close their storefronts on the same day and strike against the government.

"You may use any of the tools at your disposal," the instructor said. "You must convince our friend to let us know what he and his friends were up to."

La Baptiste eyed the helpless man, shackled to the ceiling in chains. He scanned a table filled with implements of torture. Immediately, his eyes spotted a machete. He enjoyed the hand-to-hand combat classes he had taken, particularly those where the class trained with the machete. Then he spotted some wire, and knew how he would pass his final.

"Strap him to the table," young La Baptiste commanded two army privates.

When the man was bound to the table, La Baptiste stood over him, flipping the machete into the air and catching it. "As you can see, my friend, all eyes are upon me, so let us begin with a simple question. What is your name?" The old man was too paralyzed with fear to respond.

"Very well," La Baptiste brought some wire and a pair of pliers over to the table. He took the wire and bound it around the base of the man's left thumb, where the thumb met the palm, then he swung the machete, cutting the thumb clean off.

The old man screamed, his body jolting against the restraints. To add to his horror, La Baptiste merely smiled and licked the blood off the blade, a hideous act which made even the seasoned torturers in the room flinch.

"My...n...nn...nnnn....ame is Vincent Toulane. I have done nothing."

La Baptiste replied by taking more wire and binding the index finger on the same hand. He swung again, hacking it off. The wire kept the arteries near the cut pinched closed to keep his victim from bleeding out.

The old man howled, racking his body so hard, he moved the entire table, as he fought against his bonds.

"Mr. Toulane, what were you and your friends planning to do to the legitimate government of this country?"

"Ahhhhhhhhhhhhhhhhh, you bastard. Oh, God, stop! We were going to close our shops to protest, nothing more. It is our right."

La Baptiste went to work with his wire.

"No, no, please, please, I will tell you whatever you wish to know."

The machete whistled in the air, and took off the rest of the fingers. The wire did its job, and there was surprisingly little blood.

"Who else is involved in this plot?"

The old man passed out from the pain. It took a few minutes for La Baptiste to revive him.

"Please, we are humble shop owners. I can not tell you their names; you will only torture them like dogs."

"Mr. Toulane, I am growing impatient with you. Let us proceed at a more rapid pace, n'est pas?" This time, the wire went around the man's wrist, just above the joint.

"I can not tell you any more. Stop! Pleeeeeeeeeeeeeeease!."

"You will tell me so much more, Mr. Toulane." The machete bit through the air again. The hand, what was left of it, fell onto the floor, making a soft thump.

After another ten minutes at La Baptiste's hands, Vincent Toulane gave up the names of a dozen people, including members of his own family, and then he died on the table, when his heart finally gave out from the shock and pain.

La Baptiste's instructor stared down at the body of the old man. All that was left were the stumps, where both arms were gone at the elbows. The legs had met the same fate, right up to the kneecaps. The Captain was surprised by two things: how resilient the old man was and the brutality of his student. The young man had not only passed his final exam, he would receive a permanent post at Fort Dimanche.

Book II
Chapter 5
Wilmington, New York—1982

Martial arts training did not cease in the Bonecutter home with the defeat of the Scribners. Nicholas genuinely liked the training. His grandfather had always enjoyed martial arts training, but was hesitant to teach his grandson. For him, the arts were a tool he had used in a lethal manner in the two wars where he served his country. Although he knew it was very unlikely that Nicholas would ever have to use his training in anything other than a street scrap, still he worried about the training eventually leading the boy into real combat.

George had formal training in a couple of different martial arts. Initially, he was taught Tae Kwon Do, a Korean martial art that was very popular among American soldiers during the Korean War.

After the war ended, he continued training as part of the Army's Green Beret Special Forces. He then learned a Japanese martial art called Shotokan. While he was on the base, just before the outbreak of the Vietnam War, he earned the rank of Nidan, or second degree black belt. As a Special Forces soldier, he also received exposure and training in the most lethal methods of hand-to-hand combat, coming from several other martial arts.

When Nicholas began his studies, his grandfather devised a program that would work for someone his age. Conditioning was the core of the boy's practice. Since he was only a little boy, weight lifting was not part of his regimen. He did push ups and sit ups by the dozen, though. Nick also worked on his endurance. He was expected to run two miles almost every day. School and chores always came first; training was secondary.

The boy became a very good athlete, but his school chums usually didn't want him to join in their baseball or football games. Nicholas was content with his martial arts training.

After he had done his conditioning, as well as his chores and homework, the boy would begin his lesson for the day. George taught him patience. Nicholas was not given a new technique, until he had perfected the previous one. He learned the basics well, including blocking, then punching, and finally kicking.

George was a stickler for the technical aspects of the arts. He often told Nick that the highest level of learning in the martial arts was often the simplest. A simple block and a punch, when executed at the proper time, was enough to defeat any attacker.

Nicholas wanted to learn the fancy stuff, but he eventually became more patient. He pondered the things Grandfather taught him and practiced hard. He would often spend hours working on a technique, whether it was a punch or a kick, until he had it perfect.

Nick's favorite part of training was kata. The forms he practiced were the same as they had been hundreds of years ago. He first learned a form called Taikioku. In this form, a simple pattern that looked like the capital letter "I" was traversed as a student executed a sequence of combat moves. The student executed downward blocks, followed by a second step, where a lunging punch was executed to the solar plexus area of an imaginary attacker's body.

While he enjoyed the training, martial arts wasn't the most important aspect of his life. He was still just a boy. His family situation left him with two voids. Having lost his mother at his birth, he never really knew a mother's love, and it was something he always missed. A grandmother could have filled in some of this gap, yet his maternal grandmother was dead long before he was born. His grandfather would never speak of who his father was or could have been; thus, he was cut off from that possibility, as well.

Grandfather's friend, Father Ryan, sensing this need, would always try to arrange for sitters who were very outgoing and "motherly" towards the boy, to help when George was off in the woods working. One of these women, Mrs. Jablonski, stayed with him often when Nicholas was young, and she became a part of his life. She was an older woman, even older than grandfather. Mrs. Jablonski became kind of a surrogate grandmother to him.

Nick enjoyed it when she stayed with him at the cabin. Her children were older and were gone with lives of their own. They saw her occasionally and but were never very involved in her life. She was a woman with a lot of love to give, and Nick filled a niche in her life, as well.

She taught the boy some of the things that a mother would teach a son, and George appreciated what she did for Nick.

Nick's problems in school did not end with getting Del Scribner off his back. Nick had endured plenty of foul words at school and in the town. Like many ethnic minorities at the time, he found that, in backwoods places like the Adirondacks, prejudice ran high at times. Some of the kids at school were somewhat friendly to Nicholas, and the bullies like Del Scribner left him alone, but for the most part, he never really had any close friends. As a boy, he didn't get invited to birthday parties or overnights like the other kids did.

Some of his teachers saw this, and they also tried to befriend him. One teacher in particular, Mr. Elmsford, his fifth grade teacher, saw great potential in Nicolas. Mr. Elmsford was an old fashioned teacher who wore a suit to school each day, and emphasized reading, writing, and arithmetic. He gave Nick extra jobs and arranged different scenarios, where the boy's talents would become apparent to the other children, hoping his social standing would improve. Mr. Elmsford tried, but there was only so much he could do.

Life wasn't perfect for Nicholas, but there were far worse lives for a young man. He had a grandfather who loved him very much, and who tried his best to give the boy a good life. Mrs. Jablonski loved him like a grandmother and took care of him as well as she did her own grandchildren. Another member of the family was Father Ryan. He was a frequent guest for Sunday night dinner at the cabin, and he did whatever he could for the boy with no mother and father.

Yet time has a way of changing everything. While Nick's life was as pleasant and stable as it could be, given the circumstances, things changed. Nicholas Bonecutter's life was never the same after he entered the eighth grade.

Book II
Chapter 6
Port-au-Prince, Haiti—1958

After completing his courses at the "officer's school," Second Lieutenant Armand La Baptiste received his first assignment in the Haitian military. He arrived at Fort Dimanche and reported to the commander, a woman named Madame Max Adolphe.

Upon entering the commander's office, one thing that immediately became clear to La Baptiste: this was not a woman to be crossed. Madame Adolphe took her business seriously. After returning his salute, she sat down.

La Baptiste wondered if she was ever going to invite him to sit, as she sat there reading through the file on top of her mahogany desk, his file, presumably. Ten minutes passed. Madame looked up over her "cat's eye" glasses. "You may take a seat."

La Baptiste quickly planted himself in a straight-backed wooden chair. She turned the file over and spent another fifteen minutes reading through it again. Finally, as she finished her second reading, she spoke.

"Lieutenant, my rules are simple. When I order you to do something, you will do it immediately. You work for me twenty-four hours per day, seven days per week, and 365 days per year. You are always mine, and I expect your best effort at every one of your tasks, even if I order you to clean a toilet. Do you understand me?"

"Yes, Madame!"

"Very good. Your file indicates that you have no problem inflicting cruelty on others, which is good. I myself have no difficulty doing what must be done to preserve the legitimate government of the people of this country. Anyone who stands in the way can and should be butchered."

"I understand, Madame!"

"I didn't ask for your understanding, Lieutenant. Inflicting the people's will is but one aspect of our work here. Cruelty for its own sake is of no use.

No, there must be a purpose and plan in its nature. There must be a design to all that we do. Stow your equipment and return here promptly for your first assignment."

"Yes, Madame!"

After checking in with the officer in charge of the barracks, he was given a small room. He quickly dropped his gear on the cot and hurried back to Adolphe's office.

"Lieutenant, you must learn to do field work, as well as the work done here in the fort," Adolphe said. "Report to the Captain. He is about to leave for a raid on an underground printing operation suspected of distributing brochures attacking our beloved President. And Lieutenant, be sure to bring your sidearm."

The squad captain took La Baptiste with him in a jeep, followed by an open truck carrying ten soldiers. They drove through Port au Prince and headed several miles inland. Just outside of a small village, they pulled to the side of the road. A nervous looking man met the Captain's jeep.

"Where is the printing press?" the Captain asked.

"As you enter the village on this road, it is in the third house on the left. They keep it hidden in a room toward the back of the house, just off the kitchen."

"If you have failed me, I will return. Here is your reward." The Captain reached into his shirt pocket and handed the man a plastic containing powdered heroin.

As they drove into the village, the Captain explained, "Lieutenant, never underestimate the power of addiction for keeping people in line and keeping the country running smoothly. Fools who ride the white horse, or any other narcotic, will do anything for the next taste. If the government controls the flow of these drugs, it can control the people. By way of example, the man we just met has turned in his cousin and his entire family. His need for the heroin far exceeds any familial loyalties he may have."

"Every village, La Baptiste, every city block, has such a man. They need us, and we need them."

La Baptiste and his Captain pulled up in front of the third house, a ramshackle building badly in need of paint. A dilapidated chain swing hung loosely on its mounts on the front porch, next to a pair of mismatched, weather-beaten chairs. By the time the officers climbed out of the jeep, the enlisted men had already surrounded the house and were breaking the door down.

Inside, three old men were rounded up at gunpoint and thrust onto a ratty old couch in the living room.

La Baptiste, ignoring the prisoners, went to the back of the house, immediately locating the antique printing press. The press was hand operated, and the tin type contained a drawing and article President Duvalier would not have found flattering, along with some equally provocative editorial matter.

Seizing the few printed pages stacked near the press, La Baptiste returned to the living room.

"Who else is involved in this?" The Captain slapped one of the old men with his leather gloved hand. None of the men replied. They stared at the floor, tears in their eyes, knowing it was over for them. "Very well, we will see if you will be somewhat more talkative at Fort Dimanche. My young Lieutenant here is quite good at asking questions."

Those who dared peek through their windows or from the jungle where they hid saw the soldiers throw the men in the truck. The house was set ablaze before they drove off.

Book II
Chapter 7
Wilmington, New York— 1983

The tranquility of the Bonecutter home was shattered in the fall of 1983. George was having trouble breathing and went to his doctor. A quick X-ray determined the problem and sealed his fate. George Bonecutter had terminal lung cancer and was given three months to live.

He wasn't afraid of death. He had seen it in all its forms, in peace and in war. He had long ago realized there was something in the universe a lot bigger and more important than he was—a great force of good, locked in an eternal battle with evil. What did scare him, though, was what would become of Nicky.

One day, a social worker came to the house, because Nicholas had missed too much school. The boy insisted on taking care of his grandfather, and no one dared tell him no.

George wished to die at home. He figured if he wasn't going to make it, there was no sense going out in a hospital stuck full of needles. Some of the women from the church came by and cared for him, and Father John stopped by every morning.

As Father John pulled into the driveway that day, he saw a strange vehicle with a county seal on the door parked alongside a sheriff's cruiser.

He walked into the house to find total bedlam. A social worker, the good father would later describe as a "long-haired maggot," was trying to forcibly remove Nicholas from the home, as a sheriff's deputy looked on.

"What the HELL is going on here?" the diminutive little priest shouted. At the sound of his booming voice, all activity in the cabin ceased.

"Sir, my name is Kenneth Vedder," the ponytailed civil servant said, "and I am with the Essex County Department of Social Services. I have a court order to remove this boy and place him in a foster home, where he will get the care he deserves and where he will regularly attend school."

"The hell you will, you foolish ass of a man!" Ryan replied.

"Father, he does have a court order." The deputy handed Ryan a piece of paper.

"The boy will need to be sent to foster care, anyway. His grandfather won't be around by the end of the week, and he has no next of kin. Since there is no one standing by to adopt him, he must be placed in foster care. Someday, maybe someone will adopt him, but for now, he comes with me."

Vedder reached out and grabbed Nicholas by his shirt collar, which was not his best idea. The boy smashed his heel down on Vedder's instep and spun around, swiftly snapping a kick to Vedder's groin.

The deputy stepped forward and grabbed the boy around the waist from behind. Nick pinched and twisted the skin on the man's leg until he released his grip, then smashed his foot against the man's shin bone, snapping the nerve against the bone. The deputy's leg went numb and he fell to the floor.

"Enough! Nicholas, go sit on the couch. I'll take care of this," Father John screamed. "You two make a fine pair, grown men on the floor because you tried to take a boy from his rightful home. You should both be ashamed of yourselves."

"Father, you don't understand. It's the law; I have no choice," the deputy replied.

"Yes, you do." Ryan stepped forward, between Nick and the two men. "Someone is going to adopt this boy and see too it that he lives the rest of his life in this home, and that someone is me! I believe the Catholic Church can have a New York City lawyer and a few politicians up here in a matter of hours. If you think I'm kidding, just try me."

All heads turned to Father Ryan.

"Well, this is highly unusual, but I must continue with my court order," Vedder said, finally managing to pick himself off of the floor.

The sheriff's deputy was a commonsense cop. He knew Sheriff Hollister would back Father John to the wall. As Vedder started towards the boy, he stepped forward. "Hold it right there, mister. You heard Father John. His word means a lot more to me than yours ever will. We're all done here; let's go."

"Deputy, I will have your badge for this!" Vedder's face was red with anger. He was not used to people telling him what to do.

"Asshole, you're gonna have my night stick, if you don't do an about face and get back in your damned car and leave, right now!" The deputy slid the stick from its holder on his gun belt.

Two days later, George Bonecutter died. Ever the pragmatist, he had signed the papers for Father John to adopt his fifteen-year-old grandson and had a will drawn up, giving the boy all his meager worldly goods. The lawyer even saw fit to give the title to the guiding business to the boy, in case he ever wanted to take up that backwoods trade.

Nicholas said little. He had a quiet moment with Grandfather before he passed, then he vowed to be strong and tough. He did not want to fall to pieces at the funeral.

George Bonecutter's funeral was the talk of the town. Wilmington's only Native American son would have been amazed at the turnout. Many of the residents came to see the hero to his final rest. Soldiers appeared in town, all of them wearing the Special Forces berets, including a colonel. The funeral was the best attended the town had seen in many years.

As the coffin was lowered into the earth, a tear slid down the boy's face. An Army officer handed him a folded flag, then a color guard fired a twenty-one gun salute to the fallen warrior. Nicholas would not allow himself to break down and cry. He had to be strong and carry on. Someday, he would see Grandfather again.

On his death bed, George, knowing how much the martial arts training had helped the boy, made Father John promise to see that the training continued. He provided the Father with the name of a Japanese master he knew who had a school in New York City, and another instructor in Plattsburg.

Father John moved into the home and saw to the rest of the boy's upbringing as best as a bachelor priest could.

Nicholas spent two summers in New York City with Kansatsu Sensei, training in several martial arts, including Karate, Aikido, Iaido, and Kendo. He earned his way doing chores at the dojo. Father John's friend, Father D'Arcy, at St. Cecelia's let the boy stay with him while he was in New York. During the school year, on weekends, he also trained with Cooper Sensei, one of Kansatsu's students in Plattsburg. Father John would see to it that the boy would have some pocket money and a bus ticket to get where he needed to be.

Under all the training, and through the rest of his teenage years, the boy did well living with the good Father. Cooper Sensei had told him that if he wanted to train, he had to have a B average in school and stay out of trouble. While Nicholas wasn't academically inclined, he worked hard and kept his part of the bargain.

The only noticeable change was that he became a little more withdrawn and quiet after George died. He didn't have close friends at school, but he still he got along with most of the kids; at least he had their respect.

It all went incredibly well, right up until his senior year in high school.

Book II
Chapter 8
Port-au-Prince, Haiti—1960

Captain Armand La Baptiste snapped the cylinder shut on the battered .38 caliber Smith and Wesson service revolver he carried as a sidearm. He jumped into the passenger seat of the old army Jeep and ordered the driver to move out. La Baptiste was on his way for more field work, and this job worried him.

Today, Mme. Adolph was sending him to a remote village in the mountains to capture an old woman. Typically, such things were quite simple for him, and beating an old woman to death was certainly nothing that would trouble his sensibilities. He excelled as one of the Macoutes, both in field work such as this and in extracting information in the feared basement cells of Fort Dimanche. He would kill or torture anyone who needed it, but this time, something was different.

Sweat slid down his neck, staining the starched collar of his uniform. He considered the implications of today's mission as his sergeant ground the gears of the ancient Jeep. There was much talk among the villagers that the old woman was a "lupe garou," some sort of monster. The villagers said that she stole their babies and small farm animals in the night and lived by drinking their blood.

Haiti was a country whose population was heavily Catholic, yet even more people practiced Voodoo. The ways of Voodoo were deeply ingrained in the very fabric of the country, the very reason President Duvalier played his resemblance to Baron Samedi to the hilt. It was easy for Duvalier to multiply his strangle hold over the country in this manner.

La Baptiste had enough education to realize the old ways in the countryside were nothing more than ridiculous superstition, yet in the pit of his stomach, butterflies churned away. He had been part of some of the Voodoo ceremonies all Macoutes took part in, and they disturbed him greatly.

Armand didn't believe in them for the most part. Big deal, they all got together, said a bunch of words, and drank some blood. Trouble was, during some of the ceremonies, he had seen things, scenes that scared him deeply. Once he had witnessed President Duvalier resurrect a dead man. The President made the dead man dance for him; then he had him lick his boots as he drank his whisky. Finally, he put an end to the charade with a well-placed bullet to the man's head.

As his sergeant brought the Jeep to a stop in the village, people ran out of their ramshackle huts to meet them. In contrast to a typical encounter with the Haitian Army, where people hid behind closed doors when they saw the troops approach, these poor people were clearly very happy to see the squad of soldiers arrive. La Baptiste was quickly surrounded by a group of villagers, all babbling in rapid fire Creole as soon as the vehicle came to a stop.

"Get back!" He brandished his .38 caliber revolver in the faces of the villagers. "Now one of you, tell me what this is all about."

An old man dressed in a tattered T-shirt and old blue jeans patched at the knees with pinned on scraps of cloth stepped forward on sandals fashioned out of a scrap tire. "Captain, I am Phillip Villapan, mayor of this village, and we need your help. A *loup garou* is preying on our people. Babies and old people disappear in the middle of the night. Sometimes we find the bodies. They are white, Captain, drained of all their blood!"

"Old man, who is doing this?"

"I have told you Captain, it is the *loup garou!* She comes out at night and takes the weak and the old."

"Old man, ordinarily I would tell you this *loup garou* was doing you a favor, but it seems I must rid you of this evil to restore the peace. So tell me, where can I find this *loup garou?*" La Baptiste looked at the man like he was addressing an errant child.

"She lives in the old plantation, just outside of the village along this road." Villapan pointed to the west.

"Well, old man, your *loup garou* troubles are over." La Baptiste gestured with his hand and his sergeant drove off.

Five minutes outside the village, the soldiers arrived at the remains of a once thriving plantation, an opulent remnant of wealth in an otherwise dirt-poor country. The mansion was almost completely in ruins. The roof had caved in, and the outer walls would follow soon, as the jungle reclaimed the land. It was clear from the encroachment of vines and vegetation that no maintenance had been done on the place in decades. The windows were broken, their once ornate shutters hanging in shreds, ever so much rotten wood.

"Spread out, search this place," La Baptiste ordered the men. Near the mansion, along a partially overgrown path, were more dilapidated buildings, the remains of the slave quarters. These, oddly enough, had stood the test of time much better than the mansion itself. The structures looked relatively sound, made of more solid and practical materials than the main house.

La Baptiste sent his sergeant in first, as he looked around outside. Some of the other men searched a small barn next to the slave quarters.

As La Baptiste was about to enter the slave quarters, he heard one of the privates in the barn scream like a little girl. "Captain, Captain, come quickly, help us!" Then a shot rang out from one of the ancient bolt-action Mauser rifles that the troops carried. Several gunshots in quick succession erupted from the barn.

La Baptiste and his sergeant ran to the barn. As he stood at the doorway, he could not believe what he saw. One private's head rolled toward him along the floor like a macabre bowling ball.

La Baptiste ran into the barn. Immediately his nose winced at the over-powering scent of rotting flesh, along with the undertone of the coppery odor of blood. Then he saw her, a haggard looking old woman, but obviously no ordinary human. La Baptiste had shot people who were on drugs before, the only possible explanation for what he was seeing.

The dimly lit barn was like an animal's den. Bones and rotting flesh littered the floor. Someone had hung several bodies, presumably the missing villagers, upside down. Corpses of children and old people, all with their throats ripped out, hung randomly from the beams.

The old woman had hands like claws. Her face was like a wild beast, contorted with rage, a mouth full of unnaturally sharp teeth, and blood red eyes. She had taken several bullet hits to the chest and one to the head, yet she would not go down. One of the privates, enraged at the death of his friend, held the end of an old pitchfork he had found lying on the floor and rammed through her chest. The old woman was pinned to the central beam of the barn, howling in pain and rage as she struggled to free herself.

La Baptiste saw an opportunity to increase his hold over the men who served him. Drawing his machete, he advanced toward the hideous creature pinned to the beam and hacked off its right arm; then, smiling at the old woman, he used his trademark. He licked the blood from the blade, showing her how little her life was worth, and how powerful he was, just like a voodoo priest. As he did, the old woman broke out into horrible laughter.

La Baptiste swung his machete again, hacking the old woman's head clean off. As it fell to the floor, smoke erupted from the skin of the corpse. The body started sparking and actually caught on fire, quickly burning itself to a crisp.

La Baptiste and his men backed away in terror as it continued to burn.

"You there, private, bring gasoline. I want this entire place burned to the ground. Do you hear me, to the ground! None of you will ever speak of what we have seen here again."

After the fire had erased what had taken place, La Baptiste and his men rode away. He felt odd on the ride back to Fort Dimanche. He broke into a fever and felt very weak. After reporting what had taken place to Mme. Adolphe, he returned to his quarters. The next morning, a private sent to check on him found him dead in his cot.

Captain Armand La Baptiste was buried that afternoon with full military honors, one of the Haitian military's finest.

Book II
Chapter 9
Port-au-Prince, Haiti—1960

The old drunk sat next to the large granite headstone that was his favorite, downing a swig from his bottle of cheap rum. It always amazed him that the bottom line in life was that, regardless of the differences in men's stature while they were alive, there was very little difference after they were dead.

Viewed in the daylight, the cemetery was unusual. Those who had money preferred to spend eternity above ground. There were many burial vaults, most of which were painted with the bright blues, aquamarines, and coral colors of the Caribbean. Those who did not have such means spent the rest of time buried. If their families cared enough to scrape up a little money, they had some kind of headstone.

The old drunk was the night watchman at the cemetery. The cemetery's Board of Governors had hired him to prevent the vandalism that occurred during the night in the cemeteries on the island. The cemetery, like many others in the country, was plagued with grave robbing, a common practice in Port au Prince. It was routine for a grave to be broken into on the first night of interment.

Poverty was to blame for this ghoulish practice. A thief could make a quick buck the easy way from the older graves by obtaining dried old body parts and selling them to voodoo priests for use in their ceremonies. It was also rumored that the local witch doctors would resurrect certain people, making them into zombies, who would be their slaves. In fact, there were a couple of "documented" cases of individuals becoming zombies, turning up walking around in another town shortly after their burial.

The old drunk laughed as he poured more of the dark rum down his gullet. To him, it was easy to measure a man's success after he was gone. The bigger the hunk of granite and the higher it reached up towards his God, the richer the man. The only difference between him and the rich folks was the size of a piece of simple rock. He didn't mind his job, though. Other than having to chase away the occasional bunch of kids or would-be grave robbers, he actually got paid to do something he was going to do anyway, sit and get drunk.

Nighttime on a tropical island is never silent; there is always the incessant chirping of birds and insects, continually droning on. As the old man sat there scratching his scrubby beard, he heard a dull noise, a thumping.

He took another swig of the cheap, oily rum, and the noise suddenly ceased. "I must be imagining things," he said aloud.

Suddenly, the thumping came again, and this time, the ground rumbled slightly, like a small earth tremor. The source of the noise was a hundred yards away in the newest section of the cemetery.

The old drunk rose from his seat and walked towards the sound. After zigzagging around the maze of headstones, he came to a fresh grave. As he stood there watching, the sand and dirt started cracking, like little fingers spreading out through the soil.

He stood frozen, jaw agape, clutching the sawed-off shotgun he carried on his rounds, as the sand hopped upward, like someone underneath had given it a giant shove. He tried to step back but tripped over a headstone and fell down. The sand exploded upward, as if a charge of dynamite had gone off below it. He watched in amazement, as the lid of a coffin flipped up out of the hole, turning over and over like coin tossed into the air before it landed on a headstone with a loud crack.

Mist rose from the gaping grave. The old drunk screamed, as a corpse in a full-dress military uniform, hopped out of the grave, as easily as a house cat jumps up on its favorite perch. For a black man, the corpse was very pale. Its eyes were red, eyes that glowed, but not from the reflection of the ample moonlight. No, these eyes were lit from energy within, like bright coals in a fire.

The thing in the soldier's uniform turned its head and looked about, spotting the old drunk. Leaping, it was on him in an instant, before he could bring the gun up. The foul apparition sank its hideous teeth into the old drunk's neck, tearing it open. It watched a geyser of blood spray, before it latched its mouth on the fountain, gorging itself.

After it finished, the thing in the uniform sat down next to the old drunk's body, talking to itself as it stared at the hole from which it had sprung.

"What am I, what have I become?"

The question was a rhetorical one. The thing that had burst from the grave knew what it had become. It could see the name on the simple tombstone,

Captain Armand La Baptiste, hero of the people of Haiti. The thing was once Captain Armand La Baptiste, and somehow it knew that, but now it was more. It was a *lupe garou,* a vampire.

It also knew that, just as it had hunted down and killed the *lupe garou,* men would one day come to kill it in the same way.

Book II
Chapter 10
Port-au-Prince, Haiti—1960

For as long as Armand La Baptiste existed in his new "life," he would always remember his first pitiful night as a vampire.

He buried the old drunk's corpse in his own grave and looked around for a place to hide. He had just pried open an old crypt built into a hillside in the cemetery, breaking the heavy lock as if it were made of eggshell, as the first pink rays of sunlight reached out over the horizon of the Caribbean Island. The sun in that part of the world is strong, but sunlight had never caused the reaction he experienced. It made him physically ill to look at the pink sky that foretold the coming dawn. Some of the sun's early rays touched his hand as he quickly closed the door of the crypt behind him.

He yanked his hand back. He had been burned the same as if he had stuck his hand in an open flame. He could actually smell the sickening stench of his own burnt flesh.

Inside the crypt were two caskets, covered in the accumulated dust of a hundred years. Even though the crypt was well made, and totally blocked out the accursed light of the sun, La Baptiste discovered he could actually see in what should have been total darkness. It was as if everything in the crypt gave off light of some sort; he could clearly see everything in a greenish glow.

The thick concrete walls blocked the sunlight. As the sun climbed in the sky, he could actually feel it up there. On this, his first dawn as one of the undead, La Baptiste felt himself growing weaker, as the sun rose. Finally, after an hour of pacing back and forth in the confines of the crypt, he seized one of the caskets from the slab it rested upon, still amazed at how strong he had become and dumped the corpse of a man out onto the floor. The body was remarkably well preserved. The air on the island was very dry; even the suit it had worn into the great beyond looked fairly good, considering it had been on the corpse for almost a hundred years. The flesh on the body was like dry leather, similar to an Egyptian mummy.

He put the coffin back on the slab next to the one occupied by the dead man's wife, and climbed inside, closing the lid after him.

La Baptiste felt much better, much safer in the casket. He finally slept. He could hardly keep his eyes open. His rest was fitful, as he cowered in someone else's casket, very much afraid. He feared he would be discovered and killed, just as he had killed the old woman, the *lupe garou*.

He woke as the sun began to set. He could feel it descending over the western horizon. La Baptiste had come to some realizations as he slept. He knew that if he wanted to *live*, he could not make mistakes like those the *lupe garou* he killed had made. He knew his foolishness in not believing the old legends, and he now knew that licking the hag's blood from the machete had turned him this way. There was no going back to life among the living.

In the true life as one of Duvalier's best torturers, he had learned that knowledge was power. Controlling others through fear was power. He needed to know more about his current condition, needed to find out what he could and could not do. The solution was obvious; he had to go find the old man from the village and find out everything he knew about the *lupe garou*.

La Baptiste, dressed himself in clothes he had stolen from a nearby house, then he stole a car and drove to the outskirts of Phillip Villapan's village.

The old man was easy to find. He often walked the roads at night. Like many older people, sleep did not come easily for him. As Villapan rounded the bend in the road, still within sight of the village, La Baptiste knocked the old man down and shoved a gag in his mouth. Holding him in an iron grip, he dragged him away to the old plantation where the *lupe garou* had been destroyed. The old man struggled but was rewarded for his efforts with a knockout blow to the side of the head.

When Villapan finally came to, he found himself in the burned out remains of an old barn. What he didn't know was that it was the same barn where the *lupe garou* had been killed. His wrists were throbbing and his arms hurt. He looked up to see that he was chained to a charred wooden beam by some old slave shackles. Someone had lit a few candles, providing a dim light but no warmth in the cool night air. Villapan looked up as La Baptiste appeared in the light. He saw the vampire's grinning face undergo the change. He screamed as the red eyes and sharp teeth appeared when the man changed to the monster.

"Scream, old man, no one will hear you," the thing hissed.

"You can't be real, the *lupe garou* is gone," the old man whimpered.

"Yes, old man, the old hag is gone, but a new *lupe garou* has taken her place. I offer you a bargain. Tell me what I need to know and you will be spared."

"I will never help a *lupe garou*." The old man turned his face away from the horror.

"Very well, I had planned on this difficulty. Let me show you what I have in my sack." The vampire produced a burlap bag; something was moving inside of it. He reached into the bag and produced one of the old man's grandchildren, a little boy named Remey.

"Now, tell me what I need to know, and you both shall be spared. Refuse me, and I will feast on this little one and then go retrieve another of your family." La Baptiste held the boy by the scruff of the neck, leering at the old man and exposing his teeth.

"No, please, let him go. I will tell you whatever you want to know. Just let my little Remey go." The old man cried as he looked at the little boy, paralyzed with fear, in the grip of a real-life monster.

La Baptiste spent several nights with the old man, a Voodoo priest, studying the ways of the *lupe garou*, finding out what his new strengths were and his weaknesses. One thing was clear: if he wished to continue his existence, he had to leave Haiti, a land where beliefs in the old ways like Voodoo were strong. He would go where no one believed the old legends, and he would find ways of taking blood without leaving a trail of others like himself in his wake.

When he was absolutely sure he had learned all that the old man knew, he freed Villapan from his chains and released the boy into his grandfather's arms.

"You must go away and leave here," Villapan said.

"Yes I must." The vampire moved with astonishing speed, and snatched the boy by the neck and Villapan by the arm. "First, I must feed."

"No, let me go. You, you said I would be freed!" The old man screamed, hugging his grandchild closer.

"No *monsieur*. I said you would be freed, and by that I meant you would not have to become as I am, and I will keep my bargain. Fear not, I will be sure and do as you have instructed me, none of my essence shall enter your body, and your head will be taken off, just in case. I shall honor the boy in the same way."

The last thing Villapan saw, before he drifted into oblivion, was the horrid face of a vampire. The old man died gagging and retching on the foul breath of the blood eater, knowing there was nothing he could do for his poor little grandson.

Book II
Chapter II
Wilmington, New York—
1987

Wilmington Notch High School, although a small institution in comparison to most high schools, was still an interesting case study in sociology. Like any other high school, it had its proportional share of jocks, geeks, brains, burnouts, and cheerleaders. Of course, with a graduating class of around a hundred, there were fewer of each compared to most schools.

There were also those who did not fit into any category. Some kids were total outsiders, not welcome in any of the various social groups. Some of these kids ended up badly, the isolation eating away at them throughout their schooling. Jimmy Currow couldn't pass any of his classes and became a helpless drug addict by the time he finally graduated. Fat Nancy Bass never had a boyfriend and committed suicide by taking an overdose of her mother's sleeping pills, heading to the great beyond in the same condition she hated in life, still a virgin. There were a few, though, who, in spite of a lack of popularity or a sense of belonging, didn't succumb to the misery.

High school senior Nicholas Bonecutter still didn't know where he belonged. He got along with the other kids for the most part. Most of the kids would at least talk to him, and few ever gave him any grief. Still, he had no close friends.

Girls were also a mystery. Like any teenage boy, he was certainly attracted to them. Still, he had no idea how to go about dating. Father John was no help. He had gone straight from school to the Seminary. He knew even less about girls than Nick did.

One girl, however, seemed to like Nick. Her name was Janet Early. She was no beauty queen, but she was pretty and had a very down-to-earth personality. Like Nick, she was one of those kids who didn't belong to a particular group.

Nicholas watched her in math class from his usual desk just to her left. She had brown eyes and was a just under average height at five-foot four. She had chestnut colored hair and a narrow nose that turned up slightly at the end. The only flaw in her looks was that she was somewhat flat-chested, which didn't make her one of the top targets of the popular boys.

The biggest problem with Janet was that she had been out on a date or two with Del Scribner.

Del had flubbed his way through high school pretty much unscathed. Like his father before him, schoolwork wasn't his thing. The teachers hated him. He was such a little asshole, most of them passed him just to get rid of him, with the exception of the three who were brave enough to hold him back. Del did find his niche, though. His educational achievement was booze and drugs, and he was the leader of a group of pot heads who got drunk and stoned as often as they possibly could.

Del always said, "Why should I bust my ass on this stupid schoolwork? I'm gonna party and have a good time. I don't need to know all of this shit to work in the woods logging with the old man."

Janet, in a moment of extreme stupidity, went on a date to the movies with Del. He was the bad boy, a big attraction for a young girl trying to find her own way to rebel. She got more than she bargained for. Once the movie started, Del was all over her. She decided she wasn't interested in being with the bad boy after all.

When Scribner got sick of her saying no, he drove her home. Figuring he needed to get her head on straight for their next date, he turned in the seat of his crappy Mustang and said, "Look, bitch, if you're goin' out with me, you're puttin' out, get it?" Janet had had enough and yanked the door open. As she stepped out she said, "You don't have to worry, Del, because I'll never go out with you again."

The fact that he hadn't scored didn't set well with Scribner. When he got to school on Monday morning after his big date, he went into great detail to anyone who would listen about how he had "done" Janet Early. Del painted a very vivid picture of what a slut she was. He told all his friends, who gave him the thumbs up sign for his success. He told people who weren't his friends, many of whom believed him. It made sense. Why would she go out with the king of the burnouts if that wasn't what she was looking for? Heck, he even told the janitor all about it.

If the wrong story got out about a student in Wilmington Notch High, even one as bogus as the one Scribner told, it became reality. From that day on, Janet Early was forever the school slut. The only time boys would have anything to do with her was to see if they could get what Del had gotten. Janet wasn't one of the more popular girls, but she had her share of friends until her date with Del. After Del finished with her, the other girls wouldn't have anything to do with her, either.

In a world where being popular was everything, Janet Early became nothing. She wasn't exactly an extrovert, but she became even more withdrawn, due to enduring the daily leering from the boys and the forced isolation of the girls. By the time the Senior Prom approached, she had only one person who talked to her, another social misfit named Nicholas Bonecutter.

Nick and Janet started talking to each other in math class, where they sat close together. One day, they ran into each other in town. Janet knew Nick wasn't like the other boys, who now only talked to her to see if they could get into her pants. Nick was different.

Their friendship grew and they even went on a date to the movies together. Finally, Nick asked her to go to the prom, and she said yes.

Father John drove him to Plattsburg to rent a tuxedo. The good Father snapped a couple of pictures of the kids with his 110mm Kodak camera and sent them off to the prom in George's old red Chevy truck, which Nicholas had fixed up and put back on the road.

When they arrived at the big dance at the Holiday Inn, the whispers started immediately. Nicholas was unaffected by the taunts and jeers. "I don't listen to lies," he said. "Don't worry about them, Janet, if they want to believe a liar like Del that's their choice."

For the first time in a long time, she finally felt at ease. "You're right, Nick, let's go have fun." She grabbed him by the hand and they went off to the dance floor. For someone so coordinated and balanced from years of martial arts training, Nick was a spaz on the dance floor, but she did her best to coach him.

As Nick and Janet danced, Del Scribner made his entrance to his fourth prom in classic fashion. He and his drinking buddies did not bring dates, nor did they bother to dress for the occasion. Del's bright idea was to show up wearing a tuxedo T-shirt. He and his friends had pounded plenty of Buds and schnapps on the way there.

They started right in, as soon as they arrived, harassing the geeks and the nerds. The drunken clods tried to dance with other boy's dates, shoving anyone who got in their way, until finally, the chaperons stepped in and warned them they would be leaving soon if it kept up. As he glanced on the dance floor, Del started going into a slow burn. Here was that fucking Injun dancing with Janet Early. As the night wore on, and he consumed more of the punch he'd spiked, he worked himself into a little beer bravery.

"It's time we teach that fuckin' Injun a lesson, boys. Once and for all, he's gonna learn he's not as good as a white man. Here's what we're gonna to do." Del gathered his pals and they all left the dance.

After the band had played its final song and the prom ended, and people started picking up the banquet room, Nicholas and Janet headed outside to go home. When they got to the truck, they found the tires had been slashed.

Del and his buddies stepped out of bushes, pointing at the truck and laughing as they swilled more beer. "What's a matter, Injun, got a flat?" Scribner said, as the whole group broke out into a raucous laugh.

"Go ahead and fix those tires , Chief, we'll take care of Janet," Del's fat slob of a buddy Billy Freedman said, as he grabbed Janet by the arm.

Del had four of his pals with him, more than enough to take care of the Injun, even with all his karate tricks. "Sounds good, Bill. Hell, she should be able to handle the five of us. I'll go first," Scribner reached over and ripped the top of Janet's dress, exposing the matching bra she wore underneath. She cried out and tried to move, but Freedman had come up behind her and had her by the arms.

"Go ahead, Injun, change them tires, but take your time, cause I don't want to have to rush." Del grinned as he spoke.

Nicholas, up till this point had said nothing. Now he'd had enough. By grabbing the girl and ripping her dress, he now had the right to use what he knew. "Let her go!" His shout was loud, and it startled Del and his pals, so much so, Freedman released Janet's arms.

"Get him, boys." Del swung a slow, loping fist at Nicholas, which he easily ducked. He could see one of Del's buddies coming for him out of the corner of his eye, and he slammed the point of his left elbow in the boy's face, breaking the nose and causing blood to spray everywhere. He ducked in between his enemies, confusing them and causing them to trip over each other, as they tried to hit him. As he passed between Scribner and Freedman, ducking under their punches, he shot his right hand forward, catching Freedman in the groin with the stiffened ridge of his hand, instantly putting the fat slob on the pavement.

The kid with the broken nose was all done, and Freedman was too busy throwing up to fight. That left three. Del swung again, this time connecting with Bonecutter's jaw. Unlike most people who stiffen up, Nicholas rolled with the punch, spinning away from the impact and taking most of the sting out of it, while at the same time harnessing the energy transferred to his body, as he swung his right hand in a vicious spinning back fist that caught Scribner on the side of the head. His aim was a little off, but the blow was enough to knock Scribner right off his feet.

One of Del's buddies made the mistake of grabbing Nicholas from behind, pinning his arms. Nick used the back of his skull and smashed the boy's face, breaking the boy's left eye socket. He then lashed out with a foot stomp to the boy's instep, making the attacker let him go, simultaneously ducking as Del swung at his head. Scribner's missed punch landed right on the same spot Nick had damaged with the head butt. The kid's knees turned to mush as he passed out.

That left Del and one more. As Del swung another useless haymaker, Bonecutter blocked it, smashing the stiffened edge of both forearms into the nerves that control the arm. Del's punching arm dropped to his side, totally numb. The other boy advanced, and Nick lashed out with a nasty side kick to the boy's stomach then spun around, whipping a wheel kick across the side of the boy's head, knocking him out cold.

Now there was only Del, who had produced a knife. Del swung the blade at Nick's mid-section trying to spill his guts on the pavement. Nick slid back and let the cut pass, and then he slammed Del's arm as he swung again. Grabbing the knife hand, he locked his grip on the wrist and took the knife from his hand. Del hit Nick in the face with a weak punch, causing him to lose balance and his arms swung backward. Somewhere in his mind, it registered that the hand with the knife seemed to have hit something as it swung back, but he didn't have time to worry about it. He slammed Scribner with a series of hand strikes, four in all, breaking Del's nose and the right side of his ribs. The would-be bully crumpled to the ground crying.

Nick was brought to reality by Janet's screams.

The chaperones saw the fight and immediately called the police, and Tom Quinn the high school gym teacher ran to the scene. As he arrived, he found Janet Early screaming, a huge cut on her face with blood streaming down her dress, and Nicholas Bonecutter standing there with a bloody knife in his hand. The deep gash ran from the girl's right eye socket to her lip. One of the women chaperones led her back inside the Holiday Inn to get some towels to put on the cut.

Flashing red lights lit up the parking lot as Del and his buddies fled. A young state trooper, fresh from the academy, ran from his car. Upon seeing a boy with a bloody knife in his hands, he drew his gun.

"Up against the car with your hands on the hood!" He leveled his .357 magnum on Nick's chest, before he pushed the boy around onto the car hood.

"I didn't do anything wrong," Bonecutter said.

"I said, up against the car, asshole!" the officer screamed.

Nicholas did as he was told, and was handcuffed. The trooper then took him by the hair on his head and smashed his face into the parked car.

The trooper took a statement from the gym teacher, who verified seeing the girl was cut and that Nicholas seemed to have done it. Janet was on her way to the hospital with one of the teachers and wasn't there to tell what happened. The trooper radioed his sergeant and put Nick into his patrol car, arresting him for attempted rape and assault.

The young trooper had already decided on Nick's guilt. He even roughed up the handcuffed boy a couple of times at the barracks as he booked him for trying to rape a young girl. Father John finally arrived and bailed him out. Then, the next day he hired a lawyer to defend him. Several weeks went by before the trial.

Unfortunately for Bonecutter, in spite of Janet giving the police a statement professing his innocence, Del and all of his buddies swore up and down that the crazy Indian was trying to rape the girl, and all they had done was try to help. The amount of injuries they sustained in the process made the police believe Nick had attacked them and the girl in a fit of rage. To make things worse, right after graduation and just before the trial, Janet's family moved back to Maine, where they had came from. It did not make much difference for their budding romance, because her father had forbidden her to see him. Without her to testify on his behalf, Nick was finished before the gavel hit the bench.

Justice and politics in the north woods are not the same as they are in other places. Town Justice Horace Smith, the same judge who presided over his grandfather's crooked trial, held Nick's fate in his hands. Del and his buddies, one of which was Smith's nephew, testified against him. The state police troopers also put on a good show with several of their "expert" witnesses, including the young trooper, whose story had nothing at all to do with the reality of what happened that night. They also conveniently explained that Janet's statement didn't exonerate him, because abused women often testify on behalf of their abuser.

There wasn't a lawyer in the country who could have won an innocent verdict at the trial. The only thing that went in Nick's favor was the attempted rape charge being dropped for lack of evidence.

Justice Smith gave the boy the same choice his grandfather had, enlist in the military within five days or be sentenced to five years in state prison. Nicholas tried to join the Army for Special Forces training, just like Grandfather had, but he was unable to get an appointment with a recruiter.

Father John took him to a U.S. Navy Recruiter in Plattsburg, the only other option in the area. When Nick expressed an interest in doing what his grandfather did, the recruiter signed him for a chance at becoming the Navy's equivalent, a SEAL. After he left, the town went on without him. Del Scribner and his buddies drank beer and smoked dope. Father John saved souls. And Nicholas Bonecutter went on to become a hero.

BOOK III
Old Houses

Book III
Chapter I
Albany, New York

Ed Woldman had a problem. He was only a couple of years shy of a detective's pension, one he'd worked nearly thirty years to earn. Now it looked like he had finally gotten himself into a case that, in all likelihood, would tank his career.

He simply could not believe what he had seen through his night vision binoculars. A corpse that had once apparently been the owner of the Arbor Hill Funeral Home, a body that had clearly been shot a couple of times with what could only have been a .45, judging from the sound of the muzzle blast, hopped up on its feet and tore a steel warehouse door from its hinges with its bare hands.

The perp, for lack of a better description, then ran after a speeding truck at better than forty miles per hour. The thing would have caught the truck, too, if it hadn't been shot again in the leg. The same subject went on to peel himself up off of the road and walk away, like nothing had ever happened. Better yet, the wounds Woldman could clearly see through the night vision gear, including the hole in his leg, looked like they actually sealed up all by themselves.

To top it all off, fifteen minutes later, Lavotti, the pothead he got to give up La Baptiste, had been dumped on the doorstep of Albany Medical Center, minus a few appendages. Someone had trussed him up with some primitive first aid in the form of cable ties to staunch the blood flow. Woldman had over-heard one of his numbskull counterparts saying that Lavotti's blood was also found at the warehouse on a table and on a machete found lying on the floor.

Lavotti ended up dying on the operating table, so having him explain what the hell was going on in the warehouse wasn't going to happen.

Since the guys in the truck, including the tough-looking younger dude, who was carrying Lavotti over his shoulder, were clearly being chased by the man who couldn't be hurt by mere bullets, they, in all likelihood, they hadn't cut up Lavotti. It appeared that Lavotti had been carved up by Armand La

Baptiste, the guy from the funeral home. Woldman wasn't totally sure, but La Baptiste seemed to resemble the build of the guy who ran from the warehouse; although a guy built like that certainly wouldn't be able to tear down a steel door.

Woldman sat in De Cesare's Bar trying to think the whole thing through. De Cesare's was a small neighborhood restaurant that had survived for almost eighty years. The place looked exactly the same today as it did when Woldman's mother and father had taken him there to eat dinner when he was a kid, right down to the same crappy paneling and woodwork. In fact, the dusty plastic plants hanging over his head were the same ones that had done so over forty years ago. DeCesare's didn't succeed on atmosphere. They offered a wide range of Italian dishes at a great price.

Woldman, like most regulars, was willing to overlook the surroundings, because he loved the food they served. Even though the kitchen at De Cesare's was fairly small, and lacked most of the modern amenities, like a dishwasher, the food was excellent. No one could match De Cesare's tomato sauce. Customers got a plate piled with pasta and usually walked out with leftovers, but tonight Woldman was here to drink, not to eat.

As he sat there drinking his second double scotch, he mused at just how ridiculous what he had seen would look, if it was written up on Albany P.D.'s standard crime incident database report form. The worst thing of all was the orgasm the Captain would have if he knew Woldman was the voice on the anonymous 911 call reporting the shooting at the warehouse. Reichman would finally be able to hang him out to dry.

He also knew he wasn't going to let this one go. When he was still a teenager living at home with his folks, his sister Melanie went bad. She fell in with the wrong crowd, then moved in with her drug dealer boyfriend at age eighteen. One night, she and her boyfriend were getting high, when the dealer he owed money to broke down the door and shot them both. Woldman was too young to get even with the shooter, but he spent the rest of his life as a cop trying to make sure some other family didn't have to go through the same thing. Yet, even his very best wasn't good enough to stop the drugs and all the mayhem that went with them.

He didn't know what the hell La Baptiste was, but he knew he was a dealer and, most likely, a murderer, and he wasn't going to get away with it.

A creature of habit, Woldman let his mind work on two levels, as he sought the answers to a crime. Even Sherlock Holmes did weird things while he was thinking, like shoot his initials into the wall of his London flat. While his mind twisted the mystery around and looked at it from all sides, Woldman unconsciously walked over to the nearly antique Pac Man game that Sammy De Cesare was too damn cheap to replace and dropped a quarter in. As his little yellow Pac Man gobbled up dots, while he yanked the red knob back and forth to avoid the goblins, a deeper part of his mind started spinning out his next move. When his little Pac Man had finally been destroyed by the blue goblins for the last time, he had his answer, one he really didn't like.

First of all, he needed to find some kind of rational explanation for how someone could possibly take the amount of damage that he had seen inflicted on the black guy at the warehouse and still live to tell about it. Woldman wasn't a particularly picky man when it came to his occasional female companions, but in this case, he was going to have to swallow any actual pride he had left. He was going to have to take Dr. Carter from the medical examiner's office out on a date. He'd dated nerdy women before and found the thought of listening to her life story torturous. Still, he might be able to win her over enough to get an answer without her reporting him to anyone. He shuddered at the thought of a night out with her and gulped down his glass of Johnny Walker Black before quickly nodding to Sammy for another.

The next step was to make some "unofficial" inquiries to find out who the priest and the other guy in the truck were. He had plenty of contacts and sources of information he could count on to get him what he needed to know without anyone figuring out what he was up to.

Finally, he needed to get as much information on the owner of the funeral home as he could get, but he would have to do so outside official channels and without arousing any suspicion. This was going to be the tough part. From what he had found out so far, La Baptiste had a lot of friends in high places, and it was rumored that one of them was Captain Reichman and his brother the police commissioner.

Steps two and three would be pretty easy. Woldman had busted a kid several years ago for possession, but after talking to the boy, he saw a far better use for the pot-smoking computer geek. Tommy Santone had shown Woldman how easy it was to tap into computers, including the mainframe his own department stored its data on. Tommy could hack his way into just about anything, and Woldman would use him to tap into the lives of the funeral home owner and the two guys in the pickup truck.

Two days later, after a stunning evening of wining and dining a woman who was probably the only fifty-year-old virgin he'd ever met, Woldman sat down in his apartment to look over what he had discovered so far.

From his discussions with Dr. Carter, no one could take a direct hit from a heavy caliber handgun to the leg and get up and keep running, especially if they had an obvious head wound as well. The answer to his hypothetical question on gunshot trauma was about what he figured it would be. Had he gone with his instincts, he could have spared himself a three-hour conversation with the good doctor, which included far too many details on the life of "Pebbles" the cat. Worst of all, he was going to have to deal with her again someday because of his job, and he sure as hell wasn't taking her out again, which would make the next autopsy even more awkward.

Another interesting tidbit was the fact that there had been no gunshot wound hospital admissions in the city that night. If the man who was seemingly bullet-proof was Armand La Baptiste, he certainly didn't receive any local medical care.

Woldman wasn't a religious man, but he had just seen a dead man get up and run after a speeding vehicle. Something far beyond the usual was going on here.

Tommy's illicit computer work had provided him with more pieces of the puzzle. The truck was registered to a Nicholas Bonecutter from Wilmington Notch, way up in the Adirondacks. When Tommy checked the man's background something odd popped up. Bonecutter had been charged with an assault on a girl when he was young, but the case was sealed and dismissed. He joined the Navy where he received an honorable discharge, and then oddly enough, someone in the federal government wiped his entire service record clean.

Tommy, as good as he was, could not penetrate Bonecutter's service record. It had come back indicating that it was sealed by order of the Secretary of the Navy, and was "Top Secret." To Woldman, this could only mean one thing, the guy was either in some form of military intelligence, or he was Special Forces, which would explain how he scaled the side of the building and made a silent entry at the warehouse. As far as his civilian life went, there was little to tell. He had an outdoor guide's license from the state, and also taught martial arts on a part-time basis. Apparently, Bonecutter had quite a background in the martial arts, as well. His name appeared on the website of a famous Japanese Master from New York City, as one of his senior students.

The man in the priest's outfit turned out to really be a priest. Woldman visited St. Andrews and asked if they knew of a priest from the Wilmington/ Lake Placid area who might have lost a wallet. The leader of the parish immediately volunteered that they had recently been visited by a Father John Ryan, who was in Albany on business, and resided in Wilmington Notch in the Adirondacks.

Once he had the priest's name, Woldman knew a little Adirondack vacation was in order. *I should just walk away from this thing and keep my mouth shut.* No one, including the guy who got shot, knew Woldman was anywhere near the warehouse. Somewhere in the back of his mind, Woldman knew he should just walk away from the whole deal.

After a long, sleepless night of tossing and turning, he dropped a leave slip in the Captain's mail slot the next morning and left for a long weekend upstate for a little fishing.

Book III
Chapter 2
Wilmington, New York

Jean Van Nostrand was as pale as the lace curtains on the windows in Father Ryan's spare bedroom. Her dark hair lay damp on her forehead, and she tossed and turned with a fever. She was bound to the bed by strips of cloth blessed by Father John with holy water. In the fitful moments when she had actually awakened, usually only at night, she had fought with Ryan and Bonecutter. The girl exhibited triple the strength a person her size should have been capable of mustering. Only after Ryan had flung holy water in her face and commanded in the name of God that she lie down and be silent did she finally lay and rest.

A small child could easily break the strips of wet cloth that were holding her, but they held her to the bed as if they were steel cables. Bonecutter was unnerved by what he saw. Men with weapons he understood all too well, but holy water and incantations actually having a physical effect, and such a powerful one at that, did not add up in the mind of the ex-Navy SEAL.

Ryan handed a small vial to Faye Dresden, one of the women who helped him around the church. Faye didn't gossip, and Ryan could trust her to keep quiet about the events taking place in his home on this day. "She will rest for some time, Faye, but be sure and put the holy water on her bonds every hour, and pray for her as you do. Be wary, Faye, for what has infected her is pure evil in and of itself. Do not trust what she says, she may try to trick you into freeing her. She must not get away or her soul is doomed."

Dresden, a sturdy woman who didn't take any sass from young people, replied, " "Not from me she won't, Father."

He turned from the door and walked to the living room of his small house, clumsily knocking over one of his few possessions, an autographed photo of New York Yankees player Thurman Munsen. Ryan had been lucky enough to get the autograph while visiting his friend Father D'Arcy many years ago.

Bonecutter whipped his head around at the sound of the photo frame hitting the floor and then relaxed when he saw Ryan. The priest looked pale, and for the first time, Nicholas thought he looked very old.

Ryan looked up at Bonecutter as if he were struggling with his words. "Nick, it is much worse than I thought. I have to tell you some things, things you probably will not want to believe, but you have known me for a long time, and I swear the things I'm going to tell you are all true."

"Father, before you even get started, I just want to go home and be a guide, that's all I want. I did my bit and got the girl back, now I'm done. Like I told the Sheriff, I'm no cop. I've had enough of wars and killing. I left all that behind me when I left the SEALS. I'm done, Father, I can't do this stuff any more."

"I'm afraid it's not that simple, Nick. There are some things far worse than death itself," Ryan shouted. "Now sit down and listen, because all of our lives are in danger."

Bonecutter was stunned. Father John had never raised his voice to him in all the years he had known him; gradually, he sank back into the overstuffed green upholstered chair.

"Nicholas, it all took place in 1962. Kennedy was in the White House, and I had just graduated from the seminary. In those days, most young priests were sent to do missionary work as their first assignment. My work was done in Africa in what is now called Zaire. There have been many wars, and the names of some of the countries changed several times since I was there.

"The village where I was trying to bring the Catholic religion to was as poor as any you can imagine. There was a village well, which I am sure was full of bacteria, where everyone got their water. If you had to go to the bathroom there wasn't any. The villagers did not have land suitable for raising crops or providing for themselves.

"Most of what I tried to do for them had very little to do with religion. I tried to fix things and show them what they had to do to bring modern sanitation and cleanliness to the place. The church gave me money to have a proper well drilled, and we helped them build an irrigation system that drew water from a nearby river to irrigate the land and let them raise crops. Things were starting to improve, crops started growing, livestock were doing well, and with the aid we got from Catholic Relief Services, everyone started to have enough food. Things were getting better, and then it happened.

"One morning, the people came to me screaming that I had to protect them. One of the villagers had been found dead that morning. They led me to a body out behind one of the barns we had built. The man had been dead several hours. The doctor only came to the village a couple of times a month, and I had to pretty much substitute as the nurse for the place when he wasn't around.

"We brought the body back to the makeshift clinic, and it didn't take an autopsy to figure out what had happened to him. The man had bled to death from a wound to his throat. It looked like an animal had latched its jaws around his neck and ripped a hunk out of it. His windpipe had been torn open, along with the major arteries on the side of the neck. The most striking thing about the body was that, when you look at a dead African man, you expect him to be black. This guy was extremely pale for someone of color, and he had very little blood left in his body at all.

"In Africa, a man being mauled or killed by an animal isn't uncommon. Hell, I heard that, last year, a tourist was camping out in the bush as part of a tour package and an old lion that was no longer able to hunt for food dragged him out of his tent in the middle of the night and ate him. Back then, Africa was an even wilder place, and stories of villagers being killed by lions or alligators were fairly regular events.

"The villagers kept saying it was something else. They called it a "Lupe Garoo." I told them it was an animal, and we had to stay inside at night and kill it the next morning. That night, people stayed inside their huts, but the next morning another man turned up missing. We found him out in the cow pasture, dead, with his throat torn out just like the first victim, and he was just as pale looking. It was like something had sucked the very life right out of him.

"The best trackers in the village were unable to find any signs that a lion or some other animal had attacked the man inside his hut, which had a dirt floor, or that an animal had dragged him to the pasture. There was a set of clearly human footprints, which I assumed was from the man who found him. Again, they told me it was this Lupe Garoo. The villagers had many beliefs in spirits, despite all my attempts to teach them our religion. I was a young priest, fresh from the Seminary. I didn't want to hear such talk.

"The story went on just like that. Two more nights went by, and two more bodies were found with the same wounds. By now, the village elders didn't want to hear the white priest's ideas; they had some idea of what this thing was, and they knew how they were going to deal with it. Finally, I asked one of the elders, an old man named Nukinte, what the Lupe Garoo was.

"What is it, some kind of spirit?" I asked. He told me it was a man who is no longer a man, a man who has turned himself into an evil spirit and drains the life from the living.

"I had very strong beliefs from what I had been taught and certainly didn't believe in such things, but he insisted I come with him and the men from the village. There was a man who lived well outside the village in a hut. I had never seen this man, but the villagers were sure he was this 'lupe garoo.' We arrived at the hut at noon. The sun was blazing high in the sky. Nukinte told me I must not look into the lupe garoo's eyes or listen to his words. He told me the beast would fear the symbols of what is right, just, and good, and he told me to hold my rosary out in front of me as we entered the hut. The villagers also had charms from the old ways before I showed up. The men from the village brought up the rear, armed with machetes and spears.

"I looked around the dark interior of the hut. The small window was covered by a dark cloth blocking out the light. I turned to Nukinte to tell him the man was not there. He pointed upward, and there was the man, hanging from the rafters of the hut like a bat, his feet were hideously deformed. They looked like the claws of some kind of animal, gripping the rafters and holding him there. The man appeared to be asleep.

"Nukinte called out to the Lupe Garoo, condemning it for bringing evil and death to the village, then he threw holy water from our church on the hanging man. What happened next is something I have never been able to forget, though God knows I've tried. The man's eyes shot open, and he started screaming obscenities in his native language. The eyes were horrible. They were animal eyes, scarlet red in the darkened hut, glowing eyes. This was no man. He was some kind of thing, an abomination of God's laws. He dropped from the rafters and attacked us with frightening speed. I was thrown across the hut, and he nearly broke another man's neck, because he hit him so hard.

"One of the men from the village leapt forward and stabbed the man in the chest with a spear. The creature screamed when the spear pierced his heart and struggled for a few seconds trying to free himself of the wooden shaft. Nukinte, the elder among the villagers stepped forward and signaled to one of the men who swung his machete and took the thing's head off its shoulders. It was horrible. Dark, black blood flew everywhere, spraying all of us who were still inside the hut. The spear should have killed him, but it wasn't until he was beheaded that he started to die.

"When the head left the body, little balls of lightning started leaping all over the hut, knocking things down. Then the head and body caught fire, like there was a blowtorch inside of them; the body and the hut burned until there was nothing left.

"Nicholas, most people believe in evil, but they believe in the kind of evil made by men. We all believe in the evil when we hear about a serial killer or murderer in the news acting against his fellow man. This was something far, far worse. This was real evil. The lupe garoo, as I later discovered, is the African name for a vampire, one of the living dead, doomed to forever walk the earth in the darkness of night, drinking the blood of men to exist."

Ryan turned to Nicholas, his eyes wide, his face as serious as if he were giving someone the last rites. "You've known me for most of your life, and you have never heard me lie. I've always told you the truth. Vampires are real. More importantly, the man you tried to kill is a vampire. You shot him in the head and he didn't die. Think about it. How could a man survive what your pistol did to his head?

"God gives each of us talents, calling upon us to use those talents for good. The 'calling' isn't just received by priests like myself. God calls to all men, farmers, bankers, doctors. They can use their talents for good, or they can choose to use them to do evil. I know you have had enough of being a soldier, and that's fine, but you cannot walk away from this. You're the only one with the strength and skills to help me save the girl."

"We did save the girl, Father." Bonecutter's shoulders slumped, and his face grew narrow. "It's over, it has to be."

"We have only saved her for the time being. We haven't saved her soul, which will be his if we do not stop him. The worst is yet to come. We defeated him in a skirmish, and the girl was his play toy. Vampires are vain creatures, and he won't take this lightly. He's going to come after us, unless we get him first. So you can forget all about going back to your guiding business and living life like normal. Unless we stop him, we're all in danger, including our sleepy little town if he ever comes here."

Book III
Chapter 3
Bennington, Vermont

The Forest Inn, along Route 7, just across the New York State line barely lay within the State of Vermont. The Forest was an oddity in a state that had long since gone upscale. This part of Vermont bristled with pricey bed and breakfast establishments, as well as a number of fine inns, both of which catered to clientele from New York City, touristy folks with lots of money to spend. The Forest attracted a different type of customer.

Located in a remote area in the mountains dividing the two states, the Forest was only a short drive from the Capital District. Even though it was just over a half hour from Albany, it was remote enough to be the perfect place to take a date for an evening of fun and games, without the risk of being caught.

Many famous people had been overnight guests at The Forest, including state senators, assemblymen, and at least one New York State governor, over the fifty years it had been there, although looking at the names in the guest book probably would not corroborate their stay there. The Forest was where many a politician stayed for some discreet fun.

Tonight's guest in Room 12, at the end of the west wing of the dilapidated motel, far away from the other guests and the office, was no stranger to The Forest. He had been there many times.

Captain George Reichman, commander of the Albany Police Department, sat naked on the edge of the bed. His 300 plus pounds hung loosely; a fat sausage of a man, Reichman wasn't big on exercise. He coughed as he held in the last drag of a joint and then exhaled the sweet marijuana smoke before swilling down some of his Jack and Coke. Since he couldn't see it without a mirror, he felt his penis, checking to make sure that it was already hard, while he waited for his latest present from La Baptiste to finish getting dressed.

Reichman had an equally plump wife and children waiting at home for him. He was weak in many ways, and like many men who are placed into a position of power, he envisioned himself as something far more than he really was. Reichman didn't have his pick of the girls during school, and had always wanted to be a major stud. His learned quickly that women loved power. As a cop, he had ample opportunity to score with a variety of sexual partners, usually hookers or addicts, who didn't want to go to jail. His most recent partners provided though La Baptiste, were certainly a cut above the others.

The funeral home owner had visited his office one night when he was working late, asking to speak to him alone. He slapped several photos of Reichman's fat ass up in the air with a naked hooker beneath him, onto Reichman's desk. La Baptiste made him a deal. Reichman would be set up once a month with a much higher class piece of ass than the one in the photo, and in exchange, he would provide La Baptiste with the occasional favor.

Reichman wanted to choke the little man for having the balls to try and blackmail him, but his brother the police commissioner was on his ass for his little hobby already. One of the prostitutes he let off the hook for a sexual favor went home and killed her mother with a meat cleaver the same night. When his brother found out she had been with him just before the killing, he went bananas, swearing it was the last time he would ever cover for him. Besides, as the months went on, Reichman truly began to enjoy La Baptiste's arrangement.

Tonight's "treat" was a knockout redhead, the type of hooker that could get a couple thousand for a night, and she was all his.

Reichman opened his bag and made sure that he had everything he needed.

As the redhead emerged from the bathroom, Reichman told her to get on the bed. The girl was gorgeous, dressed in thin white stockings, with a garter belt, and a matching camisole. As she got on the bed, Reichman gave her two hits of Ecstasy tablets, and ordered her to take them.

As the girl's eyes started to glaze over from the drugs, Reichman went to work. He deftly handcuffed her left wrist to the bed, flipped her over on her stomach, and handcuffed her right wrist to the bed. The girl gave him no trouble. She obviously had been briefed on his preferences.

He climbed aboard the bed, taking her from behind.

Reichman, lover that he was, came on the fourth or fifth stroke, as the girl giggled. "You think that's funny, bitch?" He grabbed her flowing red hear and yanked her head back. "Well you won't be laughing soon." Reichman moved into his favorite part of the game.

He produced two sets of leg shackles from his bag, clipping one to each of her ankles and then binding the chains to the bed posts with some rope. He then ripped a strip of duct tape off of a roll and put it over the girl's mouth.

He again reached into his magic bag of tricks, producing the first item in his repertoire: a riding crop he had purchased at an area antique store. He loved to inflict terror on his playtime partners. The terror was as much fun as watching them wince when the pain came.

He slid the crop underneath her nose, laughing aloud as her eyes widened. The girl was an expert at doing S&M tricks like the one tonight. Reichman didn't know it, but her facial expression had much more to do with what was going on behind him. A strange mist was rolling into the room from underneath the door. The cloud of mist stayed together instead of spreading like smoke from a fire would. The mist moved over to a chair in the corner.

She heard the riding crop whistle in the air and screamed into the duct tape from the stinging pain in her back. The riding crop whistled again and again, until finally Reichman's flabby arm tired.

He once again slid the riding crop in front of her face, relishing the look she had at seeing her own blood on the small whip. Reichman assumed he had her attention. Her eyes were wide open, and she mumbled into the duct tape, like she was trying to tell him something. He was unaware she had just watched the mist turn into a man seated in the chair.

"So, bitch. Is it funny now?" Reichman had worked himself up for a second round. He mounted her once again, lasting a little longer than the first time, lasting about twenty seconds, as he savored the look on the girl's face. He had her attention. *I'll have to see if La Baptiste can send this one again.*

Reichman nearly had a heart attack when he heard applause behind him coming from the corner chair.

"How the fuck did you get in here? You sonofabitch!"

"Oh, Captain, that was a most entertaining performance, though you should see someone about your premature ejaculation problem. Surely there is something that can be done?" La Baptiste smiled as he spoke.

"What the fuck do you want?"

"Well, Captain, I need to know some things. I was hosting a party the other evening, and it was rudely interrupted by two men. They drove off in a truck whose license plate number is on this slip of paper. One of them is a Catholic priest. The other is a well built man, possibly one of your Native

Americans, at least that is how I believe they are referred to now." He reached into the breast pocket of his suit and produced a slip of paper, which he laid on the nightstand.

"Why the fuck did you have to come here now to ask, La Baptiste?"

"Why, my good Captain, I came for the show. Just for the show. At any rate, I shall let myself out. Call me when you have what I wish to know." With that, he opened the door and walked out into the night.

Book III
Chapter 4
Albany, New York

"Willie, get in here!" La Baptiste screamed, as he emerged from his ebony coffin.

Willie ran to the doorway leading to the vampire's chambers, dressed in his embalming apron and gloves. He hesitated for a moment before entering. Willie feared La Baptiste, especially his rage, and yet still lusted for his power. A vampire's powers were greatest when they rose from their slumber as the sun set. Willie knew he had to be careful not to say the wrong thing and end up paying for it.

La Baptiste was dressed in a pair of black silk pajamas and matching silk robe. Willie found him sitting upright in his coffin. A vampire could sleep in any dark place, as long as it completely blocked sunlight. La Baptiste could have slept in a fine bed, but like many of his kind, the coffin gave him two things: a sense of security, and a certain power over his daytime servants. Each night when he rose, he showed that his powers transcended even death itself.

Willie was the best watchdog La Baptiste had ever had, but the vampire would destroy him in a heartbeat if it served his purpose. He was certainly mad enough to do so right now!

Willie stepped back as La Baptiste climbed from the coffin. "What you need, boss?" he asked tentatively, trying to gauge the mood of the beast who had enslaved him.

"First of all, fool, you say 'what do you need, boss.' When are you going to stop speaking like you just stepped out of a crack house? What do I need, stupid fool? Let me answer this for you, because I don't have time to wait for a dullard like yourself to hem and haw for minutes only to say something idiotic. I need to exist, to live and feed in safety, that's what I need.

"I know, Mr. La Baptiste. I been doin' my job," Willie argued.

"Doing your job? You've been doing your job? I fear that I have become too attached to you, like a man can become to a fine dog. I have spoiled you with a lack of discipline. Very well, I must remedy this now."

Willie took a step towards the door, but it was a futile gesture. La Baptiste passed right by him, before his foot hit the floor, reaching the door well ahead of him with speed of a cheetah pursuing its prey. His eyes red with rage, he grabbed Willie by the throat and easily picked the larger man up into the air with one hand. Willie was wide-eyed with terror, as La Baptiste threw him against the far wall of the chamber.

The vampire swiftly traversed the distance to the crumpled Willie and tossed him across the room again. As Willie spit out the blood from a loosened tooth, La Baptiste took his servant's left index finger in his hand and snapped it like a twig. Willie screamed in pain, staring down at the crooked finger.

"Ah good, Willie. Now I have your attention. Let us discuss what needs to be done to rectify your failures. Within the next week, we will abandon this place and move our operation. Like our facility in Mexico, I fear we have been here too long.

"It is true that you did bring me a little treat from the city, but your treat has brought me many problems. Our New York City Operation has been compromised. We can no longer move merchandise through the apartment there, nor can we move it up here, now that the warehouse has been found out."

"Mr. La Baptiste, Leshawn told me no one would come for the girl, I swear."

"Leshawn was wrong, n'est pas?"

"I know, Mr. La Baptiste, but you liked the girl. Hell, I thought you were goin' to, you know, make her like you before I even got my chance."

"Willie, you have just proven to me your judgment is not sound, yet I may have to give you that reward prematurely, we shall see. In the interim, you have brought me a problem, and as such, I will leave it to you to solve. My source will soon identify the two men in the truck who took my young companion. When I obtain this information, you will set things right. It should be relatively easy for you, since they obviously were not from the police or a federal agency."

"I'll take them out, boss, just give me a chance."

"Oh, you shall have a chance, Willie, a last chance. In the meantime, you will do the following: first take provisions to the safe house along the Mohawk

River, and see to it that adequate defenses are available there, and here as well. Secondly, you will call Leshawn and make sure the apartment and the entire operation is cleared out and moved to another suitable location by morning. After which, Leshawn will be brought to me for his punishment."

"I'm on it, Mr. La Baptiste." Willie looked at the floor as he walked past the vampire to go and do his bidding.

Book III
Chapter 5
Wilmington, New York

Faye Dresden was afraid. She was born a Catholic and spent her whole life trying to be a good one. She had always thought her beliefs were firm. Of course, like any other area of life, it was easy to have firm beliefs, until you had to lay them on the line. Her religion was now being shaken to its very core. Over the years in the pews of the church, she had heard dozens of sermons regarding the perpetual battle of good and evil, but now, she was sitting on the frontline of the battlefield.

She trusted Father John, which was not unique in the small Adirondack community. The diminutive priest was a firebrand, a forceful personality, and unlike many in his profession, he was more than willing to go to the mat for anyone who needed help—Catholic, and non-Catholic alike—regardless of what rules he had to bend to do so. When Father John asked for her help, Faye didn't hesitate to give it.

Taking care of Jean Van Nostrand scared her more than she had ever been scared before in her whole life. Every hour she used holy water to wet the cotton bonds, tying the poor girl to Father John's guest bed. Any thinking person would look at the makeshift strips of cloth and laugh at the idea of mere strips of wet fabric from an old sheet holding down a healthy teenage girl! To Jean Van Nostrand, they may as well have been steel shackles. The wretched girl would scream a litany of profanities, each time the holy water was applied.

The girl slept during most of the daytime, and it was this period when she was easiest to manage. The truly horrible part was dealing with her when she was awake at night. Father John had warned Faye that the girl would try and tempt her, make her offers to gain her freedom, but she had no idea just how tempting it would be.

The first time Jean awoke under Faye's care, the girl had been angry, using language that would have made a sailor blush. She had cursed Faye out in a manner no one had ever done before, so much so that Faye had actually lost her temper and slapped her.

That was bad enough, but Jean later tried a different strategy, bargaining for freedom from the bonds. Faye listened, as Jean told her there was a different master, one with power so great that death could not touch him. If Faye were only to release her, Jean swore the master would see to it she would never grow old and die; she would even become younger, reverting to the time when her beauty was at its peak. "You remember what it was like to be young, Faye, don't you? Wouldn't you like to be young forever?" the girl asked.

In the daylight, away from Jean, Faye knew this "master" was evil, a tempter, gaining the confidence of the weak to do his bidding. Of course, Faye knew this was evil in its purest form. The part that frightened her most was almost giving in. The girl's words became hypnotic after a time. Everything she said made so much sense. It would be nice to be young forever, instead of growing old and spending eternity rotting in the grave.

Faye didn't dare tell anyone what she had almost done.

Tonight, she was watching the girl, again, very much afraid she would be talked into something foolish. As she walked into the room and closed the door, the evil girl stirred.

Faye watched as Jean turned her head and looked towards her. "Back again, Faye?" Faye gave a small startled sound from deep in her throat. The girl's face was now very pale, and her eyes were entirely blood red, the pupils a dull bluish-white.

"Faye, we have to talk again. Sounds like I can make you a better deal than before. Sure you go to church and Father John promises, well, you know, that the big guy is going to take care of you, but have you ever thought about how? He promises your soul will have its place in his realm, but why bother? What about your body? Why must you let it rot in the wet ground, until the worms eventually find their way into your crappy casket and have their feast?"

"Be quiet, child, you don't know what you're saying."

"Oh, Faye, I know exactly what I'm saying. Why don't you just let me go, and I can see to it you never have any problems again. I know you would like to be young again, Faye, to feel your hard body become naked, while your boy-friend Kenny pleases you. You haven't had any in a long time have you, Faye? What a shame, you used to be quite a hottie in your day; too bad you married the wrong guy and he died. I can fix all that. What do you say?"

"How would you possibly know these things?"

"Well, Faye, I have some, how shall we say, insight on things. For example, one of your favorite things with 'Kenny' was the way he gave it to you in the back seat of his car. It was good, wasn't it, Faye? Now, there isn't a lot of time. If you can do something for me, I can fix it so those legs of yours get hard again, Faye, and I can also fix it so you can get back into the game, so to speak. Imagine having that kind of fun again, just like when you were young? You see, Faye, we're all living one big lie. We're told that we are born, grow old, and then we die. If we're really good all of the time, then we get our reward. Well, Faye, it's a load of crap, because what they don't tell you is the big secret. We really don't have to get old, and better yet, someone like you can be young again, young forever, Faye."

"Stop it, stop your lies!"

"Faye, it's no lie. Imagine, actually growing as young as you want to be, and best of all, knowing what you know right now. Come on, Faye. The boys are waiting, and once he returns you to your original self, the self that you want to be, you can have a Kenny, or Lenny, or Denny, servicing your every need. All you have to do is loosen up a strip of cloth. It's all so simple."

Faye, almost unconsciously, as if she was walking in a dream, reached her right hand outward. After all, it really was simple. Just let the girl loose and the master would take care of everything, just like he was going to take care of Jean. Her fingers touched the weak knot. As she was about to release the bonds, the door to the room burst open.

"Faye, get away from her," Father John screamed. He lunged forward, grabbing her hand in a grip as strong as a vise. "Get out, leave this room now."

"Ah, Father, you would still keep me from my treat?" Jean was still talking, but the voice coming out of her was not her own.

"I know what you are, vampire, and by the power of God Almighty I command you to leave this child's mind!"

"If that is your wish, but Father, you and I shall meet one day soon, and I will not be so generous then." The girl's eyes grew dark, and her body went limp, and she immediately fell into a deep sleep.

From the doorway, Faye Dresden immediately burst into sobs. She knew she had nearly failed the good Father. She had been tempted and had failed the test.

* * *

The next morning, Father Ryan called Nicholas and asked him to stop by the church. Bonecutter, sensing the urgency, complied and jumped in his truck, quickly making the drive to join Ryan on the front steps of the old Adirondack church.

"Nick, this can't wait any longer, not after what happened last night."

Suddenly, Ryan appeared to be older, weary like a man who hasn't slept in days. Bonecutter had never seen him look this bad.

"What do you mean?"

"He has power over the girl, too much power. It can only mean one thing. She must have tasted his blood somehow and she's starting to turn."

"What do you mean, turn?" Nicholas asked.

"She's turning into a vampire, and we probably only have a couple of days left to stop it. The only thing holding it off is that she couldn't feed because we've kept her locked up."

"You've got to be kidding me. You mean she's going to turn into one of those, those things?"

"That's exactly what I mean, and there is only one way to stop it. We have to break into his stronghold and kill him before she turns."

"Father, if anyone ever figures out what we've done up until this point, we'll go to jail for a very long time. Now you want to go and kill somebody!" Bonecutter was dismayed. This was the first time he had ever raised his voice to Father John.

"No, not somebody, we have to kill a vampire."

"We already tried that one, Father, remember? He got right back up and kept going."

"We didn't know he was a vampire then. That's why we couldn't kill him; we didn't do it right."

"I know you're saying these things are real, and I can't totally explain what I saw. Father. I've had to kill before, and by God none of them ever got up again!" Are these things just like the monsters in a cheap drive-in movie?"

"Well for one thing, you can't kill him with your .45 caliber pistol, because he's already dead. His body died the day he tasted another vampire's blood."

"Then how do you kill one of those things?" Nicholas asked.

"You have to slam a hardwood stake through his heart, or where his heart used to be, just like in the movies. Why do you think Bram Stoker wrote

Dracula? It wasn't exactly a novel. The poor guy went nuts because no one believed him. Vampires are basically a dead body, reanimated by what some believe is a virus or some sort of parasite. People are subject to the whims of their professions. As a priest, I don't buy the virus theory; these things are evil. I believe the blood ritual somehow opens a doorway to allow a demon to enter the dead body. Even though the heart does not beat like a living heart, wood is blessed by God, because it's pure of the earth. Their heart is the center of their power. The stake holds them paralyzed for the second phase, where the head is removed."

"Wonderful, Father, we put a stake in his heart, just like in the movies, and then cut off his head. Sounds simple. Is there anything else, no chants, or anything weird?"

"Well there is one more thing," the priest replied.

"Somehow I just knew there would be."

"The body must be burned completely, if it doesn't do so on its own."

"Hell, Father, I thought this was going to be tough. All we have to do is stake him, hack his head off, and then burn him? Piece of cake. Of course you haven't gotten to the part about what we're going to tell the cops when they show up if we get caught. I've known you for a long time, and either we've both gone gone crazy, or this is all real and there are real-life vampires out they killing people. If that's so, why isn't anyone doing anything about it? Why isn't the government or somebody handling this whole thing?

"Well, there are some who know what these things are. They will help us set things right. Vampires have always been among us, and we have always outnumbered them. Consequently, mankind won't tolerate their existence. When they're discovered, they're pursued until they're destroyed. They have always known we will not look the other way, while they slaughter us. They're very secretive because of it. They are, for example, very reluctant to create others of their kind. They're very territorial, as well, and will war with others of their kind found hunting on their turf, just like a wolf pack will turn on a wolf from outside their territory if they catch him. They don't want the competition."

"I get it, Father, they're secretive. Well, how can they go and kill people in this day and age and keep it under wraps? We've got instant news and the Internet; everyone would know what they were up to."

"My guess is this one has found sources for blood, which no one would question. After all, he's running a funeral home. The newspapers would be screaming for an investigation if dozens of people were missing. He's getting the blood without arousing anyone's interest; besides, who in today's world would believe such a thing, even though there are hundreds of novels and movies about them? People think vampires are make-believe. We know he's involved with drugs. What if he uses drugs to get what he wants and keep the victims quiet?"

"Father, what powers do they really have? I mean, is it like in the movies where they can turn into bats, or walk up a wall like a fly? What can this guy do? More importantly, what are his limits?"

"No, their powers aren't as broad as they are in the movies. They can't turn into bats or animals, but they do have some ability to change their flesh. For example, they can alter their physical appearance. They can also dissolve into a mist, and drift underneath a locked door. Vampires can communicate telepathically with their victims, and, as we have seen with Jean, they have power over them. Anyone whom they feed upon and lives is under their control. They can also communicate telepathically with others they have turned into vampires, although they rarely make others of their kind. They have limits too."

"Are they much stronger than normal men, Father?"

"Yes, although how much stronger will vary. Their greatest power is time. Imagine, instead of having eighty years to live, that you could have the cumulative knowledge of eight *hundred* years. Imagine the wealth you could gather. The longer a vampire exists, the more powerful it becomes. If they were united, instead of fighting among themselves, they could rule the world if they wanted to. The good thing in this case is that I don't think this one has been around for centuries. For one thing, he wouldn't be so visible in the drug trade or the public with the funeral home. The old ones hide deeper into the background. This one hides in plain sight."

"What weaknesses do they have?"

"God doesn't put up with them. The good Lord and the symbols of his emissaries on Earth are both feared and loathed by them. They can not look upon a cross. Holy water burns them like acid burns us. Leave a piece of the wafer in the crack of a doorway, and they cannot pass. They also can't enter into someone's home unless they are invited. The victim is given the chance to exercise free will. Fire hurts them, and silver hurts them, as well. Those who have hunted them down have come up with a variety of weapons: crossbows, shotguns filled with silver pellets, and so on. A blade blessed with holy water cuts them like a laser, but they will regenerate a hand or some other body part lost in battle."

"Well, I have a client to take fishing in the morning, and he won't take no for an answer, some cop from Albany who wants to get away from it all for a day. As soon as I get back, we can pack up and go after this thing. I need a little time to get some stuff together. I think I have just the thing for taking his head from his shoulders, and the stakes are not going to be much of a problem. I'll need all the silver you can get your hands on. I'll meet up with you after I get back from fishing."

With that, Bonecutter got back in his truck and drove away. Ryan stood by the front door of his church, his head hung low. He prayed he hadn't just doomed a young man who was like a son to him.

Book III
Chapter 6
Wilmington, New York

Five-thirty a.m. came early at the Bonecutter cabin. Even Sadie wanted to sleep in. "Come on Sadie, time to get up," Bonecutter said, as the dog opened up her droopy eyes and made a grunting noise, before she finally stood up and shook herself awake. As he stood watching her, Sadie's ears went up a little, alerting him that his client for the day was pulling into the driveway.

At the knock on the door, Sadie let out a little woof.

"Hi there, I'm Ed Woldman." A fiftyish looking man stood under the porch light, all decked out in what appeared to be brand new clothes from an Orvis shop.

Nicholas had been a guide for a long time. He only needed a few minutes to determine that Woldman didn't have a clue about fishing, or the outdoors at all. All of the clothes he wore were so new they still showed the folds from the packaging. The couple of flies the client had carelessly stuck to the patch on the spotless fishing vest were for bass, not exactly the first choice of someone on a trout fishing trip.

"Come on in, Ed. Can I get you a cup of coffee?"

"Sure, that sounds good." The man hiked up his pants, which curiously lacked a belt, and walked in the door.

"So what type of fishing shall we do today?"

"Well, I'm big into trout and salmon fishing," Woldman said.

"Really? Where do you fish?"

"Oh, down into the Catskills quite a bit; you know, Catskill Creek. We catch some real monsters out of there, twenty-inch trout all the time."

Bonecutter knew fishing as well as anyone else in New York State, and the man was a liar. Catskill Creek had marginal trout fishing at best. Were it not for the stocking truck from the state hatchery, there would be few trout in the stream. Woldman wouldn't be the first angler Nick had seen brag himself up when he didn't know how to fish. He was gathering up the two cups of coffee from the kitchen counter when he heard Sadie let out a low growl.

Bonecutter spun around and found himself staring down the bore of a Glock 17 nine millimeter handgun.

"Mr. Bonecutter, you know damn well that I haven't been fishing in forty years, so let's say we cut the bullshit and get down to business. By the way, please open the door and let your dog out, so nothing happens to her."

"Certainly, Detective. He hand signaled Sadie to go outside as he opened the door. She looked up at him, as if to make sure it was all right. "Sadie, outside!"

"And Mr. Bonecutter, nothing stupid, please."

"I hear you, Detective, I hear you."

Nicholas had to grab Sadie's collar to get her out. He told her to stay in the yard and shut the door behind him. He walked back to the table, and sat down, calmly picking up his mug and drinking his coffee. The coffee cup was in his left hand, and his right hand on his lap.

"Bonecutter, I would appreciate it if you would put your other hand back on the table," Woldman said in a stern voice.

"I'm afraid that I can't do that."

"Why's that, Mr. Bonecutter?"

"Because my right hand is holding a .410 gauge Derringer, loaded with buckshot by the way. At this distance, it will pretty much rip a hole right about where your groin is that's big enough to drive my truck through. So, Detective, I guess we're even. Well, actually, mine's bigger."

"I don't believe you, Mr. Bonecutter."

"I don't blame you, Detective, so feel free to look for yourself."

Woldman sat down in a chair opposite Nick, all the while training his gun on his chest. He pushed the chair back a little and eased his head to the side for a look under the table. As soon as he tried to look, Bonecutter slid the table across the floor, slamming Woldman right between the eyes with the heavy pine table. Blood started running down his face from a wound that had opened up over his eye. He tried to stand up straight to get the gun back on Bonecutter and looked up in disbelief as the guide leapt over the table like a cat. He finally got his wits together enough to try and get the gun back on Bonecutter, but it was way too late. Like most police officers, Woldman's sole focus was his weapon, and as he started to point it towards his attacker, he was hit in the side of the neck by a strike he never saw coming. As he tried to deal with his rattled brain, a hand as strong as a vise locked onto his gun hand. Woldman's knees buckled as he blacked out.

An hour later, the detective woke up, chained to a support beam in the cabin with his own handcuffs.

"Now, Detective, I guess I ask the questions. So what the hell brings you all the way up from Albany to see me, and more importantly, to bring you to my house where you point a gun in my face?"

"How did you know I was a detective?" Woldman was still groggy from the strike to his neck. He'd certainly need some Advil tomorrow. He reached for his wristwatch, where he kept a spare cuff key hidden, and found the watch had been removed.

"Only a cop or a wannabee cop would have a Glock, and you certainly act like most of the cops I've met." "How are you coming with the spare key?"

"Mr. Bonecutter, you have some answers that I need," Woldman said.

"Answers about what?"

"Answers about what you and your friend the priest were doing at a warehouse along the Hudson River. Answers about how a guy you blasted in the face and the knee with a .45 caliber handgun suddenly reassembled himself almost like it was magic. You might have the advantage now, asshole, but I'm not gonna stop, so you might as well shoot me."

"I don't think you would believe the answer, Detective. Even if you would, this is something you really do not want to know."

"Try me."

"Well, I guess I don't have much to lose, since you're staying here until I feel like letting you go. Well, Detective, the man you're talking about is a vampire, just like the ones in the movies. We were down there because he took a girl who lives around here, and we went to get her back. At the time, we didn't know what he was. He was in the process of cutting the limbs off of the little guy we dropped off at the hospital, when I shot him in self defense, even though it didn't do much good."

"Sonofabitch, it figures, it just figures. I've only got two friggin' years and I'll be retired, partying in the Florida Keys. But no, I have to dig too deep and now I'm mixed up in the one case that'll get me fired and tangled up with a nut like you. I saw the whole damn thing through the night goggles. I couldn't believe what I saw, couldn't explain it. No man gets shot like that and walks away. I even went to a public meeting, at night, where the same guy was guest speaker. He didn't have a scratch on him. Now you're telling me he's an honest to God vampire? Some blood-sucking ghoul going around killing people? I should've just kept my mouth shut and walked away from this one. There has to be a reasonable explanation; he has a twin and you killed the twin. Vampires aren't real, they can't be."

"You saw the whole thing. Explain to me how he took the damage he did and got himself put back together, and is now running around without a mark on him? The twin theory is good, but you certainly checked that out. You're a sworn law enforcement officer, yet you know this guy hacked the limbs off of a man and didn't arrest him. The guy died. You should have charged him with murder. If you had any idea I was involved, we'd be talking at the State Police barracks. No, you show up and try to play games with me because you know the truth. You just want to find some other way out."

"Apparently, Mr. Bonecutter, there's also more to you than meets the eye. Most people are scared shitless by a cop pointing a gun at them but not you. You've got something else going on that you're hiding. Your background has a big, blank period."

"That blank period you refer to was my time with the United States Navy, which is classified. For your information, I was honorably discharged and received medals for my service. I'm out of that business. Unfortunately, my good friend Father John has managed to get me involved with something I would also rather have walked away from, but Father John took care of me as a kid. Now I have to help. Besides, the poor girl isn't going to make it unless I do."

"You mean she's going to die?"

"No, Detective, there are some things far worse than death. She's going to become a vampire, just like he is. She's going to start feeding on people, real people, forever, until she's stopped. She'll start with her family and the people in this town. Worse yet, she's going to do so until someone shoves a hardwood stake through her heart, cuts her head off, and burns her body."

"And you're sure there's no way to stop this?"

"There's only one way. I have to take the vampire out before she turns." Bonecutter's face grew sullen, twisting into a grave expression.

"And how do you plan to do that? You'll end up in jail for murder." Woldman tugged at his handcuffs as he spoke.

"It's the only way. I have to destroy the vampire who created her. I have to destroy La Baptiste."

"Then I guess you had better undo these handcuffs, because I'm going too."

"The best thing you could do Detective is leave it alone. Why ruin your career to help a girl you don't even know?"

"Because, just as you've got your reasons, I've got mine."

"So, what are your reasons?"

"Look, Bonecutter, even though many of my peers hate my guts, I have a perfect record as a detective. I've caught every murderer I've gone after and made them pay, and up until now, the right way, by sending their asses to jail. Even though this La Baptiste is not a man, he's not going to wreck my record. And dammit, stop calling me detective!"

"Okay, Ed, if that's the way it's going to be, there's someone you need to meet." Bonecutter walked over and uncuffed Woldman, then handed him back his Glock.

"Think they'll put us in the same wing at the mental hospital?" Bonecutter asked.

Book III
Chapter 7
Albany, New York

La Baptiste sat in the elegant dining room of his apartment above the funeral home. He looked quite dapper, his hair impeccably trimmed. Anyone seeing him there would recognize a wealthy, successful man, a façade he carefully cultured.

La Baptiste looked up at a knock on the door.

"Come in, Willie."

"I've brought your drink, Mr. La Baptiste." Willie entered, carrying a silver tray with a crystal decanter filled with a red liquid, being extra careful not to spill it in spite of his bandaged finger.

"Wonderful, Willie, please serve me a glass."

Willie took a crystal goblet and poured the thick, red blood into the glass. He had done this for years, yet it still bothered him each time. In Willie's world, killing an enemy was one thing, but slowly bleeding old people to death for weeks and drinking their blood was going a little too far. He didn't want to die and had thought long and hard about becoming a vampire. He would drink like this when the time came, and he'd have centuries to get used to it.

"Willie," La Baptiste said, sipping the blood in his glass, "How are my provisions faring?"

"Well, Boss, looks like we're gonna lose one. The old ones don't last as long, and he's been around for a couple of weeks, which is about all I can get out of them."

"I want you to do your best to maintain them. We also must be ready to move them on short notice. We may have unwanted visitors soon."

"We've never had anyone come after us before. How you want to handle it?"

"Willie, it is a simple matter, really. We let them come."

"But, Boss, what if there are too many of them for me to handle?" Willie nervously looked down at the floor. His life depended on him fighting any intruders who might try to destroy La Baptiste while he rested. The problem was, if one got through, he wouldn't live to tell about it if the vampire survived.

"I don't think you need fear, Willie. At most, we will have the priest and his friend to deal with. Just make sure that my exit is available, and be sure that, from now on, our friends from our sales division join you in patrolling the grounds. Have them available downstairs, around the clock, until I say otherwise."

"I'll talk to the crew tomorrow. When do you think they'll hit us? Probably during the day while you rest?"

"My guess is they will arrive at night, even though they know I will be up and about."

"Why would they come at night, Boss?"

"We are located here for a reason. They will have to come at night. There are too many eyes during the day. White people coming into this neighborhood and breaking into a building will not go unnoticed for very long without the police becoming involved."

"I'll set things up, just like you said."

"Very well, you may leave me now. I have planning to do."

After Willie left, La Baptiste picked up the phone and called Leshawn's replacement in New York City. "Dred, I need you to bring as many men as you can and get to the summer house as soon as possible. Prepare the house for my arrival, and make sure our security is without flaw. If anyone comes on to the property, kill them immediately."

"Okay, Mr. La Baptiste. That all you need?"

"That is all. I am sure we will have intruders at some point, and when we do, you must protect the house at all costs. Do you understand? The men who are coming are not with the police, they are competitors and must be eliminated."

"Got it, Boss, I'll be on my way in an hour."

"Very good, Dred, and remember, there is no room for mistakes in my organization. Your predecessor has used up all of my good will by compromising our New York operation."

"I hear you, Boss. Fool got what he had coming; too bad about his girlfriend, though, she was a fine little bitch."

"You and your associates had better not fail me again, or this time, you all will pay." With that, the diminutive vampire hung up the phone.

After talking with Dred, he made several additional calls. Vast sums of money were transferred to offshore accounts, where the government had no jurisdiction. He also called a man he controlled, a local banker with a taste for cocaine and ordered him to empty the contents of a couple of safety deposit boxes, and move them to another bank, far across the state near Syracuse.

He made provisions to move large quantities of "product" stored locally to a small marina and boat repair facility he owned out near Utica, along the State Barge Canal System. La Baptiste was born on an island and always took a certain comfort being near water.

His final call was to Chief Reichman. "My good Chief, how are you this evening?"

"You ain't calling me at home to ask about my health, so what the hell do you want?" Reichman replied.

"I believe visitors are coming to my operation here, and I want you to make sure they do not cause me any difficulties."

"Look, La Baptiste, if the feds are down on your ass, there ain't a damn thing I can do about it."

"My dear Chief, you need not worry on that account. These people are not from a federal bureau, they are a private group seeking to interlope on my operation, uninvited. Be sure and see the funeral home is watched round the clock, please."

"One of these days, La Baptiste, I'm just gonna tell you to piss off and cut you loose."

"Is your wife at home, my good Chief? Perhaps she would like to view my photo album, or perhaps these 'feds' you speak of would enjoy some of my home movies, n'est pas?"

"Don't you dare threaten me, you sonofabitch!" Reichman's angry voice leaped from the phone.

"Listen to me, my pathetic little worm. It is you who will never dare to threaten me. There are other ways in which you could serve me, and they are far worse than your current capacity. You will do exactly as I tell you. If I do not see a police cruiser parked outside of my business in the next hour, I will come and see you personally and settle our account. Do you understand, Worm?"

"I'll get you a patrol to watch the place, but this is the last time, you prick."

"Chief, I will tell *you* when it is the last time." La Baptiste hung up the receiver and poured himself another drink, wondering what a fresh glass of Reichman would taste like.

Book III
Chapter 8
Albany, New York

Detective Ed Woldman checked in with the desk sergeant as he entered the police station, then he headed down the hall to the muster room for the morning briefing to see what was going on. He had told Bonecutter and Father Ryan he would use the day to see if anything was happening with La Baptiste's immediate neighborhood. If the place was not on the radar screen, they would hit the funeral home the next day.

It didn't take long to find out things were not going to be easy. The fat Chief himself attended the briefing, and suddenly his number one priority was a continuous stakeout of none other than the Arbor Hill Funeral Home.

This is going to be even more trouble than I thought. I'm screwed for sure. Woldman contemplated his dilemma as the Chief rattled on.

"We have it on good authority that a prominent area citizen may be the target of some sort of gang activity. I'm reassigning several of you to a round-the-clock surveillance of the Arbor Hill Funeral Home. You are to observe the building and intervene if you detect any criminal activity. I also want you to observe the people going in and out of there for known perps."

Woldman raised his hand. When Reichman looked his way, Woldman said, "Uh, Chief, does that include checking the coffins for known perps, too?"

Reichman's face went red, as the other cops in the room chuckled. "All right, asshole, since you think this is so funny, you can have the first watch. You've got the day shift, and I don't want any screw-ups. You make sure your ass is sitting outside of the funeral parlor in your car for the entire eight hours of your shift. I don't care if you've got the screaming shits, you make sure your sorry ass is out there the whole eight hours!"

"Absolutely, Chief." Woldman did his best to conceal an absolutely shit-eating grin forming on his face. "I'll be there, just like you said." The other detectives seated near Woldman looked at him like he had just sprouted another head on his shoulders. The last thing they thought he would do was go along with Reichman's stupid surveillance of a funeral home. *This guy is absolutely the dumbest of all asses*, Woldman thought.

As soon as the morning briefing was over, Woldman, for once, anyway, did exactly as he was told. He parked his unmarked patrol car right outside the Arbor Hill Funeral Home, and then got on his cell phone to Bonecutter and Father John. "I want you guys to meet me at De Cesare's Restaurant and Bar on Central Avenue at 8:00 tonight. You'll really like the pasta."

Woldman then sat back in front seat of the Crown Victoria, and spent his shift staring at the funeral home, observing the people who came and went. At 10:00 a.m., a number of vehicles pulled up for the funeral of an old man who had recently passed away. Woldman saw an opportunity. After all, he was here to protect La Baptiste, and he could do that more effectively from inside the home. He grabbed a hand-held radio and headed up the steps with the rest of the mourners. He was greeted at the top step by a scowling Willie.

"What you want in here, man?" Willie asked, sticking his chest in front of Woldman.

"Hey, I'm only here to protect you and your boss." Woldman lowered his left shoulder and pushed right past him and entered the funeral parlor.

Once inside, Woldman, out of respect for the mourners, took up a position in the back of the funeral chapel, near one of the windows, so he could look out to the street for trouble. As he sat in the back of the room, he marveled at the proceedings. The man who had passed away was a small black man who appeared to be in his eighties. The man apparently had a pretty good-sized family, judging from the number of mourners. It looked like a couple of sons or daughters and their families were in the front row, along with at least fifty other people.

The minister got up and went through the man's life, telling those in attendance how he had helped the community, and every time he hit one of the highlights, the people wailed and carried on.

Man, these folks really loved this guy. I'll be lucky if I have anyone at my funeral. Woldman was no racist and certainly didn't hold any predisposition against black people. The world he had grown up in was a lot different, funerals in particular. He always admired people like these, the honest, hard working people. These were folks who lived their lives in peace and honor.

Finally, the service was over. Slowly, the throng of the mourners left, except for Willie. Woldman knew Willie very well. He had personally slapped the cuffs on him once when Willie was only fifteen years old. "Well, Willie, I'll be out in the car if you need me."

"I ain't gonna need your white ass," Willie replied.

"Is that any way to talk to an officer of the law, Willie?"

"Fuck you, Woldman."

"Willie, I had no idea you had that type of interest in me, probably from your jail time, huh? Like I said, I'll be right outside in the car."

The rest of Woldman's watch over the funeral home was uneventful, except for a couple of body deliveries by various ambulance services and hearses.

Later that evening, at De Cesare's, the three would-be vampire hunters compared notes over plates of linguini and white clam sauce.

"I watched the place all day long. There doesn't seem to be anything unusual going on there. They had two funerals and a couple of body deliveries." Woldman expertly twirled his linguini with a spoon, loading up his fork for his next bite.

"Are there any funerals tomorrow?" Bonecutter asked.

"No, nothing scheduled."

"That's good, because that's when we're going after him," Nicholas said.

"Do you guys have some sort of plan?" Woldman asked.

"Our expert certainly does," Father John said, as he poured everyone another glass of wine.

"And what exactly is this plan? I would love to know how two armed white guys are going to waltz into that place during the daytime." Woldman said.

"Very simple, Detective. We, or rather Father John here, will deliver a body, complete with body bag. I don't think whoever unzips this bag is going to be very pleased, either." Bonecutter said, with a devilish twinkle in his eye.

"And where do you two figure on laying your hands on a hearse or an ambulance?"

"We already have one," Bonecutter replied.

"Where the hell did you come up with something like that?"

"Father John used his connections and got us a black hearse with no other identifying features. It also comes complete with a brand new set of license plates, which, by the way, are off of your captain's wife's car, extra little touch I thought you would enjoy."

"Oh, you two are a couple of beauties, but it's not going to be as easy as you think. In addition to his watchdog, a couple of local gang punks are hanging around the home around the clock."

"Don't worry, they're going to take a nap," Bonecutter said with a smile, as he dug into his plate of food.

"And how is that going to take place?"

"Well, we have a couple of military issue stun guns. The good Father here is going to give them a jolt or two."

"It might work, Nick, but I doubt it. One of those gang members is going to mess up your plan and start shooting."

"Well, Ed, granted Father John isn't a trained cop or soldier, but the gang kids have no training either. La Baptiste surely knows we're coming. That's why he has them around, and that's why he has you sitting outside in a patrol car. What he doesn't know is who he's dealing with. I've broken into fortified installations before, many times, and these were facilities guarded by elite soldiers. I can certainly handle a couple of gang bangers. There'll be so much confusion in the first thirty seconds, they're not going to know what the hell is going on until it's too late."

"Look, Ed," Father John said, "I've known this young man his whole life, and he does what he says he's going to do, and that's that. We have to stop this thing soon. A young girl's immortal soul is at stake, and there's no telling how many people have died from this beast feeding on their blood. These things have to be destroyed, as soon as they're found out."

"Okay, you guys, I want to get him, too, but I think you still need some sort of diversion." Woldman said.

"That's where you come in. You're going to make sure we get at least a half hour undisturbed in that place, by any means possible. We can't have somebody show up, and we can't, God forbid, have the police come busting in."

"I think I can take care of that. I have a few little dirt bags who owe me their freedom, and one of them may be just the ticket."

"What do you have in mind?" Bonecutter asked.

"Well, how about the whole street getting closed off for the day because of a sewer overflow?"

"Outstanding, Ed, absolutely outstanding," Bonecutter replied, grinning at the idea. Apparently the detective was a cut above average.

Book III
Chapter 9
Albany, New York

Tommy, known as "the Hacker" to all his friends, sat in front of his Apple notebook computer at the end of Tivoli Street, near the Hudson River in a parked van with a logo from a local construction company. Tivoli Street was directly downhill from the neighborhood where the funeral home was located, the lower part of the Arbor Hill section of Albany. From where he sat, he could see the construction project where 250 low-income-housing units were being built. His van looked like just another subcontractor parked at the site.

At precisely 12:00 noon, using the wireless broadband on the notebook, he routed his connection through enough other servers so that it could never be traced, then tapped in to the City's Department of Public Works computer. It took him only a few keystrokes to drop down through the menu of the SERVICEPAC program that controlled the automated portions of the sewage collection and treatment system. He issued commands ordering the computer-controlled gate valve at the end of the Hudson Street, where the Arbor Hill Funeral Parlor was located, to close. He then issued encrypted commands to simulate a password protected order issued by a member of the supervisory staff to block anyone from overriding the command to control the valve.

Ordinarily, the valves were only routinely closed for maintenance, but none of the necessary preventative measures were in place. Within ten minutes, raw sewage started backing up on the street, just as a large hearse passed. In another five minutes, a geyser of sewage blew the manhole cover off at the end of the street, and sewage was rushing everywhere.

The residents of this area typically tolerated problems with the DPW, but sewage flowing down the middle of the street was well beyond the limits of their patience. Within minutes, the Department of Public Works had both ends of the street blocked off to traffic, while they frantically tried to pump the sewage around the closed valve.

From his unmarked car, Detective Ed Woldman could see Willie Robinson looking out the window of the Arbor Hill Funeral Parlor. Robinson appeared to be muttering something to himself, as he watched the crews erect temporary barriers to keep traffic out of the way, while they tried to repair the sewer line. Robinson stepped back from the window closing the curtain, probably to answer the bell from the back of the home, where a hearse had just pulled up for a delivery.

A grizzly-looking old man in a cheap suit that didn't fit him right, stepped back as Robinson answered the door.

"Where you from, man?" Willie asked.

"Delivery from the County Home."

"You ain't the regular driver."

"Clyde is sick, I'm his Uncle Jim. I'm filling in for him."

"Well, get the damn stiff, and bring it in here."

The old man walked back to the hearse and wheeled out a gurney with a black, zipped-up body bag strapped to it. Willie helped the old man get the gurney through the back entrance, and into the small elevator that led to the basement. As he was about to push the down button, the old man said, "Hey, you got a john I could use, I really gotta take a wiz."

"Down the hall and to the left, let yo'self out when you done." Willie said.

"Thanks, buddy."

"I ain't yo buddy, dum son of a bitch," Willie replied, as he pushed the down button. Once he got in the basement, he wheeled the gurney into the embalming room. "Might just as well see who we got here." He undid the straps securing the body to the gurney and unzipped the heavy black plastic bag.

As the bag opened, he saw it contained a long haired street person, the same one he had seen in front of the home the other day. It looked like there was nothing wrong with the guy; he didn't look dead at all. The face had color, and there were no signs of lividity. Then it happened, something most in the funeral profession have nightmares about, the long-haired guy opened his eyes and sat up. This corpse held out his hands; in the right was a wicked looking .45 caliber Colt handgun, and in the other a pair of handcuffs. Anyone who has ever stared down the barrel of a loaded gun can easily attest to how big the business end of a .45 looks up close.

"You," the corpse said, "put one of the cuffs on your right wrist before I ventilate your head."

"Fuck you, you ain't gonna shoot; nobody robs a funeral home," Willie replied.

"This isn't a robbery. Now do what I told you. My guess is your skull won't put itself back together like your boss' did. The corpse took off his ratty wig and the fake beard, revealing himself to Willie as the same man who had blown off a big hunk of La Baptiste's head at the warehouse.

Willie knew he didn't have an option and clipped the handcuff to his wrist.

The intruder hopped down off the gurney and pointed at an upright support beam. "Go over to the beam and sit with your back to it."

Again, Willie did as he was told. Bonecutter walked around behind him, pressing the .45 to the back of Willie's shaved head and snapped the other cuff on Willie's left wrist.

Upstairs, Father John was busy too. After he came out of the bathroom, he found one of the two gang members La Baptiste was using for watchdogs in the hallway. "Hey, buddy," he said to the street hood, "where'd Willie go? I gotta get him to sign the paperwork for the stiff."

The gang hood turned his back on him and pointed towards the elevator to the cellar. A big mistake. Father John hit him in the back of the neck with a high voltage stun gun, dropping him like a sack of potatoes.

As the first hood fell, a second, who was watching the front of the funeral parlor, came running. "What the hell you doin, old man?" he yelled, as he reached behind his pants and drew a stolen Smith & Wesson 9mm handgun from his waistband.

He started to swing the gun towards Father John, but he should have been paying better attention to what was behind him. Bonecutter slammed the butt of the .45 into the base of his skull, knocking him cold. He then took plastic handcuffs and bound the hands and feet of the gang bangers before searching them for weapons.

"Not bad for a priest, Father."

"I wondered where you were. I was starting to think you were going to be a little too late."

"It all came together; now we have to get to the tough part," he replied. "Where do you think he'll be?"

"Sunlight will kill them in the most horrible way possible. Knowing how much they fear sunlight, I would guess he's in the cellar, somewhere nice and dark."

"It's just after noon, and we have lots of time; besides, since he knew we were coming, he probably isn't here. Let's do a quick rip through the upstairs, just to be sure before we hit the cellar."

"He's here, Nick."

"How do you know?"

"Look at this." Father John produced a small vial of liquid which gave off a bluish green glow."

"What is it?"

"Don't you watch the movies? It's Holy water; it glows when a vampire is near."

"Father, someday it really would be nice if you filled me in on all of this stuff before we get into these things, not during. I still want to hit the upstairs first."

Father Ryan was truly amazed as he watched Bonecutter rifle through the upstairs apartment. In less than ten minutes, he had systematically gone through the place, looking in the weirdest places, finding things in each of them. He pulled out a number of hidden weapons, including a pair of machetes. La Baptiste had a safe hidden upstairs. Bonecutter pulled a little spray can from the inside of his jacket and began spraying brown foam on the hinges and lock of the safe.

"What are you doing, and more importantly, who the hell taught you to do this stuff?" The good Father looked on in amazement, as Nick took out what appeared to be a fuse and stuck it into the brown foam on the safe.

"The United States Government taught me how to do this stuff for the same reason I'm about to break into our host's safe, because I need as much information as I can get. If our pal gets away, this may tell us where he's heading. You probably want to step back, Father." Bonecutter lit the fuse with a cigarette lighter and stepped back a few feet.

The foam on the safe lit up like a welder's torch; sparks flew in every direction. There was no banging noise, the safe door fell right off after the sparks stopped. Bonecutter stuffed all of the contents of the safe into a satchel.

"Well, Father, it's time for the big show."

The two went down to the first floor and opened the door, just as Detective Woldman hopped up the porch steps.

"Looks like things are going smoothly so far, gentlemen," Woldman pointed towards the two trussed-up gang members lying in open coffins in the display room of the funeral chapel.

"He has to be downstairs, so let's go," Bonecutter said.

Nicholas led the way down the elevator, and he and Woldman, guns drawn, stepped out onto the floor of the embalming room. Willie looked up at them.

"I gave him the chance to tell us where his boss is, but I think he's less afraid of me shooting him than he is of his boss getting to him if he told us, so let's see, I'm guessing there's another room somewhere, right Willie?"

"Don't know what you talkin' about, man." Willie glared at his captors, eyes filled with hate.

"Well, I know what he's talking about, Willie, because I happen to have the plans for this building in my hands, and I also have the plans for the sewers and the storm sewers. Guess what? If someone was going to build a secret room for this place, it would be on that wall," Woldman pointed to the back wall, where an entire rack of embalming materials and supplies were stored on a metal shelving unit.

Willie didn't say anything. He didn't have to. The look on his face said it all. The street hood's eyes went wide, as if he had seen a ghost.

"Ah, I see you're right on the money, Detective," Bonecutter said, as he examined the storage shelving. Along the end of the shelf, he found a hidden latch, by feeling around the back side with his fingers.

After popping the latch open, the shelf rolled along on a set of wheels, revealing a large, oak door. Bonecutter worked the door over with his spray foam, taking it off its hinges. The door fell, revealing a hidden room. The three companions were completely unprepared for what they found next. In the room, lit by an overhead fluorescent light, they could see several gurneys, all of which had old people strapped to them. They looked like living skeletons, barely alive. Each had intravenous fluids being dripped into their veins, and all of them looked horribly pale, as if their life was being slowly milked out of them.

"What the hell is this?" Woldman asked. "What kind of sick sonofabitch would do something like this?" A career cop, Woldman had seen the worst of the worst. Even he was cut to the core at the sight of the old people strapped to gurneys, bleeding into blood bags like some twisted parody of a Red Cross clinic. He had loved both his parents, and when they got old and withered away, it hurt him badly. He always respected old people. As a cop, he went out of his way to help them. He just couldn't believe this.

"This is how he exists beyond death, Detective," Father John replied. "He's keeping these people alive and using them for a food pantry, slowly bleeding them dry."

"How's it possible?" Bonecutter asked. He too, could not believe what he was seeing. "Someone would miss these people, wouldn't they?"

"Look at them. They're all old. He must have gotten them from a senior citizen's home," Father John said.

"So what, Father? Someone would know," Woldman said.

"Think about it, Ed. Old people die every day, and not all of them have someone who cares." He walked over to one old soul and held his hand as he spoke. "He could have taken them here when they weren't dead, and then buried some bricks in a casket for the funeral."

"We can figure that out later." Bonecutter pointed to a low, steel door in the back of the room. "I think all of the answers are behind door number one."

"And this bastard is gonna die," Woldman replied, as the three turned towards the door in the back of the room.

The door was stout, made of reinforced steel. "How are we going to get in there?" Ryan asked.

"I thought you would never ask, Father. We're going to walk in after the door falls down." Bonecutter produced a doughy brick of C4, a powerful explosive, and worked it back and forth in his fingers to make it more pliable. He stuck a blob of it on the hinges and on the lock to the door. Then he took out some wires with detonators attached and inserted one into each blob. "You boys might want to get those poor folks out of the room."

Woldman and Ryan made short work of wheeling the gurneys full of victims into the embalming room. When they were clear, Bonecutter punched a button on a little remote detonator. For an explosive charge, the blast did not make much noise, just a little whoosh and down went the door.

As the door fell, Bonecutter threw a concussion grenade into the darkness beyond which detonated with a huge roar. He entered the room, .45 ahead of him in a classic shooter's crouch with a small Maglight flashlight in the other hand. Woldman brought up the rear, his Glock sweeping the room in unison with a flashlight of his own.

"Looks like our buddy isn't home," Bonecutter said.

"Get out of there, back up now!" Father Ryan held the vial of holy water in his hand. The vial was glowing so much the blue phosphorescence actually lit up the dark chamber.

Bonecutter knew where to look. As he craned his head upward, he was horrified. La Baptiste was clinging to the ceiling of the chamber like some kind of a bug, and his face was anything but human. While he should have had the drop on the vampire, the other's unnatural speed overcame him. The .45 swung around too late as the creature dropped from the ceiling and grabbed him.

Woldman saw the commotion and swung his gun around to help, but he couldn't get a clear shot. Just what La Baptiste was counting on, as he threw Bonecutter at Woldman like a child's toy. Both went crashing to the floor, and Woldman lost his grip on his Glock.

Ryan wasn't out of this fight. He had weapons of his own, which were far less conventional. He uncapped the vial and splashed the holy water on the vampire.

La Baptiste screeched like the damned as the skin on his face started to melt away. The holy water peeled his face, as if he had been hit by acid. "You win this round, fools, but when we meet again I shall dine on each of you in turn."

He seemed to shimmer in front of them, gradually melting away into a mist.

Bonecutter fired the .45 through the hazy cloud, but it was too late. The mist floated toward a crack in the ceiling and was gone.

"We hurt him. Next time he's going to be much harder to kill," Ryan said. "He won't be coming back here, look at this." He opened the coffin the vampire used for his daily rest and took out a small wooden cross. He stabbed the cross into the silk pillow. It made a hissing noise, before the entire coffin burst into flames.

"Gentlemen, you two have to disappear. I'll handle the rest, including booking the asshole you have chained up out there for attempted murder of these old folks on the gurneys," Woldman said. "Now get the hell out of here before someone else shows up. I'll meet you at the restaurant tonight. Get going!"

Book III
Chapter 10
Albany, New York

The mist that was Armand La Baptiste drifted through the huge brick sewer lines beneath the streets of Albany, until he came to the tunnel where the regulator valves were located, right near the bank of the Hudson River. He had discovered the nearby tunnels when he set up his enterprise in Arbor Hill, and had plotted this escape route soon after relocating there. For his kind to exist, they always needed a way to hide during the day in complete safety and security, and have an escape if discovered. Those who perished usually failed to follow this simple rule.

The basement of the funeral home gave him access to the large sewer lines, and thus, gave him a multitude of ways to escape in darkness in the event anything ever went wrong during the daytime. He was clever as a young man, and as a vampire, he did well for one who did not yet have centuries of existence under his belt. He learned long ago that men would not tolerate his existence. Sooner or later, men like the three he had just escaped were always going to come and try to destroy him. He also knew it would be when he was weak, when he had to sleep. He was ready, and yet, even with a plan, he had barely escaped.

His mist passed through an overhead grate into the valve chamber under an unmanned control room. The valve room would be a good place for him to ride out the rest of the day. As he started to re-materialize from the mist, he felt the pain. He could still feel the burning where the miserable priest's accursed holy water had melted the skin on his face. Even though he was nearly mist when they hit, he could feel the burning bullet holes from the pistol the bastard with the priest shot him with. He was the same man who had shot him before at the warehouse. Apparently, they had learned conventional lead bullets did not work. Judging from the burning pain, these were made of silver. Fortunately, they had passed through his flesh and were not lodged inside him.

His misery was bearable, and only temporary. It would only take a few hours for his undead flesh to heal itself.

The physical pain was not the problem. His mind raged, screaming with the hate and anger only the undead were capable of. He had not felt like this for a long time, not since his days in Haiti. When he had first become a vampire, he raged. Initially, he did not see the vision of how wonderful it was. He dwelled on being a monster and was enraged with those who had caused this condition, one in particular.

Once he'd had a week or two to discover his new powers, he'd vowed to put them to use. As the equally evil Duvalier had slept peacefully in the grand bedroom of the presidential palace, La Baptiste had drifted over the balcony and through the open French door into the room.

Doctor Duvalier, like many senior citizens, did not sleep very well at night. As the old man's eyes opened, he stared in fascination as the mist drifting into his room materialized into a man in an army officer's uniform. Duvalier thought it was one of his loyal soldiers come to check on him as he slept, but somehow this man wasn't one of his guards. Finally he recognized him. This was the young Captain from Fort Demanche, who had been buried a couple of weeks before. He had personally attended the military funeral.

"How can this be?" the old dictator asked.

"Come now, doctor, you are a trained voodoo priest. You know as well as anyone what I am and how I came to be. Rest assured, though, I am no parlor trick accomplished with a drug. I am the real thing, old man," replied La Baptiste.

"But that was only a trick; it is only the zombie powder. You were really dead, killed on a mission for your government. How can this be?" Sweat beaded on the little doctor's forehead.

"My dear doctor, you have lived on this island your whole life. Have you never met a Lupe Garou?"

"No, no, it can't be, you can't be real. I am dreaming. You are only a nightmare. Go away, leave me alone."

"Doctor Duvalier, it was you who made me this way. It was all your fault, and now your nightmare will show you how very real this is."

Duvalier's eyes were like saucers as La Baptiste let the flesh of his face transform, revealing his true, undead self. His nose became elongated, flattened, like the nose of a wild animal. His ears grew in length, changing shape to those of a bat. His eyes were the worst, a crimson rage glowing in his skull.

The diminutive dictator, murderer of thousands, lost control of his bowels as he stared at the gaping jaws of death, smiling only inches from his eyes. Duvalier awoke the next morning with only a vague recollection of his nightmare. He was very weak, barely able to ring the bell for a nurse to come and change him.

Several nights came and went, and always Duvalier's nightmare was the same, until the morning when he finally died. His nightmare did not end there. On Duvalier's last night among the living, the nightmare apparition made him taste its blood. After he drank the foul liquid, the nightmare made him tell his secrets. He simply couldn't stop; the other's will made him do it. He gave up everything. He even told the monster where fortunes remained hidden in other countries, knowledge the rulers of his country kept just in case their rule was cut short.

Duvalier truly came to understand La Baptiste's agony and suffering. He awoke in his coffin, locked inside, flailing away to escape. The fright of being 'alive' and waking in a sealed container built to contain its occupant for all eternity was the worst horror imaginable.

Duvalier's agony ended after he finally broke the latch and was able to sit up inside the casket in its rightful place within the Presidential crypt on the palace grounds. La Baptiste was there to greet him into undeath, with a stake and a machete.

La Baptiste slammed the stake through the pathetic chest at the moment the little doctor's undead eyes opened, as he sat up. He laughed as the geyser of black blood from the fledgling vampire shot upward. The undead hands clutched the stake, but it had already done its work, paralyzing the dictator. Then the machete sliced through the air, cleanly hacking off Duvalier's head.

La Baptiste would always remember what happened next. The frail little body started to glow, a slightly greenish, phosphorescent color, then sparks of electricity dancing up and down, particularly on the flat slab of oozing flesh, where the head used to be attached. Then all hell broke loose. The body burst into flames, but the poor little dictator wasn't truly dead before the finale. The body writhed in agony as it burned. The face looking up from the head as it fell back into the coffin grimaced in agony, though it could not scream with its vocal cords no longer connected. Flames eventually consumed the body, but it continued its macabre dance for quite some time.

La Baptist laughed aloud in the crypt. He relished the twisted revenge he had taken upon Duvalier, vowing to extend it to others. When his lust for getting even was finally slaked, he realized it was time to get away before anyone realized who had done these things and sought his resting place. No one would do to him what he had done to Duvalier.

He had moved through various countries in South America, settling where life was cheap, and death went unnoticed. Sometimes, he would set himself up as a small-time businessman, sometimes as a drug dealer. He would always find a place where no one asked questions, where his existence would never stand out. Whenever his anonymity started wearing off, he would move on, long before men put all the clues together and came for him.

Always, he had his watchdogs, all vampires did. Sleeping without protection during the daylight was foolish. He would quickly gain control over someone and enslave him for just this task. He always selected those who were as evil as he was, just not as clever. He would get rid of them when he surmised they were about to turn on him. By frequently changing his guardians, none ever became a real threat.

La Baptiste was a survivor. He had learned much in life, and much more in undeath. He had killed thousands, bleeding them dry as they met his needs. No one had ever come this close to getting him before. The old priest and his friends were different, though. They knew exactly what he was and had the nerve and knowledge to take on one of his kind.

He was a vampire, and by his very nature, arrogant, yet somewhere deep inside his blackened soul, for the very first time, he was afraid.

Book III
Chapter II
Albany, New York

"We almost had him, Father. Now what are we going to do?" Bonecutter pushed at the plate of pasta in front of him. Ordinarily he would have enjoyed a good plate of De Cesare's linguini and clam sauce, but tonight he was in no mood to eat.

"I'm not surprised we didn't get him," Father Ryan said. "You have to remember, he's been around far longer than most people. A vampire's strength is time and the knowledge they accumulate. He chose his hiding place wisely. We did damage him, though, and now his operation is shut down. He's cut off from his income and the things he had stashed at the funeral home. The good news is, according to our friend Detective Woldman here, all of the old people he was feeding on have returned to their nursing homes and will recover. It'll be interesting to see how the local officials explain people who were supposed to be dead now living and breathing." Ryan buttered another slice of the home-made Italian bread, no loss of appetite evident.

"How are we going to find him now?" Bonecutter asked.

"I'm going to make a few phone calls," Detective Woldman said, "and I'll cut my friend the computer expert loose on the stuff you pulled from the safe. This thing is no different than you or me. He had bills and bank accounts. Tommy will be able to trace any other properties La Baptiste has in the area. He's hurt and on the run. My guess is that he's not very far away." Woldman raised his hand, as his favorite waitress, Maria, came by, and signaled her to bring another round of drinks.

"What else do you know about these things, Father? I need to know everything," Bonecutter said.

"They have powers mortals don't have. As you have seen, they can dissolve into a mist and travel that way. They also have the ability to change their flesh; thus, the stories about men turning into werewolves or vampires turning into bats. They don't really turn into these things, but they can will their flesh to change into poor mimics of these other creatures, if they want to be able to fly like a bat or run like a wolf. They can also change their appearance in the same manner, appearing young or old with the same face."

"What else can they do?" Woldman sipped his scotch as he listened.

"That's about it, but there is something in the way they think that you should be aware of. As I mentioned before, they're very territorial and don't want any competition. That's why the world was never overrun with their kind; they simply won't tolerate it. They rarely make others of their kind and only seem to do so in the case of wanting a companion of sorts. One basic trait they always have is the need to have a watchdog guard them during the daytime. It's said they have the ability to corrupt weak-minded men. In some cases, they develop the ability to enter the minds of certain types of animals to force them to do their bidding."

"Speaking of which, what about his watchdog, Willie? He gave up and took to the handcuffs, instead of dying for his boss," Woldman added. Don't their human helpers have some powers too?"

"They're people, just like you or me, but they have basically given themselves to evil. There have been instances through history where those trying to destroy a vampire have encountered human watchdogs, as you put it, and have had considerable difficulty killing them. It's almost as if they have developed some of the vampire's powers. I think this was not the case with Willie. This usually takes place only in those who have been with the vampire for many, many years."

"So, all we have to do is take out the new watchdog or watchdogs, and we're okay, right?" Bonecutter pushed his uneaten food away and sipped his beer, which had already gone flat.

"Well, not exactly," Ryan replied.

"What do you mean, not exactly?"

"I'm afraid he'll be much more prepared this time. He can also make others of his kind to use against us, and those he creates will be under his total control. If he has done this to protect himself, any of them will be compelled to die for their boss, if called upon to do so."

"Wonderful, Father, now there're going to be more of those things?"

"Probably, but the good news is they won't have the full range of powers he has, yet they will be far stronger than the average man, and their bite is just as deadly as his."

"Great, Father, just great.

"There is one more thing."

"What's that?" Woldman asked.

"As I said, they also have a certain dominion over some types of animals. They can use animals, like rats, snakes, or especially dogs, as 'familiars.' It's possible he has done this to guard his new hiding place."

"You've got to be kidding me. Now we have to fight animals, too?" Bonecutter shook his head in disgust, and the three finished their meal in silence.

* * *

Tommy the Hacker sat doing his favorite thing—secretly prying open sources of information most people could not access. He checked the mainframe computer at the county offices. After spending an hour in the files of the Real Property Office, he had a good start. The Arbor Hill Funeral Home was owned by a corporation named Maglior, Inc.

He sat on his ratty couch in his parent's cellar, eating his favorite snack— Cheeze Doodles, as he hacked into the next site he needed to look at. He didn't mind the orange crud he got on the keyboard and simply bought a new one when the keys got gummed up. In his mind, he had a cool apartment, even if it got damp at times. The couch folded open into a sofa bed. He had a cheap, twenty-three-inch color TV, complete with cable, a dormitory refrigerator, and a hot plate. He had always thought the chicks would dig him, having his own place, but as of yet, none had stopped over.

He opened his Internet browser and did several searches on the word, "Maglior." While there was no website for a corporation called Maglior, Inc., he did determine this was the name of a former Haitian president. He downloaded a document that listed a brief history of Haiti, including a list of its presidents and public figures.

He then tapped into the records of all the area banks and located a couple of accounts listed under Maglior, Inc. He was also able to obtain account numbers and on-line access information as well. A quick hack into the records of VISA, MASTERCARD, and American Express yielded a couple more account numbers for the same corporation.

Then he tapped into the account histories on the credit cards. It seemed, based on the transactions, a number of charges for gas, food, and other items had been made in the Fonda-Fultonville area of Montgomery County.

On a hunch, he hacked into the Montgomery County Tax department. Although there were no listings for Maglior, Inc., a large estate outside of Fultonville was owned by a Mr. Duvalier, another of the Haitian Presidents on his list. From the same computer, he was able to download GIS files showing the precise location of the old house, and all the information the tax office used in billing the property owner.

After he had all of this data, he sent an e-mail to Woldman telling him what he had found.

* * *

In a very old house overlooking the Mohawk River Valley, on the end of a one-lane gravel road, a meeting was underway. The house had been built before the Revolutionary War and had a rich, dark history.

The structure was constructed with a post and beam design, with an elaborate brick exterior. The building was two stories high, with the exception of a central turret structure that projected above the roofline. Many of the bigger homes built at the time had a similar structure, to give the owners a lookout point in case of an Indian raid. Several hundred feet from the house, there was a smaller carriage house and a barn on the grounds. The house was built by an early settler named Van Schuyler, who was rumored to have been an ex-pirate and smuggler, before retiring to his estate in the Mohawk Valley.

Throughout the years, many terrible things had taken place in the house and on the grounds. Ten years after it was constructed, a tribe of Mohawk Indians had led a raid on the home and its occupants, killing those who were unfortunate enough not to escape or hide. The oak banister leading up to the second floor still had a hack mark from a Mohawk tomahawk.

The home's grisly history did not end there. The residence had been used as a meeting place for the few colonists settling in the Mohawk Valley, during and after the Revolutionary War, and became a sort of community house where trials were held. Sometimes, prisoners were executed by hanging them from the ancient oak tree in the front yard.

As the years went by, other horrors took place. There were two suicides in the house. There was also a murder that made headlines in the biggest newspapers in the country in the 1920s. The house was purchased by a star of silent movies. The movie star had lots of money, and his prize was an underwear collection from his romantic conquests. He was killed by a jealous lover, and it took the police a while to figure out why his naked body was covered in women's underwear, each item containing a different name written in ink.

Most who owned the home did not keep it for very long. It had been sold many times. Most owner/occupants preferred to sell it for whatever they could get and move elsewhere.

In recent years, the house had fallen into disrepair. Inside, a fine layer of dust blanketed all of the rooms. The curtains and carpets were frayed and tattered, and there was a musty smell throughout.

In the great room at the front, left side of the house, Armand La Baptiste, like any great general, took stock of his troops before the battle that was to come. He stood in front of the gang bangers he ordered sent up from New York City, sizing them up.

Six tough looking hoods from the Latin Kings had been hired for the job. La Baptiste had opted for a gang with no current ties to him or his operation. The other reason for his choice was that this was farm country, and many of the farms hired Hispanic workers, as did some of the area construction companies. His "crew" could be explained away to questioning locals as laborers who were hired to repair the house.

"Do what I ask and you will be paid well. Your mission is simple. One of my, shall we say, competitors, is going to try to take over my operation. You shall see to it that he does not, and that all of them end up dead."

"Why you want us to bring these dogs?" The gang leader, a skinny, pock-marked young man with eyes like a weasel and his hair done up in a hairnet pointed, to a pair of huge Rottweiler's lying obediently in the corner.

"The animals will help you guard the property," La Baptiste replied. "If my enemies come, I expect you to deal with them, using any means possible. If you serve me well, you shall also receive the bonuses I described. For now, go upstairs and get settled in. Divide yourselves up so four of you watch during the day, and two at night."

"Why only two at night?" the gang leader asked.

"Because I shall be around in the evening. Now, do as I have asked. I have business this evening back in Albany. I will give you further instructions tomorrow night."

* * *

In the detective's office of the Albany Police station, Ed Woldman was going over his paperwork. Woldman was an atypical investigator in a lot of ways. In addition to being the king of all misfits in the department, and drawing the constant ire of his supervisors, he also had a different problem. Woldman was at his absolute worst when he was right, especially if things were not going his way when he was right.

He would go out on a limb to keep another cop from throwing the book at a suspect who truly deserved a break. He could just as easily pull every string, when he was trying to put away someone he thought deserved a trip to jail, especially if those at the top were telling him to go light on the suspect.

Woldman's parents had brought him up to do the right thing at all costs, and they taught him that those in authority were not always trying to do the right thing. They also ingrained in him the idea that he would sink or swim on his own merit. No one was going to hand him anything in life. He would have to earn it.

When he joined the police department at age eighteen, it didn't take him long to figure out that right and wrong didn't have a lot to do with everyday police work. The only reason he had stayed in it as long as he had, was that he had talent. He could solve the most difficult crimes, the cases others gave up on. He was a thorough, patient investigator with an intuitive skill for judging character. It didn't take him long to size people up, to figure out what they were made of.

While Woldman's talent helped him eventually make detective, it was also a curse. He could just as quickly size up his superiors, identifying the ass-kissers and the weasels who wormed their way into positions they didn't deserve. Most of his bosses did not like him. It wasn't his wisecracking, and they knew he did his job to the best of his ability. They disliked Woldman because they knew he could see them for exactly what they were, not what they were supposed to be.

Such was the case when Captain Reichman was appointed to the force by his brother the commissioner.

Woldman looked up to see his fat boss waddling his way.

"Woldman, have you got the new reports for manpower in your section done like I asked?"

"Why no, Captain, I don't. You told me to drop everything and get over to the morgue, and I just came back."

"Listen to me, you dumb sonofabitch, you ain't at the morgue now, and I don't have the reports in my hand, do I? Now you can sit there at your friggin' desk, until you get them done."

Woldman had finally had enough, especially after going through the contents of La Baptiste's safe and finding out what Riechman did on his off hours. "Okay, Captain," he replied. "I'll get them to you faster than a cop can whip an S&M hooker's ass."

"What did you say?" Reichman said, all color draining from his face.

"Why nothing, Captain." Woldman could scarcely keep his poker face and not break out laughing, "nothing at all."

"You just make sure I get those damned reports!" With that, Reichman stormed off in a huff.

Oh you'll get your reports, and a whole lot more.

* * *

Ryan called his friend Father D'Arcy to tell him all about what was going on. This wouldn't be the first time the Church had become involved in fighting vampires and certainly wouldn't be the last. He asked D'Arcy to wire the money they needed to purchase the expensive, and illegal, items on Nick's list of supplies.

"Why do we need all this money?" Ryan had asked Bonecutter.

"Father, like I told you, I don't mess with the whole saving souls business, and you don't mess with my part of the show."

"What is your plan?"

"Don't have one. It depends on what information our friend the detective comes up with. Right now, we don't know enough."

Ryan watched as Bonecutter unloaded his purchases. From a locked wooden box, he removed two wicked looking semi-automatic shotguns, and a semi-automatic .50-caliber sniper rifle, complete with scope. From a smaller box, he unloaded three Glock .40-caliber handguns, equipped with laser sights and several spare clips for each. Another box contained a mixture of concussion grenades and anti-personnel fragmentation grenades. From a third case, he unveiled six stun grenades, and enough C-4 explosive to level a shopping mall. Rounding out the collection was none other than a World War II vintage flame thrower, complete with tanks.

"Father, I hope your connections have plenty of money to bail us out after this whole mess hits the fan. I'm guessing the local cops are not going to be happy with us, after all of this is finished," Bonecutter said.

"The church assures me it will take care of us."

"I hope so. Now, Father, come on out back with me. It's time for your crash course in combat firearms."

* * *

Albany County Jail, like most county jails throughout upstate New York, was not built to be an architectural wonder, but rather to be laid out for functionality as a modern incarceration facility. The brick facility, located near the county airport on Albany Shaker Road, looked exactly like a small prison. Passing drivers had no trouble figuring out what the building was, given the three rings of fencing surrounding the building, each topped with razor wire.

The current Sheriff, a no-nonsense lawman, ran a very tight ship. Under his watch, there had been only one escape, and the con had done so with the help of a guard on the take. Fortunately, the deputies found the escapee the next day, and the Sheriff personally locked his former employee in a cell right next to him.

Since the escape, things had been even tighter around the jail. as even more procedures were put in place and strictly enforced.

Third shift guard Calvin Smith checked the monitors of the high security wing, as he did regularly from his post. Smith was new to the job and was a little edgy for some reason. His wing held the worst of the worst, which he had gotten used to over the first few weeks, but the new prisoner, some nut named Willie who had been busted in the funeral home raid in Arbor Hill, was getting on his nerves.

Smith's wife had shown him the newspaper article. Apparently, this Willie was a whacko who, along with his boss, was stealing old folks from the area nursing homes and doing something weird with them in the cellar of the place.

Smith cued up camera three and zoomed in on the door to Willie's cell. He could hear the pathetic goofball through the speaker saying over and over again that someone was coming to get him. Just who he figured was going to get through several locked doors and manned checkpoints to get to him, in a locked cell used for solitary confinement, was a mystery to Smith, but the guy wouldn't shut up, especially at night.

As Smith viewed the monitor screen, something strange happened. The camera suddenly started cutting out, eventually losing the picture entirely as the speaker spewed white noise.

Since the Albany County lockup was a relatively modern jail, he was the only guard needed on the wing through the night when the prisoners were locked down. He radioed the command center to report the problem and left his post to enter the wing. As he unlocked and opened the security door, he noticed something strange. A mist was coming from Willie's cell and rolling along the floor toward an open window. The mist moved as if it had a purpose, and it slipped out of the window through the welded steel bars and mesh grate that covered it.

Smith thought there might be a fire in Willie's cell. Prisoners sometimes set fire to their mattress as a stunt to cause trouble. None of the training he'd received as a guard could have ever prepared him for what he saw when he reached the cell door and looked inside through the view port. Willie was hanging from the cell window, where his skull had been wedged between the bars, crushing it entirely. In the center of the cell floor, the man's still beating heart lay in a pool of blood.

Smith tried over and over to report to the command center but kept having the same problem. He had to stop screaming first.

Book III
Chapter 12
Fultonville, New York

The Mohawk River is an unusual body of water, largely due to the fact that, through much of the year, a series of movable dams operated by the New York State Canal Authority keep the water level high enough to move barges and boat traffic through the river. In the winter, the dams are removed, and the river flows like it did for thousands of years.

The stretch of the river to the west of the quiet little village of Fultonville is a relatively placid section. A big, sweeping bend gives way to a flat area where one of the major feeder streams enters. In some ways, the river banks are not much different than they were during the birth of the United States. Old farmlands with barns going back hundreds of years, milk cows peacefully grazing in the green fields, and many old historic homes dot the landscape. Icons of modern times, power lines, a small oil storage terminal, and two highways line the banks, but for the most part, the area still looks like a snapshot from another time.

Looming above it all was the Van Schuyler mansion, currently owned by a front company that few could trace back to the sole owner of the property, former Haitian Army Captain and torturer, Armand La Baptiste. Angel Aquinto stood in the turret portion of the mansion, using this unique architectural feature for its original purpose. Aquinto scanned the area below, using a powerful set of binoculars to survey the surroundings. Angel was a handsome youth, whose looks were potentially good enough to land him a movie role, although his current occupation made it unlikely he would even live much past thirty.

As he adjusted the focusing knob on the binoculars, he saw a fishing boat come into view from around the bend. The boat looked like any of the other half-dozen similar rigs he had watched that morning. The Mohawk was a popular water for tournament bass fishermen, and this boat held two anglers. They appeared to be slowly working the flat area out in front of the mansion.

The boat did not seem to be a threat, just another pair of fishermen trying to catch bass.

* * *

On the boat, one of the anglers, an older gent of small stature, sporting a gray beard, checked the precision chronometer attached to his wrist. As he checked the watch, he wished he had spent some time in the military, because his training as a Catholic priest wasn't helping at the moment. According to the waterproof Doxa diver's watch, Bonecutter had insisted he wear, there was only ten minutes left until the show started. As Father Ryan sat there pretending to fish from the front seat on the deck of the bass boat, he wondered how things were going down below.

Beneath the surface, in the relatively clear water of the Mohawk River, a school of decent sized smallmouth bass scattered, fleeing from something they had never seen before. Bass this size had little to fear in the way of predators in the river, but these fish had never seen anything as big as the two objects swimming towards them.

As the two divers approached, the lead swimmer could see the fish. The second diver, Woldman, was as far out of his element as a man could be. In his early fifties, he was not in his athletic prime, and swimming along behind Bonecutter, while inhaling air from a scuba tank, wasn't his idea of a good time. Bonecutter had rigged both of them with Draager breathing devices borrowed from a buddy of his from the SEALS. These scuba tanks were developed for stealth operations and did not leave any telltale bubbles rising to the surface where they could be seen. As Bonecutter kicked effortlessly along, while Woldman tried his best to swim directly behind him, all the while wishing he had spent some time at the gym because his legs were starting to burn from the effort.

The plan was relatively simple. There was a forty-eight-inch, round, corrugated-metal storm water pipe from the road and the property that emptied into the river. They had identified the pipe from plans Tommy the Hacker had obtained from the computer system at the Department of Transportation. The blueprints showed that the pipe surfaced close to the barn on the Van Schuyler Mansion property. The pipe was the only way inside the property through the security fence, which was undoubtedly rigged with sensors.

Bonecutter and Woldman had dropped over the side of the bass boat just before it rounded the bend, making sure that they were not seen by anyone.

Bonecutter led the way up the river channel and counted the anchor cables on the buoys to navigate them to the right spot. He had memorized the river map, and it was easy to spot the 4X4 concrete anchors and cables rising to the surface as he swam along. After he passed the third anchor, he turned towards the southern shore, using his compass to guide him on a bearing that would bring him to the pipe. The bottom of the pipe was in about ten feet of water. He guided Woldman into the pipe, and they slowly swam upward in the dark pipe, until he broke the surface into the air.

Bonecutter flipped on a small light and looked up the pipe, as Woldman crawled up behind him. He hand signaled for Woldman to stay quiet. Sound would amplify in the enclosed pipe and could give them away. Hearing nothing, he was happy with the situation. Even if they were watching on the riverbank, they would not see divers enter the submerged end of the pipe, and they had encountered no security devices on the way in.

They shed their scuba gear and put it into a mesh bag and left it in the pipe. Bonecutter took the lead and told Woldman to stay at least fifteen feet behind, proceeding in the darkness. The trip up the 200 feet of pipe was going well, far too well. Bonecutter's instincts took over and he stopped. Every mission he had ever been on, no matter how simple, never went a hundred percent according to plan. As he moved up through the pipe, he could see daylight from around the bend. Inside the pipe, the sound from every little pebble they hit with their boots echoed as they crawled along. He had gotten used to the noises he and Woldman made, but he could hear something else, a tiny scratching noise coming from another location in the pipe.

He signaled for Woldman to stop at the same time he saw them. Rats! Dozens and dozens of rats were running down the pipe toward them. *Father John said he had a power over animals, and he wasn't kidding.* He had prepared for this eventuality, and he looked back at Woldman. "Get your mask on!"

As the dozens of nasty-looking river rats continued their advance, he reached inside a satchel and pulled out what looked like a can of spray paint. The can contained enough high strength pepper spray to stop a charging grizzly bear. He pointed the spray at the rats and fogged them hard.

Even though a vampire has influence over his animal familiars, the level of pain that the capsaicin spray caused the rat's eyes and lungs was enough for them to turn and run away.

I wonder what else he has planned for us, Bonecutter thought.

He continued crawling along, past the bend in the pipe and into the daylight shining in the last section of the pipe. *Now the fun starts*. He signaled back to Woldman to come up behind him.

"What did you see?" Woldman whispered.

"A few dozen of the nastiest looking rats I've seen in awhile."

"What's next?"

"Chances are, he has some more animal surprises. If you were in his position, how would you guard the place during the day?" Bonecutter asked.

"Well, most drug pushers use dogs."

"Exactly," Bonecutter replied as he reached into the satchel again, pulling out two short metal tubes, and what looked to be a long, skinny whistle.

"Give me your Glock."

"For what?"

"Just do what I tell you and give me your Glock."

Woldman handed him the Glock that Bonecutter's 'supplier' had procured. Nicholas then proceeded to screw a silencer into Woldman's gun, as well as his own.

"Wonderful, if we get caught, not only can I forget all about my pension, but I'll spend part of my retirement in a Federal Prison."

"Don't kid yourself, Detective, chances are we either won't make it out of this alive, or at the very best, we're going to spend the rest of our days in a mental institution. Besides, how bad could Federal Prison be? They sent Martha Stewart there. Anyway, this is your last chance, in, or out?"

Woldman thought about the haggard, gray faces of the old people the monster had been feeding on. "I'm in."

"Me too. This thing needs to die before he kills anyone else."

"I agree. I can only imagine if that was one of my folks strapped to a gurney in his little shop of horrors, thank God neither of them ended up in the nursing home. Besides, I hate pushers."

"Then get ready, because the show is about to start. You take out anything on the left and I have the right," Bonecutter blew the dog whistle.

From the other side of the property, a pair of wicked looking Rottweiler's ran towards the sound of the whistle, right to the front of the drainage pipe. From the other side of the property, an ugly mongrel that was part pit bull came running. As the dogs approached, they heard muffled puffing noises from the pipe, and that was the last thing their sensitive ears ever detected.

The silenced .40 caliber rounds did their job, and the lead dog went down in a crumpled heap. Woldman took out the other Rottweiler, and he fell within a foot of his buddy. The Pitt bull mutt saw the other dogs crumple, and smelling dog blood, it turned to run but wasn't quick enough. A slug from Bonecutter's Glock killed him instantly.

"I've seen plenty of vicious dogs when I've kicked down the door to crack houses on the job, but there was something different about them. Did you see their eyes?"

"He did something to them, Ed, just like Father John said he would, and I bet there's more to come."

With the canine guards eliminated, Woldman and Bonecutter left the relative security of the pipe. Woldman had done a brief stint in the Army, and he knew from watching the fishing guide thus far, that Bonecutter knew a whole hell of a lot more than Woldman had ever learned in the service. If he wanted to live through this, best bet was to jump when Bonecutter said jump.

Bonecutter was here to kill a vampire, not people, and he wished there had been another option with the dogs, although there was little resemblance between these beasts and his buddy, Sadie. The next part of the assault would be the hardest. Bonecutter dragged the dogs off into the bushes and slipped away into heavy cover near the end of the pipe. Woldman played his part and stepped out into the open. It took only a couple of seconds for the sentry in the turret to spot him and radio his two fellow gang members who were patrolling the grounds.

Woldman stood there, seemingly helpless, as two youths, armed with Mac 10 machine pistols approached. As they started screaming at him to get on the ground, two sets of wires suddenly appeared, running from their chests up into a nearby tree. The two twitched like a couple of marionettes, trying to free themselves of the darts delivering the electric shock from a pair of Tazer stun guns. The gang bangers dropped to the ground, and Woldman quickly cuffed their hands and feet with plastic handcuffs and slapped duct tape over their mouths.

Bonecutter was already on his way to the back porch, while Woldman secured the still twitching gang hoods. Trained soldiers, particularly those in any of the Special Forces, would never have fallen for the next trick Bonecutter had up his sleeve, but untrained gang hoods with no military experience were predictable.

Angel came running out the back door, right on cue, without checking first, ready to empty his machine pistol at Woldman. As he breached the door, he heard a whistling sound. His wrist erupted in pain, causing him to drop his weapon. As he bent over to retrieve it, he was smacked in the back of the neck with a solid shot from the ex-SEAL's stiffened right arm and crumpled in a heap.

It took Woldman and Bonecutter fifteen minutes to sweep and secure the house. Finding no other resistance, he radioed Ryan to come ashore with the boat.

"What have you found?" Ryan asked, still huffing from running up the steep lawn to the house.

"Nothing so far, Father," Nicholas pointed to Tommy the Hacker, who had just joined Ryan on the back porch, lugging a duffle bag with the shotguns and explosives. "Tommy, go back and run the boat up the river a mile or so and wait. Keep your ears on. If you hear us call on the radio, get here as quick as you can." Tommy didn't ask any questions and ran back down the lawn and launched the boat.

"He must be hidden here somewhere," Ryan said.

"How do we know he's even here, Father?" Woldman asked.

"Same way we knew at the funeral home." Ryan reached inside his jacket and produced a small vial of liquid that was glowing a phosphorescent bluish green. "This vial of holy water, properly blessed in the church, is telling us he's here. Gentlemen, we are in the presence of a vampire, and he's quite close."

"Then let's find him. We have about four hours of daylight left." Bonecutter and his two companions entered the house.

"Let's split up; it is only him left, and he can't do much in the daylight," Woldman said, "but if you find something, radio everyone else before you check it out, no sense giving him the chance to pick us off one by one."

"Here, Father, I have something for you," Bonecutter said, as he handed the diminutive priest his grandfather's well worn .45 caliber Colt Model 1911 handgun.

"Oh no, I don't want it."

"We do this my way, remember, Father?" Bonecutter replied, as he handed him the gun. "It's real simple. The hammer is cocked, and the safety catch, this little button here, is on. All you do is push the button down with your thumb and start shooting, understand?"

"If you say so, but let's get going. We're losing daylight while we're talking." Ryan shoved the handgun under his belt and walked towards the kitchen.

The old house, nearly void of all furniture, was almost empty. They checked each room, including the attic and cellar and found nothing. They tapped on walls and floors looking for false panels, and even knocked holes in the old lath and plaster walls, but there was no hint of where the vampire could be hiding. The only thing in the basement was a furnace and an oil tank from when the house was converted from wood heating in the 1920s.

The three searched for nearly two hours, without results, yet all the while the vial of holy water kept its eerie glow. Bonecutter searched the barn and the carriage house with the same results. As he walked back to the house to join the others, he noticed something. The house, since it was built during a time when wood fireplaces were the only source of heat, had five chimneys showing above the roof. Two were on the ends of the house, and there were three on the side walls, two in the front, and one in the back.

As he noticed this, Bonecutter had a thought. There were five chimneys, yet he had only seen four fire places on each floor, even though he had been all through the house. One of the chimneys didn't seem to open up inside the house. Then he looked back toward the carriage house. There was a chimney on the outside of it, yet there was no fire place inside.

He ran towards the house, yelling for Woldman and Ryan on the radio. The three met in the great room in the front of the house. "Look, there's a fireplace here, and somewhere over on this wall, there's a chimney, but it doesn't open to the inside of the house," Bonecutter said. "Father, didn't you say it was rumored that this house was built by a man who had dealings with pirates?"

"That's what Tommy came up with on the computer when he researched this place."

"Then he must've had a way to store the loot and move it without anyone noticing. More importantly, didn't you say he and his family somehow escaped an Indian attack? Well, how would you get out of here without someone outside seeing you? I think the answer must be upstairs."

"What are we looking for?" Woldman asked.

"You'll see."

The three ran up the large wooden staircase to the second floor, and Bonecutter ran into the room where the chimney should be. He looked along the wall. There was an area along it where he could see a couple of handprints in the dust covering the old walls. There were a couple of old candle sconces attached to the wall right next to the handprints.

Bonecutter touched the candle sconce on the right, trying to move it. The antique candle holder turned to the right, as a gear inside the wall moved an iron catch. He turned the sconce several times, and the panel with the hand prints on it made a slight clicking noise.

"This is where he's hiding," Bonecutter pushed the panel inward and took a flashlight from the holder on his belt and shined it down the chimney. Along the outside wall of the chimney was a set of wrought iron ladder rungs.

"Father, you stay here and guard the door. If it's one of us coming through the door we'll whistle three times before we open it. If you see the door open and don't hear anyone whistle, shoot anything that comes through."

"Shouldn't I come down there with you two?"

"No way. First, Ed is trained on handling guns, and second, if we don't succeed, you will be our last chance at killing this thing. Okay, Ed, stay behind me and remember to keep checking behind us too." Each of them holstered their handguns and grabbed a shotgun from the duffle bag.

"Let's just get this over with. I don't want to be caught down there with him in the dark." Woldman pointed out the west window towards the sun, which was sinking ever farther toward the horizon.

Nicholas started down the iron ladder, as Woldman lit the way with his flashlight. The chimney dropped down below the basement of the house into a tunnel that seemed to lead in the general direction of the barn and carriage house. Woldman made his way down the ladder with the shotgun pointed forward over Bonecutter's shoulder, as the two crept forward. The inside of the tunnel looked like an old mine shaft, reinforced every few feet with hand-cut timbers.

"Be careful, Ed; I would guess he has some surprises left for us. I know I would if I was him."

The first surprise wasn't left behind by the vampire. It was the handiwork of the original owner of the home. Crypts cut into the tunnel walls held several skeletons.

"I wonder who these guys were?" Bonecutter asked.

"My guess would be the people who built Van Schuyler the tunnel, because as they say in the pirate business, dead men tell no tales." Woldman moved one of the skulls toward the beam of his flashlight and showed Bonecutter the hole in the forehead where a bullet had entered. "The Egyptians did the same thing with their workers when the pyramids were built; no need to worry about someone coming back and looting the goods."

The two continued moving cautiously down the tunnel, until they came to a spot where the shaft forked. Now there were two tunnels, and time was running out.

"Now what?" Woldman asked.

"Unfortunately, we have to split up. We have to finish him before sunset."

"You want left or right?"

"You pick, Detective."

"Left it is," Woldman replied.

"Give me a yell on the radio if you find anything." Bonecutter moved into the right branch of the tunnel, off into the darkness.

* * *

Ryan's nerves were getting the better of him. He kept looking out the window, watching the sun sinking into the trees. He guessed there was only about fifteen minutes left before it would be down. La Baptiste would soon rise and have the full range of his powers available to fight with. He kept pacing back and forth, just about jumping out of his skin, with every creak and groan of the old house. He couldn't stand the temptation any longer. Ryan went over and twisted the candle sconce and opened the hidden door. He thought he could listen and maybe hear what was going on in the darkness below. As he shined a flashlight down the shaft made by the phony chimney and listened intently, above him, about ten more feet up the chimney, a pair of glowing scarlet eyes opened.

* * *

Woldman's tunnel continued along for another hundred yards, ending in a shaft leading upward. "Nick," he said into the microphone on the headset.

"Yeah, Ed."

"Looks like another fake chimney going up into the barn."

"Well, check it out, I haven't found anything yet."

Woldman walked over to the iron ladder on the shaft. He couldn't climb and carry his gun at the same time, so he slung the shotgun across his back. He grabbed the ladder and climbed up a couple of rungs, putting his head into the shaft. He fumbled with his flashlight, before he could finally position it in his mouth to shine upwards, so he could see how far he would have to climb. As he finally got the light in his teeth and pointed it up the dark shaft, it reflected off a hideous face only inches from his own, at the same instant, something grabbed the back his skull and smashed his forehead into the iron ladder.

* * *

Bonecutter eased along the walls of the right tunnel. His flashlight was attached to the barrel of the 12-gauge shotgun. He swept the light along the tunnel walls and checked the ceiling as he went. He stopped every five feet, the paused to listen. He could hear nothing from up ahead.

After he covered another forty feet of the tunnel, he felt the air change. The temperature suddenly dropped five degrees or more. Sweat ran down the sides of his face despite the cold. He thought he had been scared in combat before. Nothing in the SEALS matched what he was doing now. Going up against something that could change into a mist and rip your throat out to drink your blood was something else entirely.

The tunnel opened up into some kind of a room just ahead. As he played the flashlight around, he could see that the room was quite large, at least ten feet high and nearly as big as the foundation of the carriage house on the property, which was exactly where he figured he was.

As the flashlight beam swept along, he couldn't believe what he was looking at. Several chests lay on the floor in the center of the room. Bonecutter was no antique expert, but the wooden chests were obviously hundreds of years old. He walked over and threw the lid back on the nearest one. It was filled with gold and silver jewelry, cups and goblets, and even some crudely fashioned ingots and coins, although some of it was tarnished and dusty. The other trunks he opened had old silver and gold chains, piled to the rim. One was filled with old coins. Behind the pile of loot was a large object, lacking the layer of dust on the old trunks. The new coffin looked like it had just come from a funeral director's show room.

Bonecutter knew that he was almost out of time, and he would much rather deal with a sleeping vampire than one who was awake. When he flung back the coffin's lid it was already empty. Something grabbed him from behind and threw him thirty feet across the room. He was upside down when he hit, his back slamming into the stone wall. The strap on the sword slung across his back snapped, and it clattered to the brick floor.

After what seemed like an eternity, Bonecutter crumpled to the floor. Somehow, he managed to hang onto the shotgun, and was sweeping the light around trying to find a target. He was at a huge disadvantage in the darkness, and it was only a split second later before the gun was knocked from his hands. He reached for his holstered pistol, and that too was batted away. Something grabbed him and slammed him into the wall again, and he was knocked nearly senseless. Then he was picked up off the ground by a hand that latched onto his shirt with an iron grip.

"Gentlemen, please light the room for our guests," a voice said, as Bonecutter was carried to the center of the room by his throat.

As Bonecutter struggled, unseen hands lit up several propane lanterns and hung them from hooks on the stone wall. From what Nicholas could see, this would surely be the end. There were now three of them: La Baptiste and two others that appeared to be from the Hispanic gang guarding the house. Their eyes glowed crimson in the dim light. His hopes dropped even further, as he saw his companions tossed onto the dirt floor of the room, their hands bound behind their backs. *We're all done. Best thing I can do is piss him off so he kills us instead of turning us into vampires, bound to serve him for eternity.*

"It is good that you intrepid hunters of the Nosferatu could join me again. I regret my leaving so soon when we last met. As you can see, this time I was able to prepare a more fitting welcome. You can see my research on the previous owner of my estate paid off. I now have his fortune, in addition to my profits from other enterprises. Of course, I must relocate, but in my profession, this is often necessary."

Bonecutter was thrown to the floor. "Glad to meet you, asshole," Bonecutter replied, as he fought to catch his breath.

"Oh, well, since you must be crude, let us conclude our business. First, pardon me while I reward my recruits for a job done very well. Come forth my friends and receive your reward." La Baptiste reached out with his left hand and picked up two gold ingots and held them before him. The two fledgling vampires stepped forward, imagining the riches they would receive, as well as the fact that they would be able to enjoy them forever.

"Gentlemen, though you are new to existing as I have for many years, you did well." La Baptiste smiled and handed each an ingot and said, "this is but a down payment. I shall give you each a vast share of the treasure you see before you."

Then, to the horror of Bonecutter and the other members of his failed raid, the vampire produced a machete from behind his back. One quick swing and the heads flew from the shoulders of both gang members. As the bodies hit the floor they erupted into flames, as if they were made of rocket fuel. It took only a couple of seconds for them to be reduced to ashes.

"I'm sorry for that unpleasantness, gentlemen, but when one exists as I do, one should not make others of his kind, unless it is absolutely necessary. Now, let us conclude our business," La Baptiste's grin was abominable, the sharp fangs of his upper and lower teeth clearly visible.

"You my friend, you are obviously a soldier, a warrior of some sort. I shall give you a chance to save yourself and your friends," La Baptiste said. "I offer you this chance, because you are the strongest. Where I am from, my job was extracting information. It shall be much easier for me to learn the things I must know to survive from your friends, once I kill you and they no longer have any hope. Yet, if you do defeat me, then you and your friends leave with your mortal lives and souls intact. You will die, whether we fight or not. At least this way you can die with honor as a warrior, a common courtesy among soldiers. Shall we get started?" The vampire stepped back as Bonecutter stood up. La Baptiste spun him around and untied his hands before stepping back.

Ryan and Woldman could only watch the unfolding spectacle. Ryan was obviously dazed, probably from a solid crack to the head, as some blood ran down his face from above his left ear. Woldman struggled with the ropes binding him, as Nicholas fought for all their lives.

Bonecutter circled to the left, trying to buy some time to figure out his opponent. As the two circled each other, La Baptiste made some odd moves, almost like he was crawling around on the floor doing some strange kind of dance. Father John and Detective Woldman were puzzled, but Nick had seen this before. Obviously, La Baptiste had training in Capuera, a Brazilian Martial Art. *Great, the style I know the least about.*

Nicholas thought he had the vampire's timing, and launched inward with a combination kick, first low to draw the other's guard and then high at La Baptiste's head. The vampire easily evaded both, and ducked low, putting his hands on the floor, then he swung a circular kick smashing his heel into the side of Bonecutter's face, knocking him backwards. A bloody gash opened up from the impact.

Fortunately, the ex-SEAL was smart enough not to stiffen up and rolled with the blow, or he would have been knocked cold. The vampire twisted in an arc, and the leg swung again, this time connecting with Nicholas's left side, snapping a rib. The second shot knocked him over a trunk full of silver.

* * *

From where he sat, Woldman, who had been slammed around pretty good himself, tried his best to even the odds. The vampire gang members hadn't searched him very well. Woldman, like many detectives, always carried backup weapons, in case he was ever tied up or handcuffed. There was a knife built into his belt, and he always kept a spare handcuff key stuffed into a little pocket in his shoe. It was fairly easy for him to draw the small knife, but using it to cut the ropes was proving difficult from the awkward way he had to hold his hands. He only hoped he could get through the ropes in time.

* * *

Nicholas had taken a couple more hits from fists and feet. He had also gotten some shots of his own in, after learning that, because of the vampire's speed, he had to punch or kick where he was going, not where he was. Trouble was, on La Baptiste they had little effect. Under ordinary circumstances, there were very few people who could take him in hand-to-hand combat. He had never fought anyone with reflexes and speed like this. Although he had taken damage, he was still connecting when he had the chance. As La Baptiste moved left, Bonecutter shot out his stiffened hand, correctly anticipating the other's timing and connecting with a solid palm heel to the jaw.

La Baptiste's head rocked back, as the hand strike connected, and he bit through his own lip. He roared with rage. One trait all vampires have is their vanity, and his little fighting exhibition was not supposed to be an even affair. The vampire dove forward and grabbed Bonecutter's left leg. Using it as a handle, he threw him across the room as if he were made out of straw instead of flesh and blood.

"My friend, I grow tired of this. I am afraid it is time for you to learn what I taught to many in Haiti, the reality of the machete." La Baptiste bent down and picked up his blade.

Bonecutter barely had time to move out of the way of the first cut, aimed at his throat, and though he got back from the second, the machete left a wicked gash across his cheek.

* * *

Woldman finally freed his hands of their bonds, and just in time, for the vampire had cut Bonecutter's side, causing him to fall to his knees. La Baptiste stood back, gloating at his prize, as he prepared to deliver the final cut and behead Bonecutter. Woldman desperately looked around for a weapon, and his eyes fell on Nicholas's sword. "Nick, catch," he yelled, as he tossed the sword.

* * *

Bonecutter caught the sword, still in the wooden saya that served as its sheath.

"How unfortunate for you, my blade is out, and yours is still in its sheath, oh well." La Baptiste advanced to kill his victim, yet the other did not move to draw his sword. As the machete started downward towards its seemingly helpless opponent, Bonecutter rose straight up to his feet, moving into the machete's cut. He twisted his body as he stood. Bonecutter's katana appeared in his hand as he moved. Instead of hitting the skull of his opponent, La Baptiste's machete struck the finely crafted sword on the shinogi, the strong side part of a hand-forged Japanese blade. The block did not stop and absorb the strength of La Baptiste's cut, it stole it. The machete slid off of Nicholas' sword, and the energy being deflected caused La Baptiste to lose his balance and lean forward. Bonecutter's katana sprang upward, and he harnessed the strength of the other's cut, pulling the katana downward with the full momentum of the attack, now redirected at the back of the vampire's exposed neck.

As La Baptiste's foot hit the floor, he could hear an odd whistling noise, the sound of a Japanese blade in the hands of its master. Bonecutter's katana bit deep, cleanly severing the vampire's head from his body.

The end of the fledgling vampires paled in comparison with how La Baptiste's remains left the world. The head writhed around on the floor, its mouth kept moving as if to scream, but there was no sound. Small streaks of electricity leapt across the body and head, and then the two parts started to burn. The fire was intense, glowing like the flame from a dozen traffic flares, consuming the writhing vampire until there nothing was left.

* * *

Detective Woldman walked over and cut Father Ryan free. The little priest was groggy from being knocked unconscious, but he snapped out of it as Woldman helped him up. Then he scrambled over to check Bonecutter, who was clearly in bad shape. Nick was kneeling on the floor, bleeding in several places. There was a good sized gash in his side, which fortunately only cut the flesh and did not penetrate his ribs to the internal organs, but Ryan could see some of the ribs in the cut. The gash on his face was bleeding badly, but any facial cut usually did. He and Father John helped Nick to his feet.

"Well, Father, how'd we do?"

"No more vampires, and we are all alive. Sounds like a banner day." Father Ryan handed Woldman a handkerchief and grimaced as Woldman covered the wound and put Nick's hand over it to hold it in place.

"We still have to explain the two guys we have trussed up outside," said Bonecutter.

"I think I can take care of that one," Woldman replied. "But what do we do about all of the old pirate treasure our buddy seems to have gathered?"

"Detective, there are plenty of needy people in the world, and I know just how to distribute it." Father John smiled as he thought of all the people this amount of wealth could help. "Now, let's close this place up and call our young friend on the boat. We need to get my adopted son to the hospital and come up with a good story along the way."

Book III
Chapter 13
Wilmington, New York

In the bed in Father Ryan's guest room, Jean Van Nostrand sat upright, waking quickly from a nightmare. She no longer looked beautiful. Her raven hair was covered in sweat and hadn't been washed in days. She wore no makeup, dark rings were nearly black around her eyes, and her skin was still quite pale. Jean looked like a victim of some hideous crime or catastrophe, and indeed she was.

Though her general appearance was ratty, the biggest change was her facial expression. Gone was the malevolent look of evil. It was replaced with the tears of a scared little girl who needed her mother. Deep inside, Jean had changed direction. She had learned the hard way that life was a proving ground, and she had nearly failed the test. The quick rush of drugs and sex had almost cost her far more than her life. For the rest of her days, she would carry the awareness that there are some things in this world far worse than death.

Her mother entered the room. They cried as they held each other, knowing it was finally over, and for the first time in many years, things were right between mother and daughter.

* * *

In August of that year, Father John Ryan sat in the office of his church, attending to his visitors. Ryan had spent most of his years as a simple country priest and had never dealt directly with the Vatican. Now he was sitting face to face with two Cardinals who had traveled all the way from Rome to see him.

"Our lawyers have purchased the property in Fultonville, Father," said the tall, gaunt Cardinal, a dark-haired man with a thick Italian accent. His assistant, a bull of a man with a brush cut and a blocky appearance was apparently from one of the former Soviet Bloc countries, although which one, Ryan could not be sure. Neither of the two gave their names to him, claiming they could not for security purposes.

"How could we purchase it when we basically murdered the owner?" Father John asked.

"One of our Franciscan friars from Somalia sat in for Mr. La Baptiste at the real estate closing," said the Slavic cardinal.

"What will happen to the treasure we found there?" Father Ryan asked.

"Well, for one thing, your friend Father D'Arcy will have a much better budget to run the programs he has in New York City. The value of what you found was only ten million dollars, and it will be used where it is needed until the money is gone."

"This may be a silly question, but how do you plan to do that? This country really frowns on not paying taxes."

"After a suitable period of time, we, as the new owners of the property, will discover the treasure, and then we shall declare our find to the government and pay all of the appropriate taxes. We shall also offer some of the rarer pieces to the New York State Museum," the Italian cardinal replied.

"Then what happens?"

"As we said, Father Ryan, the rest of the money shall go to helping the poor where it is needed."

"Well, if we are going to help the poor, I could use a few extra dollars here. I would appreciate some extra money for this church, particularly for the youth programs."

"That seems fair enough, Father," the blocky Slavic cardinal replied. "I will see what can be done. We must be going, but before we leave, I must re-iterate, no one must ever know what you and your companions have done and seen. We simply cannot tell the world that vampires are real, and worse yet, we cannot tell them the church has secretly been destroying them for centuries." The look in his eyes made it quite clear he wasn't kidding.

* * *

The Bistro De Lachambre was one of the finest restaurants in the City of Albany. Located on Pearle Street, the Bistro was a favorite of political insiders in the New York State Capital. Photos of governors and mayors adorned the walls above the mahogany chair rail surrounding the perimeter of the main dining room, which also featured the largest crystal chandelier in the State. At a table in a side room, the mayor of Albany sat with his lunch companion for the day.

"Detective, you're probably wondering why I asked you to lunch," Mayor Flanders said. The mayor was a good-looking man, with dark hair, just slightly graying at the temples, and a thin, neatly-trimmed mustache. Like the other mayors of the city before him, he was part of a political dynasty. His party had ruled the city for almost a hundred years, and as such, he controlled everything that happened in the city from this very room. There were many lunch and dinner meetings at the Bistro with the power brokers who ran the town.

"No, Your Honor, I have no idea why we are having lunch. I do appreciate a free meal, though," Woldman replied. The detective had dealt with the mayor only a couple of times, usually when a big case was solved and it was time for the press photo-ops. He personally had nothing against the mayor and nothing for him. Woldman simply viewed authority as a necessary evil, but an evil nonetheless.

"Detective Woldman, I didn't get to be mayor of this city by being an idiot." Flanders face flushed red as he raised his voice. "So you can cut the horse shit with me right now! You know damn well what I'm talking about."

"No, Mayor, really I don't. I thought maybe you invited me to lunch because you were trying to get to know some of us cops better."

Flanders wiped the corner of his mouth with the linen napkin and regained his composure. "Woldman, there are times when you really disappoint me, and this is starting to be one of them. Since you want to play games, let's play. A package arrived in my office mail. This package contained photocopies of some material that is very damaging to my police chief and his brother, the commissioner, both of whom happen to be your bosses."

"Still don't know what you are talking about, Mayor." Woldman shoveled another forkful of rice pilaf in his mouth to give it something to do besides smiling.

Flanders slammed his utensils down. "Listen to me, you stupid asshole, you're not the only one who can get things done behind the scenes. It only took me an hour to have someone check the envelope for fingerprints, yours by the way. You're here because you just dumped a pile of shit in my lap, and you're going to help me get rid of it."

"Okay, Mayor, you're right, I sent you the stuff," Woldman said.

"No shit! The city doesn't need another major scandal. You have my assurance this situation will be taken care of." Flanders said.

"Taken care of how, Mayor? Those two assholes were in bed with someone who was stealing old people from the county home and, shall we say, performing some rather sick rituals with them. The same guy was also the biggest drug dealer in the city, probably in all of upstate New York. It's all there. They were taking bribes and filling various bank accounts with money, in addition to getting freebie upscale hookers at their favorite hotels in Vermont. And I have a spare copy of everything."

"I figured you would. Here's how it is going to go. The Captain and his brother are going to take an early retirement. Seems they both have a rare disease, and it is ruining their health. They're going to quietly go away," Flanders said.

"That's not good enough, Mr. Mayor!"

"I didn't finish, Detective. One year after they have gone, and they will be gone well away from this city, the Feds, the same Feds who found your fingerprints on the envelope by the way, will be given the financial records you provided me. The good Captain and Chief of Police will spend many glorious years in a Federal facility for their crimes. No one gets more pissed off than the Feds when they don't get their cut in taxes."

"Well, Mr. Mayor, the man they did business with is all done, so I guess it's wrapped up," Woldman said. "Pity though, because I didn't get to order a fancy dessert yet."

"Oh, by all means, Detective, order whatever you like. You and I aren't finished. "As I have said, you disappoint me. You're a brilliant detective, but you're also a major pain in the ass. You're not very big on following the rules, but all that is about to change."

"Don't tell me you're firing me after all I've done for this town." Woldman couldn't believe his head would be on the chopping block.

"No, Detective, you're not getting fired, although the thought did cross my mind. You're going to hold a new position—Chief of Detectives. Don't worry, though, you're going to keep up your detective work, but you will also make sure the rest of the jackasses under you solve their share of crimes and keep the city running right."

"I suppose I don't have a choice in this."

"No, Detective. No you don't."

* * *

That October, in the middle of a pool on the Salmon River, New York State's best known salmon fishing destination, three friends sat anchored in a green wooden McKenzie-style driftboat. Although the river drew crowds of anglers, the guide at the oars knew its waters well, and had anchored his two anglers on a good run, far away from the crowds.

On the back deck of the boat, Sadie the dog lay with her chin on her paws, looking toward the bow. The angler there was hopelessly entangled in his own fly line. Even Sadie knew this guy was not going to catch a fish and hunkered down as close as she could to the deck because more than once a salmon fly had winged by just missing her head.

"Detective, it is not a hammer. Just use your forearm to cast, and let the rod do the work, it is not a muscle thing." Bonecutter moved forward from the rowing seat to help Woldman untangle himself.

"I thought you said I was the worst fly fisherman you ever had in the boat?" Father John chuckled.

"Today is Ed's first day, you've been at this for years," Bonecutter replied.

"But it still is possible that he's the worst?" Father John reached back and scratched Sadie behind the ears.

"Father, I predict that Ed here is going to catch one on the next cast," Bonecutter said.

"Bet you five dollars, Father, because I have confidence in my guide," Woldman added.

"You're on, Detective, you're on," the good Father replied.

Woldman told himself to relax, and let the rod do the work. While the next cast wasn't textbook perfect, the fly dropped right where Bonecutter wanted it to. As the line tightened and the fly drifted through the run, a king salmon of about twenty pounds grabbed it, and the race was on.

"Just let him run, Ed, make him work against the rod," Nicholas said. "Make him work against the bend in the rod."

The big salmon bolted upstream, until it could go no more, and then it pulled the usual salmon trick, turning and running downstream as fast as it could.

"I think I lost him," Woldman said.

"Crank the reel, quickly!"

Woldman, though momentarily startled, did as he was told, and again the rod bent double.

"Keep him working against the bend of the rod, Ed."

The salmon put up quite a battle, which lasted another ten minutes, before it was brought to the net. Sadie barked when the big king salmon flopped in the boat.

"Can I keep him?" Woldman asked.

"Sure you can." Bonecutter put the big fish on the stringer, while Father John dug in his pocket to produce his five dollar bill. "I believe you're up next, Father, and not to put any pressure on you, but I'll bet five more dollars you lose the next fish."

As the sun set, while the three anglers reached the downstream boat ramp and packed up for the day, all of them had become fast friends. On the ride back in the truck, Father John sat in the back seat with Sadie, the happy dog occasionally giving him a big lick across the cheek. "Nick, I'll buy dinner, but I want to go to the new restaurant in Lake Placid."

"Why can't we go to the diner by the house where we always go?"

"I want to go to try the new restaurant. It's coming up on the left."

Nicholas had trouble pulling the truck and trailer into the parking lot, but he was able to find a spot in the back where he could fit in. Bonecutter, if nothing else, was a creature of habit. He always took his clients to the same diner after fishing. As he walked along grumbling, he noticed Father John and Woldman whispering like they were up to something.

The three friends walked into the restaurant and sat down at a corner table. Woldman dove into the seat by the wall, and Father John grabbed the seat by the window. Now Bonecutter definitely knew something was up. He had a habit since the SEALS of hating to be in a public place and seated so he couldn't watch people coming in the door or walking up to the table.

Woldman had a shit-eating grin, and Father John had all he could do to keep from giggling, as the waitress approached the table.

"Would you gentlemen care for drinks before dinner?" The waitress was a sweet young woman about the same age as Bonecutter. She was cute, except for the scar on her face.

Bonecutter knew that voice! He quickly stood and turned, coming face to face with the high school sweetheart he had lost years ago.

Upon seeing him, the little waitress' eyes filled with tears, as did the eyes of the tough as nails Navy SEAL. Bonecutter and the girl latched on to each other in a hug that even the strength of a vampire could not pry apart.

"Well, Ed, I can see we'll have to have our first drink at the bar," Father John said, and he and Woldman walked away from the happy scene.

* * *

Inside a mountain in Northern Colorado, deep within an abandoned silver mine, the master rose from his gilded coffin. He could hear water dripping in the lower levels, as he took a match and lit the lamps, although his scarlet eyes certainly did not need the light to see, even in the complete darkness of the mine. Awakened early from a fitful rest, he knew one of his bloodline had been destroyed.

His was an ancient race that had existed as long as man. While he did not go back all the way to the beginning, he had walked the earth for almost a thousand years, preying on the mortal sheep, as he thought of his prey. He was one of the old ones, the truly powerful among the undead. He had created the old woman on the pitiful island of Haiti. Similarly, he also knew the moment when La Baptiste had destroyed her. How he had laughed when he sensed another of his bloodline had been born in the process. The fool who had destroyed the old woman was just as much his.

He admired La Baptiste, after all, not only did he succeed in his new existence, he thrived! The master had followed his progress through the years, always from a distance. He loved how the fledgling had used drugs to enslave his victims. After all, who would miss the junkies? Yes La Baptiste was a promising one, and he had potential to be an asset to the master with a little training, but now all that had changed.

His mate's coffin lid slowly crept open, as he pondered the situation. "What is it my love?" she asked.

"It would seem, my dear Cassandra, that we have lost one of our line. Now leave me while I decide what to do. Enjoy the hunt."

The truth be told, many of his kind had been destroyed through the centuries, but they were always the greedy ones, the foolish ones. The drug lord was not like this, and it was impressive that a mortal could kill one who was so careful, so strong. What mistake could the drug lord have made to be discovered and vanquished?

"Perhaps, after all of these centuries, a worthy opponent has finally come along." The dull echo of his voice in the mineshaft was his only reply.

Epilogue

From the journal of Father John Ryan

So ended the first of our adventures.

It is unfortunate that destiny could not have left us alone at that point. My adopted son finally found the woman he loved. And our friend, the detective, well, he finally found what he was looking for all along. He found satisfaction and a little justice in his career. For me, I always had what I wanted, my small Adirondack church.

Sadly, though, as long as man has walked the earth, the world has always been at war. Not the wars of men, although there have been far too many of them throughout history. No we have always been engaged in a different kind of battle.

Christ, to whom I gave my life in service, was the greatest, but not the only casualty of this war. Good and evil have fought for the hearts and souls of mankind since he first trod upon the Earth. It will never end.

Most of us, at some point in our lives, must make a choice. Oh yes, the degrees are different. We can beat our wives, or not. We can cheat in our business dealings, or be honest. We can kill, or protect life. We face these choices every day. The scale and gravity of the decisions are different for all of us, but the choice is always there.

Most of us are bit players in the war between good and evil; few ever have to actually go into battle. But as long as there are undead demons that feed on the blood and fear of the living, a handful of good men must always be called upon to put them down.

Yes, our first adventure ended happily, but we only won the battle. We sure as Hell didn't win the war.

Father John Ryan